UNSPORTSMANLIKE CONDUCT

An Aviators Hockey Novel

SOPHIA HENRY

Krasivo Creative

Cover design: Amanda Shepard, Shepard Originals

To every single person who lives their life with love, respect, and compassion for all. We can change the world. Together.

#BeKindLoveHard

CONNECT with Sophia:
SophiaHenry.com

AMAZON // BOOKBUB

#BeKindLoveHard
I stand with Ukraine 🇺🇦

Chapter One

KRISTEN

DAY 1 - CRUISING IN THE CARIBBEAN

IS THERE anything more perfect than breathing in the salty scent of the ocean while jogging around the top deck of a cruise ship in ninety-degree weather?

Well, sure, seventy-five degrees would have been a better temperature for running, but I'm not complaining.

Sweat glistens on my arms and a gentle wind blows the flyaway strands of hair away from my face as my feet pound the track.

Mental fist bump to my parents. They'd succeeded in their quest to find me the perfect college graduation gift, even if I hadn't realized it at first.

When they presented me with a printout of an itinerary for a cruise a few months ago, my first reaction was complete and utter terror. At that time, the mere thought of being in a large body of water with no land in sight gave me hives. But I didn't want my amazing parents to think I didn't appreciate their generous gift, so I kept it inside and went along with the planning.

So here I am. Sea breeze in my hair, a cardio remix of Lil Wayne's "How to Love" blasting through my earbuds, and a tropical destination.

Nothing could ruin this moment.

Except the familiar face of the person running toward me. Which sends my version of personal paradise plummeting to the ocean floor. Because, in this case, "familiar" and "welcome" are not synonymous.

Maybe Spiros hadn't recognized me. Maybe I can pretend I didn't see him.

"Kristen!" he calls.

Not even paradise can deter Murphy's Law.

So I do what any smart girl who wants to avoid her friendly stalker would do: I spin around and run the opposite way, putting more distance between us.

Note: When the self-proclaimed "smart girl" is unfamiliar with the territory where she's running, glancing over her shoulder to see if Spiros is still there is not the best idea. Because within three strides, I smack into another runner.

Not a light, whoops-sorry-I-bumped-you collision. A head-on, semi-to-semi crash, where both bodies lay crumpled in a pile of twisted, burning limbs.

Burning, not only because the scorching Caribbean sun pounds on us from above, but also because the other semi has the body of a Greek god.

No joke.

As a good Greek girl on a singles cruise set up by my Greek Orthodox church and paid for by my straight-off-the-boat Greek parents, I know my Greek gods.

And the hunk of muscle I'd knocked into is Adonis in the flesh.

Instead of scrambling to my feet, my gaze freezes on his face, particularly on the sexy scruff dusting his upper lip and jawline. His twelve o'clock shadow is a distinct contrast to the absence of hair on his chiseled chest. Even the sweat rolling off the tip of his nose doesn't detract from his perfection, nor does the red undertone on his sun-kissed skin, flushed from running in the heat.

"Dude!" I exclaim, yanking the earbuds from my ears. Then I break into a cough and can't stop.

Adonis picks up his sunglasses, which must've fallen when we crashed, and replaces them over his eyes. He waits until I finish my coughing fit before speaking. "Maybe you need to pay attention since you were running the wrong way on this track, yes?"

"I didn't—" I can't finish my thought. I'm still trying to catch my breath as I consider the situation: Adonis knocked me down, and he has the audacity to blame me?

"Well, if you were going the right way, why didn't you run around me?" I ask breathlessly.

"I play chicken."

"Excuse me?" Who says something like that?

He jumps to his feet. "I wait to see if you will stop first. You call this game chicken, yes?" He bends down and holds out his hand.

At least he has some manners. I clasp his hand and allow him to pull me up, impressed at the lack of effort it takes him to lift me.

"Common courtesy dictates that people don't usually play chicken while running." I brush a palm over my butt, even though the track seems relatively debris-free.

He draws the back of his hand across his hairline, wiping away a film of moisture. "I think this same common courtesy say that people don't look over their shoulder when they run."

True. Technically, my poorly planned attempt to escape Spiros's approach caused the collision.

"I'm sorry I ran into you," I say.

"Are you also sorry because you are running the wrong way?"

"Who are you, the track police?" I ask, resting my hands on my hips and leaning away from him, my breath finally under control.

"This track has rules. Today, we run this way." He points in the direction I'd initially started running. Then I follow his finger as it travels in another direction, stopping at a red sign with the heading track rules in thick white letters.

Who pays attention to what day it is or obnoxiously large signs about rules when they're on a cruise?

"Well, I'm really sorry. I got flustered trying to avoid that guy running toward us." I nod slightly toward Spiros, who'd caught up.

Yep. Spiros Loukas, my annoying admirer, didn't take the hint and stands at my heels, just like at home.

Paradise lost.

Chapter Two

PASHA

I CAN'T EXPLAIN WHY MY PROTECTIVE INSTINCTS KICKED IN FOR THE gorgeous girl who just slammed into me, but when the out-of-shape oaf she'd been avoiding reached out to place his thick, dirty hand on her, I jumped into action.

Without a second thought, I step forward and slide my arm around her slim waist, placing myself between the girl and the man who'd chased her straight into my arms.

"Kristen, are you okay?" the guy asks, panting.

The slob must've jacked up his speed when he saw the collision. It's sad that such a short burst took so much out of him. He needs to get in shape if he wants to impress anyone.

"I'm fine. I had this rock of a pillow to fall on." She swats my stomach with the back of her hand, and my muscles involuntarily contract under her touch.

"Wanna join me for a few laps?" the man asks her, completely disregarding me.

But I'm not the type of guy who lets himself be ignored. "Who are you?" I demand.

"I should be asking you that question," he counters.

"I'm her boyfriend," I say.

Kristen, as the huffing man had called her, stiffens. I pat her waist, silently asking her to follow along with the scheme I'd quickly concocted.

"Excuse me?" He runs a hand through his unkempt brown hair as his beady eyes shift back and forth between me and Kristen.

"You will tell him, or I smash his face?" I ask.

"We've been, um," she stammers, "seeing each other?"

Her voice rises slightly, which would have made me smile if I hadn't had to scare off the stupid fuck who doesn't realize this poor girl was running away from him. At least she's quick enough to go along with the story I'd created to help her.

"What? Since when?" he asks. "Who is this guy?"

I squeeze the tiny girl into my sweat-soaked side and feel her bare skin against mine. A glance down tells me her hot pink shirt has ridden up, revealing a tight, toned waist. It makes me want to get sweaty *with* her. And I don't mean by running together.

"He is not your business. What are you even doing here?" she asks, effectively taking the spotlight off me.

The quickness with which she regains her composure intrigues me as if she's a pro at going along with crazy schemes with no preparation.

"I signed up for this cruise months ago," the man says defensively. "After your parents—" He stops and shakes his head. "I hoped we could spend some time together."

My body tenses, but I keep my arm around Kristen, my hand still resting on her hip. She allows me to stay close.

"It's a singles cruise. Go meet someone." She pauses. "Someone new."

"Or I smash your face," I promise.

My fingers slip down and skim her backside before curling into a fist behind her. Kristen reaches around and swats at my hand until I return it to her waist. She obviously got the wrong idea about my accidental ass contact.

Dough Boy doesn't speak, but his eyebrows slide closer together as his head swivels from Kristen to me. I try to keep my expression neutral, which is hard because this guy has to be an idiot not to realize that she doesn't want him to bother her. It had taken me less than two minutes to figure it out.

When neither Kristen nor I cave, his sloped shoulders drop. Then he sighs and spins around, heading straight for the elevator instead of resuming his run.

Once he's out of sight, I reluctantly release my hold on her waist. "Why are you trying to avoid him? Other than obvious."

A soft, sweet laugh escapes from her deep pink lips, a trait shared by many of the beautiful Greek American girls surrounding me on the ship.

"What does that mean?" she asks.

"Possessive creep."

"Kinda like a stranger who randomly puts his arm around my waist and claims to be my boyfriend?" she counters.

Her sarcastic comment doesn't put me off because there's no conviction in her delivery. None of the animosity she'd been projecting toward Dough Boy comes across toward me, just a feistiness I appreciate. I enjoy people who challenge me.

"I saved you," I remind her.

"You did, actually." She adjusts the front of her shirt, peeling the fabric away from her sweaty skin. "Why would you do that?"

"I am gentleman," I say. The words remind me to lift my gaze from her tight stomach to her beautiful face. "American girls, they are not used to this," I add before abruptly leaving her to continue my run.

I don't pursue women. They come to me because it's their foolish goal to "land" a hockey player. No challenge. No connection. No love. Just a girl who wants the status of being with me. Needless to say, we have fun, but there's no future. There's never even a second time.

Usually, my protective instincts emerge only when it comes to my family—including my sister, Irina, and her best friend, Svetlana, who is like a second sister.

But something about Kristen made me jump between her and Dough Boy. She didn't know who I was or what I did for a living. And she'd never stood outside the team's locker room or waited for me to show up at my favorite bar, so I had anonymity on my side.

If Irina had been here, she would've teased me for the caveman-like growls that had rumbled in my throat as I stood toe-to-toe with Kristen's stalker.

The Caribbean sun must be melting my brain because this Kristen girl is not my sister, just a stranger in obvious distress. And I can't blame Dough Boy for trying to get with her because she's by far the most gorgeous girl I've seen on this boat.

When Blake Panikos, my good friend and teammate on the Charlotte Monarchs hockey team, first invited me on a cruise set up by a conglomerate of Greek Orthodox churches in the metro Detroit area, I immediately declined. Despite being raised by Russian Orthodox parents, I'm not a religious person. The thought of being stuck on a boat with a group of religious fanatics made me want to chop off my dick with a hacksaw.

But Blake, who recently divorced, kept needling me to go. After various attempts to sway me into taking the trip with him, he finally sold me when he showed me some of the women who would be on the cruise. He pulled up his Instagram account and scrolled through pictures of people he'd met at the church he frequented when we played together in Detroit on Charlotte's minor-league affiliate team. Flipping through photo after photo of the most gorgeous Greek girls Detroit had to offer sealed the deal.

A week in the Caribbean surrounded by sexy singles looking to hook up was worth the effort it took to relearn the sign of the cross.

Chapter Three

KRISTEN

AFTER RUNNING AWAY FROM SPIROS AND CRASHING INTO A gorgeous Greek god, I'm famished, so I stop for a quick breakfast before changing into my swimsuit for a glorious morning catching rays by the pool.

I could win medals for eating and sunbathing since I'm equally exceptional at both activities.

We have a full day of sailing before the ship docks in Barbados, our first stop. Though my lifelong fear of water always made me wary of taking a cruise, now that I've taken the plunge, I plan to thoroughly enjoy everything the ship offers—*after* savoring a day lying by the sparkling pool.

When I arrive at the Lido deck, I scope out the seating situation, looking for three open chairs next to each other. My cousin Lena and our friend Sia will join me when they wake up. Being the early bird of the group means I get the super-important yet not-so-glamorous task of securing a group of lounge chairs for all of us.

The deck is set up with stadium-style seating, with rows of chairs crammed next to each other on multiple levels. My eyes lock on the closest area with three consecutive empty loungers. At the end of the row, next to the empty chairs, with his body stretched out in all his fabulously muscled, glistening glory, lay Adonis.

Damn.

I'm not usually an ogler, but I'm also not used to seeing guys who are so cut. Most buff guys I know are thin and relatively smooth, not ripped and jacked. He makes wearing nothing but sunglasses and swim trunks borderline indecent.

I make the bold decision to set my towel on the chair next to his before securing the other two seats by tossing my beach bag on one and an extra towel on the other. I don't even bother asking if he's been saving the seats. I have a feeling he'd let me know if I wasn't welcome.

"So, what's your story?" I ask.

"My story?" He lowers his head and gazes at me over his sunglasses.

My heart flutters fast, waiting for him to tell me to move or ask why I chose to sit next to him, given all the open seats surrounding the pool. But he doesn't.

Did I really choose this spot because these were the only three empty chairs next to each other? I could've dragged another lounger next to two others.

"You're not Greek. I can tell that by your accent." Under the ruse of trying to figure him out, I twist my torso and lean toward his chair. Subconsciously, I relish the opportunity to study his features more closely. "So you can't be one of the Detroit-area Greek singles I'm supposed to hang out with."

"I am. I came here with a friend."

"Who's your friend?" I ask, tucking my hair behind my ears.

"Blake Panikos."

I don't recognize the name. After spending the majority of my life around people in Detroit's Greek Orthodox community, I know almost everyone close to my age, whether we went to the same church or not.

"How do you know Blake?" I settle back into the lounge chair, flicking back a corner of the towel that had fallen onto my shoulder.

Adonis's lip curl into a smirk. "Panikos work with me when I live in Detroit."

"Where do you live now?"

"North Carolina."

"Really?" I sit up. "My best friend just moved to Charlotte."

"Charlotte. This is where I live."

"What a small world. She lives downtown, in the Artisan condos." I pause to correct myself. "Well, I guess you guys call it *uptown* instead of downtown."

"Why she move to Charlotte? She get job there?" Adonis leans sideways, picks up a plastic cup from the ground next to his chair, and brings it to his lips.

"No. She moved in with her fiancé. He's a hockey player."

Adonis doesn't respond but chokes on his drink and diverts his eyes toward the pool.

"His name's Aleksandr Varenkov," I add, thinking his response holds recognition. "Do you know him?"

"No," he answers quickly, adjusting his aviator sunglasses, which had slid down his nose. "I never hear of this guy. Maybe I see him, I know his face."

"If the Internet worked here, I'd show you a picture on my phone."

"This ship have Internet," Adonis corrects me.

"Yeah, I know. But I can't afford the hundred dollars a minute they charge to access it."

A hundred dollars a minute is only a slight exaggeration—but the ship charges enough that I don't feel the need to waste my money. I'll wait until we dock somewhere with a restaurant or a bar that offers free Wi-Fi. "So what do you do?"

His gaze veers from my lips to my eyes before he answers. "I am Aviator."

Aviator is a weird way to say he's a pilot, but he's obviously foreign, so I'll let it slide.

I grab my water bottle from the tiny table beside my lounge chair. "Really? So you're always traveling, eh? Do you love it?"

"I like to fly. To travel. Is, um, is good job for me." Adonis takes another swig from his drink, something clear with a cluster of crushed ice floating in it. "You have job, yes?"

I lean back in the chair and bend my knees slightly—perfect position to soak up the sizzling sunshine. "I'm the assistant to one of the owners of Motor City Bar Management. It's a company that owns a group of bars and restaurants around Detroit. I coordinate all the volunteers and employees for events our venues host or sponsor." I finish my water and set the empty bottle on the table.

"What kind of events?"

"Concerts. Promotional events at bars," I say, rattling off a few of the things I helped plan recently.

"Maybe I see you around," he says. "I go to many concerts."

"Probably not," I say. "I just started two months ago. Before that, I was at Central State."

Adonis's eyes dart toward something behind me. "You like this party life?"

"It's fun right now." I wiggle my toes, watching the pink glitter polish sparkle in the sunlight. "My goal is to learn the ropes of event planning, then turn it into something more professional in a few years when being immersed in the bar scene isn't my thing anymore."

Suddenly, he sits up and swings his legs over the side of the chair, planting them on the ground facing me. Then he leans close, his face inches from mine.

Is he going to kiss me?

My heart hammers, excited and eager to accept a kiss from this stranger. I lick my lips and close my eyes. But instead of feeling his mouth on mine, I feel his breath against my face.

"This guy you try to avoid is behind you," he says.

My eyes flicker open. "Huh?"

"The guy you run from." Adonis nods. "He is behind you now." He leans back, resuming his original lazy, reclined position. Then, he tilts his cup and drains his drink.

How does this man already have my heart pounding and my brain begging for his lips on mine? The salty ocean air must be permeating my mind and breaking down my common sense.

I sit upright and swivel around, pretending to be interested in scoping out the pool scene so the hottie next to me won't notice my disappointment at not being kissed.

True to Adonis's report, Spiros plods toward us, clad in navy blue board shorts with a matching navy and green striped towel draped around his neck.

"Is this seat taken?" he asks. Without waiting for an answer, he tosses my beach bag onto the next seat and covers the chair with his towel.

"You're gonna have to move when Lena and Sia get here," I warn, refusing to let him feel welcome.

Adonis stands up. "I go get drink. You need one, yes?"

"I'll go with you," I say quickly.

He puts a hand on my head to stop me from standing. "Is okay. I go. You relax. Tell this friend about me."

What happened to the heroic guy who "saved" me on the running track?

"Can you please grab me a vodka soda with a couple of lemon wedges? "

Adonis winks and retreats toward the huge bar, spanning the entire length of the pool.

Spiros leans over, speaking through the corner of his mouth like he's conveying a secret. "Is it smart to let a stranger get you a drink?"

"He's only a stranger to you," I remind Spiros. *Though, I really should ask Adonis his name. Just not when Spiros is around.*

"Well, I'm watching him."

Spiros might be watching under the guise of a cautious friend convinced that Adonis will slip something into my drink, but I'm watching every step the man takes for the pure pleasure it gives me.

And believe me, watching him walk away is quite the view.

Adonis doesn't wear boring navy blue. He screams 'exciting' from the top of his perfectly coiffed Euro-sexual undercut hair to the hem of his swim shorts—red laced with fine white lines bouncing across the fabric to create star-shaped flowers. His trunks show off his incredibly muscular thighs.

Which is another way I could tell he wasn't one of the second-generation Greek American guys on the cruise. Most guys I know wear board shorts or longer swim trunks. Europeans wear shorter shorts—or Speedos.

"Can you please hand me that bag?" I point to the chair next to

Spiros. I shoved the new Richelle Mead novel in there somewhere. Pretending to read will save me from talking to Spiros. Under normal circumstances, I rock at small talk, but I can't even fake it with him.

When I find my book, I lift it in front of my face but leave myself a clear line of sight. With my eyes concealed by oversized sunglasses, I have no shame in watching Adonis's every move. As he strolls back to our chairs, I swear his stomach shoots me multiple smiles. At least, it looks that way when the hard curves of his eight-pack crunch with each stride.

I squeeze my eyes shut, willing myself to stop thinking of him as a piece of man candy from the newest *Magic Mike* film.

"Let me know if you need me to save you," Spiros mumbles.

I bite back a laugh, which turns into a cough. Adonis and Spiros are on opposite ends of the same wavelength.

Adonis returns with our drinks, carrying plastic cups in his hands and dangling a water bottle loosely from his pinkies.

"You okay?" he asks. His eyebrows draw together in concern as he watches me cough into the bend of my elbow.

I nod. "Thank you."

When Adonis holds the drinks out, I set my book down and reach for the cup with two lemon wedges perched on the rim. Suddenly, Adonis drops the water bottle into my lap. Ice-cold condensation hits my inner thighs, and I jump.

"Whoops." He reaches between my legs. His fingers skim the inside of my thighs when he grabs the bottle.

"Holy shit!" I gasp, trembling from the innocent yet sensual touch.

Adonis's lips quirk up on one side, diminishing the innocence of his actions.

After he sets the water on the table next to me, he reaches out and presses two fingers on the skin of my breastbone. Then he lowers his head and brushes his lips across my cheek. "You need lotion."

I drop my gaze to my chest, trying to control my breathing. When he lifts his fingers, two light spots appear before quickly returning to a darker olive color. I can't believe he doesn't feel my heart bursting under his touch. I nod because I can't speak, which rarely happens to me.

"I'll help you," Spiros interjects. He snatches my beach bag from the chair and reaches inside, which pulls me out of the moment with Adonis.

"Hey!" I jerk the bag out of his hands and clutch it to my chest. "Don't go through my stuff."

Adonis's shadow covers me as he leans toward Spiros with fists clenched at his side.

Spiros throws his hands up. "I was getting her sunscreen."

"No good man dig in woman's bag," Adonis growls.

Adonis continues to impress me with his manners. He has a way of stating things that diminish Spiros to the size of an ant.

After I fish out the can of SPF 30 spray, I shove my bag under Adonis's chair, out of Spiros's reach. Then I stand up and hand the bottle to Adonis. "Can you help me, baby?"

"Ridiculous," Spiros grunts under his breath.

It *is* ridiculous because I've never called any guy "baby" in my life. It actually makes me gag a little.

Instead of reacting, I ignore Spiros and step behind our chairs, giving Adonis room to cover my skin with a mist of sunscreen. "It's the kind you have to rub in after you spray," I inform him, sprinkling salt into Spiros's wounded ego.

He starts with my arms, spraying from one wrist up my arm and straight across my chest and neck down to the other wrist. Then he holds the can between his knees and uses both hands to work the lotion into my skin.

When we stand face-to-face, my forehead comes to his chin. I look up at him, which causes my heart to race, so I move my gaze to the side, watching him work on my arms. When he squats to spray my legs, I close my eyes and enjoy his hands.

Though Adonis acts like a perfect gentleman as he sprays and rubs, I'd be lying if I said I wasn't affected by his touch. Before he stands up, he pinches the back of my knee playfully, causing a shiver to ripple through me.

Chapter Four

PASHA

Out of all the gorgeous girls who could have knocked me down on a cruise ship in the middle of the Caribbean, it had to be Auden Berezin's best fucking friend.

And I can't keep my mind—or my hands, evidently—off her.

Her body quivers, visibly affected by my teasing nip to her knee.

"Let's go in the pool. It's hot out here." My words come out between quick pants as if in desperate need of water. I am—to immerse myself in, not to drink.

Kristen must feel the heat from the sexual tension, too, because her eyes are wide when I reach out to her. Instead of answering, she nods and places her hand on my forearm, allowing me to lead her to the pool.

What the fuck am I doing?

I need the shock of Lake Baikal in a Siberian winter to knock some sense into me. Instead, the lukewarm water of this solar-heated pool lulls me into continuing with this horrible decision I've made to pursue Kristen—or KK, as Auden calls her.

I knew exactly who Kristen was talking about when she mentioned friends in Charlotte.

Aleksandr Varenkov and I have been friends since age six when we learned to skate together at a hockey program in Russia, where we hail from. In some strange twist of luck, after playing for different teams during our teenage years, we were both drafted by the NHL's Charlotte Monarchs in the same year. Before going to Charlotte, we played together for the Detroit Aviators, the Monarch's minor-league team.

But I can't tell Kristen any of that.

Though we've never met before now, I know she hates me.

Girls don't like it when a dickbag tries to break up their best friend's relationship.

Shortly after we joined the Aviators, Aleksandr fell in love with Auden Berezin, the translator his agent had found for him. During a regrettable period in my life when anger and jealousy fueled my actions, I attempted to break them up—to ruin my friend's happiness —because *I* was miserable.

If Kristen knew who I was, she wouldn't be speaking to me right now. And that would suck because of the stupid primal, selfish tug I'm feeling that makes me want to get to know her, to protect her.

Fuck me.

As she approaches the water, I take a second to look at her. I noticed her figure on the track this morning, but now that I have a chance to study her in-depth, I realize she's thin, too thin; though her muscles are toned, she seems frail.

My gut tightens with the urge to pick her up and carry her into the pool. I want to inspect her gorgeous mouth and glowing cheeks up close—with my lips.

Kristen holds on to the railing and dips a foot into the water. "Shit," she mumbles and steps out.

"What is it?" I ask, walking backward slowly without taking my eyes off her. The gorgeous Greek girl screams sex, from her thick brown hair to the pink polish on her toes.

"This is my tanning suit, not my swimming suit," Kristen responds as if that answer makes any sense at all.

"So take it off," I tease.

"Funny," she retorts, placing a hand on the sparkly silver fabric covering her chest. She lifts her head and catches my eyes, still looking at her chest.

I don't mean to stare, but the sunlight bounces off her swimsuit every time she moves, creating quick flashes that draw my eyes to her assets.

She looks over her shoulder, back at the lounge chairs we'd vacated a few moments ago, and seems to quickly resign herself to staying in the pool with me.

I cup my hands, digging into the water, then splashing it over my face. Kristen lowers herself to the edge of the pool and lets her feet dangle instead of meeting me in the deeper zone.

Guess she wasn't kidding about not getting her suit wet.

I wade toward her. When I get close enough, I reach out, put my hand on her hip, and skim my thumb over the scratchy fabric of her one-piece swimsuit. "What is point of wearing suit that does not get wet?"

I know pursuing her is trouble, but I can't shake the instinct to keep her away from the guy from the track. The one she obviously doesn't want to be around but who seems to keep popping up everywhere she is. Over Kristen's shoulder, I see him watching our every move like a hawk stalking prey from its perch on a tree branch.

Maybe that guy should be protecting her from me.

Though I pretend to struggle internally with the situation, I've already made my decision. Despite the epically fucked-up way our paths intersected, I want to see what could happen if she got to know me as the person I am rather than as the bastard I was at a particularly low part of my life.

"What's the point in wearing sequins if they get covered by water?" she counters. "Sparkle is meant to be seen."

I cock my head and squint at her, assessing whether or not she's being serious. Did I misinterpret her feistiness and quick wit? Maybe my fascination with her will end before I'm forced to confess my identity.

"I'm not an airhead," she snaps, evidently having noticed my reaction. "I just like things that make me happy."

"I, um, well . . ." Surprised by her vehemence, I take a step back and search for words to apologize, even though I hadn't said anything.

She reaches out and grabs my biceps to stop my retreat. "Sorry. I suppose that reaction was a bit dramatic."

"A bit?" I grin and lean toward her again.

She rolls her eyes and smiles, obviously amused by my teasing. "So, what's your name, hotshot?"

I think quickly. "Pavlos," I say since I can't tell her the truth. The fictional name fits since I'm supposed to be a young Greek professional.

This time, she's the one who leans away. She knows I'm lying, especially since she's already called me out on my non-Greek accent.

I place my other hand on her hip, holding her in place, and take another step closer, situating myself between her legs. "But you can call me Pasha."

"Pasha," she repeats. "Well, that's better than Adonis."

"Who is this?" I ask.

"The Greek god of hot."

I laugh, though part of me wants to puff out my chest and smirk. "Why you call me this?"

"I had to call you something since you ran off without telling me your name." Her slender fingers skim the top of my swim trunks.

I clench my abs, trying to keep my mind off how much her touch affects me. She'll be in for a show if she keeps that up. The slight contraction must make her realize what she's doing because she drops her hands and grips the edge of the pool again.

Her stalker keeps shooting us daggers behind her back, so I grab the outside of her thighs and squeeze them to get a reaction. Maybe I'll make her suit wet without water.

Her breath catches. "Don't you want to know my name?" she asks.

"I know your name," I tell her.

"How?" she asks.

"The stalker call you Kristen. This is your name, yes?"

"Oh, well, yeah," she says.

"Speaking of him, he stare too much. We move over there?" I nod toward the bar along the pool with stools inside the water.

In all honesty, I would've preferred to hang out between her legs for the rest of the day, preferably with our clothes off, but that's not the kind of impression I want to make after we just introduced ourselves.

"We just got—" She pauses, remembering we've left our drinks at our seats. Then she nods and says, "Lead the way, Pasha."

Before following me, Kristen glances back at our chairs. Two girls have joined her stalker. Instead of leaving or finding another chair, Dough Boy took mine.

Not that it matters because I'm in the pool with the girl he wants.

Kristen jumps off the pool edge and follows me through the waist-deep water toward the pool bar. I gesture for her to sit on one of the underwater stools before I slide onto the one beside her.

"Your suit is wet." I skim my fingers over her stomach, where the water line hits.

She flinches, and I drop my hand immediately. I know I can be too touchy-feely sometimes, but I didn't intend to be disrespectful.

She gives me a flirty smile, her demeanor flipping back to cool and calm in a split second. "What's the point in having a suit if it can't get wet?" she asks, throwing my earlier question back at me.

I smile, relieved she wasn't offended by my touch. "Why you don't like this guy?" I nod toward the other side of the pool, where the creepy guy sits.

"Spiros is boring and annoying." She reaches for the plastic tray the bartender set in front of us that holds the bill for our drinks, but I snatch it out of her hand. She's crazy if she thinks she'll pay for anything when she's with me.

"I'm not saying I want a guy that plays hard to get, but he's been hounding me since I was four."

"So young?" I ask while scratching numbers and my signature on the receipt before sliding it back toward the bartender.

"It's been eighteen years—you'd think he'd get the point by now." She nods toward the bill. "Thank you for the drink."

"He need to live a little. Find a girl interested in him."

"Exactly," Kristen agrees. "But tell that to my parents. They've been encouraging him the entire time."

"Do you get along with them?"

"My parents?"

When I nod, she continues, "Oh, yeah. They're great. A bit over-protective, but I know it's because they want me to have this super-fulfilling, amazing life. Too bad our definitions of 'amazing' and 'fulfilling' don't match."

We have that in common. My father's definition of an amazing and fulfilling life never matched mine.

Kristen gathers her thick brown hair in her hands, twists it to create a long ponytail, then flips it behind her back.

Without thinking, I reach out and smooth back the stray strands she missed. "What do you mean?"

"I don't know," she admits as color flushes her cheeks. "I want to travel and skydive and swim with dolphins. They want me to have a boring desk job and marry a boring lawyer. My motto is: Don't waste your precious time on earth with someone who makes you miserable."

If she only knew.

The bartender sets our drinks on the bar in the space between us. I allow her to take her drink before I take mine. She pinches the lemon wedges off the rim, squeezes the juice into the cup, and then twists toward me.

I raise my drink. "To avoiding this boring lawyer."

We clink cups, and I take a long sip.

"You don't seem boring. I mean, anyone who chooses to be a pilot has to be somewhat adventurous, right?" she asks.

I almost choke but catch myself. "New city all the time. New people. Nothing hold me back." I avert my gaze, staring at the water for a few seconds to regain my composure, before focusing on her again. "I like this life."

Technically, it's not a lie. I play for a team called the Aviators. And travel to different cities is a constant part of my life as a hockey player.

Still, I feel like a horrible person deceiving her.

"Why settle? There's too much to do before we die." She presses her lips together and stares at her drink as if she's said something wrong.

"Some people, they die before they live," I agree. I try to keep my voice light, but I can't. Though my mother had been an internationally acclaimed dancer, I don't know if she ever really lived because my father held her back.

I shake my head to clear my thoughts. "So, let's live." I raise my glass and wait for Kristen to raise hers before downing my drink and slamming the cup on the bar.

"Let's live." She smiles and takes a breath before tilting her own drink back.

Chapter Five

KRISTEN

TALKING TO GUYS HAS NEVER BEEN A PROBLEM FOR ME. I'M NOT SHY. I'm not insecure. But for some strange reason, being with Pasha feels too easy, like hanging out with my best friend, Auden. Experiencing that deep bond with someone so soon gave me a false sense of familiarity and trust.

Unfortunately, I can't keep my big mouth shut around my friends. It's what I'm known for.

On a regular basis, my mouth gets me into more trouble than Kanye West's. Though this time, I'm the only one who realizes it. I don't usually blurt out comments about my short life span to hot guys at pools, whether they're pretending to be my boyfriend or not.

We're all going to die. I just know my time is coming sooner than others.

It's the reality of life with cystic fibrosis, the genetic disorder I was born with. It affects my lungs and digestive system. CF has no known cure, which sounds super scary, and it is, especially for people who have more severe symptoms. But in my case, though still serious, it's not an immediate death sentence. With daily maintenance and healthy lifestyle choices, I should live into my thirties or even forties.

The healthier I keep myself, the longer I live—in theory. In reality, the common cold could take me down. Though, I try not to dwell on that.

I don't even realize how much time Pasha and I have spent in the pool together until my stomach starts growling. I'll have to eat soon, which means getting away from my new friend so I can take my medicine without questions about what and why.

I have no shame about the everyday things I have to do to keep myself healthy. Managing my particular case of CF is relatively easy since I've been doing it for so long. It's also expensive and grueling. Hotties with Adonis bodies aren't usually the type to hang around and get involved with everything that goes into keeping me healthy.

Boring lawyers are the type for that.

"My work is done," Pasha says, nodding to the pool deck.

I twist to see Spiros, who had barely crossed my mind while I was hanging at the bar with Pasha, stand up and throw his towel over his shoulder.

"Well, hot damn!" I rap my hands against the bar a few times.

Pasha stands up. "I should find Panikos."

"Oh, yeah. I should go hang out with my friends, too." I catch my bottom lip with my teeth to stop myself from blurting out how much I want him to stay. Because saying things like that to a fake boyfriend is as ridiculous as going along with the charade in the first place.

Pasha and I wade to the stairs. I stop, remove my sunglasses, and lift my face to the sun.

Always take the time, no matter how brief, to stop and enjoy the moment when you're in it—that's one of my many self-help mantras.

As I slide my sunglasses back on, I catch Pasha's eyes on me.

"What did you do just then?" he asks, extending his hand to assist me on the stairs. Spiros is already gone, so his sweet gesture isn't for show. Maybe he likes me. Though, it's more likely another example of his exceptional manners.

"I stopped to appreciate the moment," I say.

"You do this often?"

"At least once a day." I inadvertently squeeze his hand as we walk.

Pasha stops next to Lena's chair, grabs my towel, and hands it to me before pulling his off his seat. He rubs his shorts and legs quickly.

"Thanks for saving me again," I say.

"Is fun to piss that guy off." Pasha smiles. "See you later?"

My heart flutters inside my chest as I nod.

"Bye, ladies." He throws his towel over one shoulder, winks at my friends, and walks away. Water drips off his swim trunks, leaving a trail of blotches across the ground. My friends and I stare at him until he's out of sight.

"Where's your boyfriend going?" Lena asks.

"Probably the weight room. He looks like he needs to lift more," I deadpan.

Sia frowns and glances over her shoulder to check Pasha out again. "He's not as jacked as Spiros."

The confused expression on Lena's face must have mirrored my own.

"What?" Sia asks. "Spiros has a nice body."

"If you like thick and flabby," Lena quips.

"Oh, come on," I interject, patting my legs with a towel. "He's not flabby. He's just smooth. There's no cut to define his muscles."

"Because he doesn't have any." Lena adjusts the brim of her floppy hat over her face.

"You're so mean." I turn my head to cough into my elbow, then wrap the towel around my hips and tuck the corner to secure it at my waist.

The way Spiros's body has transformed over the years reminds me of what happened with Anthony Michael Hall, who played the Geek in *Sixteen Candles*. When Spiros left for college, he had been a short, skinny teenager. But when he returned, he'd gained a healthy weight and shot up to a six-foot-four hulk, like Hall in his *Edward Scissorhands* days. It didn't make me any more attracted to Spiros, but the change was decidedly better than his geeky phase.

"Lunch?" Lena asks.

Sia and I agree.

"Come to my room after you drop your stuff off," I tell them. "I have to do a treatment before we eat."

We gather up our gear and leave the pool for our respective rooms. As much as I want to see Pasha again, I hope it isn't during our meal.

One of the significant health issues of people with cystic fibrosis is the buildup of mucus. The ducts in my pancreas, the part of the body where enzymes break up food before sending it to the small intestines, get clogged by all the excess mucus. Sometimes, this causes blockage in the small intestine, where food is digested. Every time I eat, I have to take enzymes to help my pancreas break down the food. Technically, it's only popping a few pills, but there's no point in explaining that to Pasha since I won't be around him for very long.

Any relationship built around withholding information and deception is a recipe for disaster.

Chapter Six

KRISTEN

"That thing creeps me out." Sia visibly shudders as she eyes my upper-body gear.

"Dorky and overprotective" would be my first thought if I saw someone sitting in an interior room on a cruise ship wearing a vest resembling a life jacket. But not creeped out.

My vest, with pink and purple flowers swirling over a teal background, couldn't be less scary. It's childish and cutesy because I've been rocking it since middle school. I have a newer, more sophisticated pattern at home, but I always bring this old one to travel.

"Good thing I'm done, then. I wouldn't want one of the treatments that keeps me alive to creep you out," I mutter.

I've just finished my vest therapy, also called chest wall oscillation. It's a treatment that helps me breathe better. It doesn't hurt. It's not freaky. It's a bit gross because it makes me hock loogies, but I can't think of many glamorous parts of living with a health disorder.

"Will you two please stop bickering?" Lena demands. "Kris needs to tell us more about the hot guy she met."

I press the clasps to undo the straps across my chest and shrug out of the vest. "It's not that big a deal. He saw how creepy Spiros acts around me and asked if I wanted him to be my fake boyfriend to get Spiros off my back."

Sia sits on the other bed. "Fake boyfriend? What does that even mean?" she asks.

"I don't know." I hang the vest over my compressor. "Someone to spend time with and prove to Spiros that I don't want to be with him. I want to pick my own partner. A guy with a personality."

"Spiros has a huge—" Sia stops mid-sentence, catching her bottom lip with her top teeth. "Wallet. He doesn't need a personality."

Lena grimaces. "Why would you want a fake boyfriend on a singles cruise? The whole point is to get to know all the unattached hotties Detroit's Greek Orthodox population has to offer."

"Maybe I don't want a nice Greek boy." I mimic my mother's accent as I deliver her favorite three words: "Nice Greek boy."

Both my cousin's and Sia's eyes widen as if I'd just bitten the head off a kitten.

Nom nom nom.

"Your parents are gonna be so pissed," Lena says. "You know they knew Spiros would be on this trip. They probably thought it would be a vacation for the two of you alone. Pre-wedding honeymoon planning."

I stand up and walk to the bathroom to brush my teeth. "You think?" I ask, glancing over my shoulder as I flip on the light.

Since early childhood, my parents have had this grand plan for me to marry Spiros Loukas, the son of my mother's best friend. My childhood photo albums overflow with pictures of Spiros and me as kids, learning to ride bikes, at each other's birthday parties, and on joint family vacations. There are probably as many pictures of Spiros and me as of my older brothers and me.

Because our families hung out so much while we were growing up, some people thought Spiros was one of my brothers. Or thought that I saw him that way.

He wasn't, and I didn't.

He was a dull, stuffy tool who used to pick his nose and eat it. Not my type at all.

It didn't help my case against him when Stuffy Spiros graduated from an Ivy League law school before moving back to Detroit for a job with one of the city's top law firms. And it certainly didn't help that he'd recently been named the newest—and youngest—partner at Manos, Manos, and (now) Loukas.

Why would my parents waste so much money on a cruise to push me into "falling in love" with Stuffy Spiros? It didn't make sense when they could do it at home for free.

"Come on, Kris! Don't play dumb. Of course, that's why they sent you on this cruise. I'm pretty sure your mom would marry Spiros herself if she could."

I hold up a finger, asking for a minute while I finish brushing. Then I turn off the light and join my friends again. "She can have him. He's not my type. He's boring and annoying, and there's no chemistry."

"He's cute, stable, and rich. Fuck chemistry," Lena counters.

Fuck chemistry? That's something people say about their high school class schedule, not about the person they marry. Chemistry is everything. Well, chemistry and the willingness to understand and support someone with a disorder like cystic fibrosis, with symptoms that could rear their ugly heads at any time.

"Take Spiros out of the equation," Sia finally pipes up. "Why would you want a fake boyfriend? What about all the other guys on this cruise? Don't you want to have fun?"

"I've been thinking of all the fun I could have with my fake boyfriend since the second I set eyes on him. The kind of fun I wouldn't have with multiple people on a seven-day cruise."

"Kristen Katsaros!" Sia exclaims.

"What?" I ask. "Did you see him at the pool? He oozes sex."

"Which is another reason to be concerned. He probably works his magic with a lot of girls," Lena warns.

I shrug. "My parents sent me on a singles cruise to find a boyfriend, right? I found one."

"A fake one," Sia interjects.

"Real, fake—who gives a shit?" I ask. "I refuse to have Spiros breathing down my neck the entire week. My parents wanted me to meet a single Greek guy to marry and pop out gorgeous Greek babies with. As far as they know, that's what I found. Everyone's happy. Especially me. Since he's funny and hot and has the body of Adonis in the flesh."

"At least it's believable." Lena rolls her eyes. "Because everyone knows all the hottest guys in the world flock to you, no matter where we are."

"Oh my gosh, you're such an idiot." Laughing makes me cough.

"What? It's true!" Lena ignores me and continues with her fish tale. "Anytime we go anywhere, you get the hot guy, and we get the wingmen." She removes her sunglasses from the top of her head and holds the lenses up to the light.

"A lot of hot guys have hot wingmen," I say, grabbing my beach bag and peering inside to ensure I have everything I need.

"That's true." Lena rubs her glasses against her bathing suit cover-up. "I've never gotten the raw end of any wingman deal. Remember Derek? He far surpassed Evan in hotness."

The hair on my arms stands up, a gut reaction upon hearing my ex-boyfriend's name, though it's been years since I've had any contact with him.

"Back to the fake boyfriend in question," Sia interrupts. "Does he live in Detroit?"

"Nope," I say. "He lives in Charlotte."

"Yanni and Helena will never go for that." She shakes her head.

"I think it's perfect. My parents are too overbearing and involved in my life. A fake long-distance relationship will keep them off my back."

"Not for long," Sia chirps. She stretches her long, tan legs and crosses them at the ankles.

"I know, I know. But Pasha's a pilot. He travels constantly. I'm sure he can swing a trip to Detroit for a quickie."

Lena jumps up. "Dude! Get ready to join the Mile High Club."

Joining the Motion on the Ocean Club has already been on my mind; I can't believe I haven't thought of doing it on a plane yet. Not while Pasha was at the helm, of course. I'd heard of autopilot, but would that feature really fly the aircraft if no one were paying attention?

I should ask.

"Your parents are still going to shove Spiros in your face. They're hell-bent on the two of you getting together. It's like they signed the arranged marriage papers with the Loukas family when you guys were kids," Lena says.

"Why are they so determined that it has to be Spiros?" Sia asks.

I shrug, feigning ignorance, though I know the answer. The Loukases are a well-known, respected family in the community—and they're wealthy. My parents aren't gold diggers, nor am I. But they *are* worried about me. They obsess about the future and who's going to take care of me. Cystic fibrosis takes a significant toll both emotionally and financially. Since Mom and Mrs. Loukas have been best friends for years, she trusts their family. In Mom's mind, Spiros equals security and stability.

"As long as you two don't snitch on me, this Pasha thing should buy me a little time. Thank God I'm out of the house."

After graduating from Central State, I'd moved back in with my parents for two weeks while waiting for my apartment to open up, and Mom had hounded me every day. Though, if you count the calls, texts, and drop-in visits to my new place, she still does.

"Are you really going to have sex with him?" Sia asks.

I shrug. "I don't know. I was joking." Sort of. Who wouldn't want to get naked and straddle a living god?

Lena squints, then shakes her head. "I don't like the look in your eye."

"What look? I've slept with two people in my life," I say. "Men find this thing super-sexy," I joke, patting the top of my compressor.

"I just think this is a bad idea." Lena replaces the sunglasses on her head, using them as a headband to hold her dark brown hair out of her eyes.

"It's becoming increasingly apparent why you guys hang out with me. I'm the positive one."

"He's not Greek," Lena warns.

"But he's hot," I counter, hooking my bag onto my shoulder.

"Super-hot," Lena agrees. "Spiros is gonna be pissed."

Cultural expectations still take precedence over love in our community. Despite living in the twenty-first century, my parents expect me to marry another Greek. Which is probably why they happily shelled out the money for this cruise. It seemed like a sure thing. Even if I didn't hook up with Spiros, hundreds of other young professional Greeks are here as fallback suitors.

Leave it to me to pick the black sheep in a sea of cyan and white. As if I didn't cause my parents enough stress.

"Spiros can find another girl who wants what he has to offer," Sia says.

"Exactly. I hope he does it soon because he won't like what he sees if he keeps lurking," I say.

Sia rolls her eyes, visibly disgusted that I'd even joke about hooking up with a guy I'd just met. I admit sleeping with a random guy wasn't something I'd planned before the cruise. But everything about Pasha intrigues me. Especially when his full pink lips lift into that sexy little smirk. My heart races just thinking about him.

I haven't felt this way about anyone in a long time.

THAT EVENING, as we walk the deck looking for a place to party, I stop and gaze out into the immense body of water surrounding the ship. An involuntary shiver ripples through my body—a not-so-subtle reminder of why I've avoided the ocean my entire life.

All I see is a dark, vast abyss that could swallow a person whole. It's a reminder of how I could feel about having Cystic Fibrosis if I let myself.

"Let's take a picture," Sia suggests.

"Sure," I agree, despite my fear. "I haven't done enough to document this trip yet."

"Good idea," Lena says. "We should stand in front of the rail and have the water behind us."

I take a deep breath, trying to ignore my cousin's suggestion to get closer to the edge—closer to falling to our watery deaths.

I pluck my phone from my wristlet and turn it to the camera setting. At least the camera works without having to pay the ship's ridiculous Internet rates.

Lena and Sia stand against the rail. I step in front of them.

"What are you doing?" Sia asks. "Get on the other side of Lena."

"Hell no. Trying to take a cute selfie is hard enough without the added pressure of falling over the rail as I lean back."

"Oh my gosh! It's not that bad," Lena says.

"Maybe you don't care about falling to your death, but I sure do. I can't swim well enough to stay afloat in creepy black water with who knows what kind of creatures circling below waiting to eat me."

Sia stares at me with wide eyes. Her lips, which had been turned up in a smile a second ago, have morphed into a thin line. "You're crazy, you know that?"

"I'm not getting near that rail. I'd rather be crazy than shark food."

Sia shakes her head and holds her hand out. "Give it to me."

"With pleasure." I relinquish the phone.

We cram together, and Sia extends her arm, expertly holding the phone in a grasp that leaves her thumb free to hit the shutter button. "One, two, three!"

My entire body slides into the practiced photo pose I rock every time someone holds up a camera—shoulders down, neck out, eyes wide, with a slight pucker and lift to my lips. I've had the same facial expression for every photo since I learned it during my modeling days in high school. If I'm really happy or laughing and not thinking about it, I end up with squinty eyes and too much teeth.

After the picture, I shudder and step away from the rail. Once I've gotten a few feet from it, I relax again.

"Let's take one more, just in case," Sia says.

I back up into my place and accidentally knock into her. The phone slips from her grasp and flies over the rail.

"Oh, no!" she howls.

I watch in wide-eyed horror as my phone plunges toward the ocean. My stomach drops with it. The deck is so far from the surface that I don't even hear a splash when it hits the water.

"Oh my God, Kristen. I'm so sorry," Sia says quickly. She looks over the rail, but the phone isn't visible. Obviously.

"It's—it's okay," I assure her. My heart drops, though I don't blame her at all. It was a complete accident. Thankfully, I'd backed up my phone and all the pictures before leaving for the cruise. Lena and Sia had taken a few photos of the ship as we stood waiting to board so I could get theirs later.

"I feel horrible." She peers over the rail again.

"It's okay, seriously. I mean, it sucks, but it happens." I pause, racking my brain to find something positive to say. "You guys will just have to follow me around snapping pictures like the paparazzi I deserve," I joke.

"Let's do it again," Lena says. She's already pulled her phone out, ready to re-create the shot.

I glance down at the water, mentally saying goodbye to the photos I'd miss out on because I didn't have a camera with me. I'll have to focus on making the kind of memories I'd remember even without capturing them.

Chapter Seven

PASHA

I EYE THE ENTRANCE TO THE LATIN DANCE CLUB BLAKE AND I CHOSE tonight, hoping Kristen and her friends walk in. I know the odds are low that she'd pick this particular club out of all the options on the ship, but I keep glancing over, just in case.

"Dude," Blake says after I've checked the door for the tenth time in two minutes, "I invited you on this cruise to help me get into the swing of dating again. I need you to be your usual love-'em-and-leave-'em self."

"What does this mean? I do not love any girls." I down a double shot of vodka and motion to the bartender for another.

"Hook up and walk away? I don't know the singles lingo. I was married for the last five years."

"You sound like an asshole. Women don't like assholes."

"Actually, they do. Or you wouldn't get any," Blake quips. Then he taps my arm with the back of his hand. "There's one for you, Gribsy."

I follow his gaze to a smokin' blonde with red lips, huge tits, and legs for days. Exactly the type of girl I'd be making a beeline for if I hadn't met Kristen earlier. "Time to wheel," I tell him.

"I'll save your spot."

"I was talking about you." I shove his shoulder. "Get over there."

Blake straightens up after almost falling off the chair when I'd pushed him. "She's not my type."

Blake Panikos is one of those guys who wants to be married. He likes dull women whose idea of a perfect night is snuggling and watching movies on the couch.

His ex-wife fit that mold. They'd been together since high school, and she moved with him when he was assigned to Detroit. With no friends around and no job to keep her occupied, she gave in to the loneliness that can come with being the partner of a hockey player.

I get it because being with a professional athlete is hard. We're gone most of the time. Even if we aren't traveling, we're at our home rink or one of the organization's various community or promotional events. It can be lonely.

That's why it takes a strong, independent woman with goals of her own to be with one. It makes sense that guys with an intense professional drive would be attracted to girls with the same.

Unless you're Blake. He wants the barefoot-and-pregnant girl who'll wait for him. Which is why his ex-wife cheated on him with their neighbor, the stable guy who was always around when she felt lonely and neglected.

"She doesn't have to be your type. It's just for the night," I remind him. Maybe I'm reminding myself.

"Is that why you keep checking the door looking for the girl from the pool?" he asks.

"Yep."

Kristen has everything I'm looking for and more. Beauty, body, fun: check, check, check. And she chirps better than some guys I've played against. Since sarcasm creeps into most of my sentences, having someone who gets it and can give it back is essential.

Blake takes a long pull on his beer and slams the bottle on the bar. "All right. I'm going over there."

I raise the new glass of vodka the bartender had set in front of me. "Go get her!"

He stands up, then sits back down. "Ya know, I'm just gonna wait for someone a little more low-maintenance. She's got a ton of makeup on, and I like girls who are a little more natural."

Blake isn't a chirper. He's a talker. And though I love the guy, sometimes he's annoying as fuck.

"Do you know how much I want to punch you?" I ask.

Blake lowers his head. "Yes."

"Good. Now go talk to someone because I'm going to dance."

Chapter Eight

KRISTEN

"LATIN DANCING?" SIA WHINES AS WE STAND IN THE DOORWAY OF one of the ship's many nightclubs. "Do we have to go here?"

"Yes," I whisper, closing my eyes and letting the music penetrate my ears. After spending my entire childhood in dance classes, I still get lost whenever I hear an infectious beat.

"Did you think Kristen would let us walk by this place without going in?" Lena asks. She knows my love affair with any dancing.

The room explodes with flashing lights, pulsing strobes, and glowing neon backdrops. Across the way, multiple people dance on a huge stage. A few at the front of the stage seem to be giving instructions. My limbs itch to get up there and help, but this is my vacation, so I fight the urge to teach and set my sights on the floor instead.

"They have a lesson going on up there." I point to the stage. "Why don't you try it?"

Sia purses her lips and shakes her head. "I'd rather watch you."

With a smile, I grab her hand and weave through the crowd to the dance floor, where I let the pulse of the music take over. Who can hear a Latin beat and not want to shake something? The compelling pull makes it impossible to stand still.

Though I knew it wouldn't be anything like the sultry Latin Fridays back home at Diablos in Royal Oak, I thought a Latin club on a cruise had promise. Within thirty minutes, I realize the dance floor holds far more people with Sia's skills than mine. Instead of expecting to find a partner who can keep up with me, I slip into instructor mode and teach Sia and Lena a simple salsa.

Tons of bodies bump, bounce, and gyrate around us. It's hard to loosen up and let the music take hold while trying to sidestep each predatory pelvis. I'd much rather groove with a guy who stays in his zone than someone who tries to grind every girl in the vicinity.

As I put weight on my back foot, rocking away from one particular creepy dude, someone catches my hand and tugs me forward into his hard chest.

What kind of guy had the audacity to grab me when I hadn't been giving off those vibes?

I press my palms against a soft black button-down shirt to brace myself. Pasha stands in front of me with an adorably arrogant smirk on his face. Instead of speaking, he holds his arms up in a formal dance position. Intrigued, I take his hands, and he immediately leads me in a succession of smooth salsa steps.

It isn't intricate choreography that only two dancers who have practiced together would know. It's a series of basic Latin dance steps. He leads, and I follow. But nobody else on the dance floor knows that. It probably looks like a scripted routine straight out of a musical to them.

And damn! Pasha can move.

Instead of keeping the typical position, he releases my right hand and steps closer to me. He places his hand on my waist while keeping his eyes locked with mine. His slight change in position makes the moves harder for me to complete since I'm accustomed to being led by a partner with a rigid form who leaves space between us. That's how I learned during my eight years of ballroom classes and competitions.

Pasha's steps are flawless as we float across the floor. I have to pay attention and count steps for the first time in years. Our intense eye contact and proximity make every seductive move a million times sexier.

A trickle of sweat rolls down my back as I heat up from the exercise and being so close to him. Every time he steps forward, our bodies are inches from mashing together. I've seen couples perform sexy salsa dancing in competitions and practices, but I've never participated. Probably because I've never been with a partner who had the effortless confidence Pasha has.

If I take my gaze from Pasha's, I'll lose my count, so I can't tell what the rest of the crowd is doing, but when hoots and claps thunder around us, I know we've gained an audience. The song morphs into another, and I finally close my eyes, breaking the intensity of his gaze. Pasha tugs me into his arms and hugs me.

"You surprise me." Despite our proximity, Pasha has to yell over the music.

His comment makes me laugh because he's the one who surprised me. Outside of the studio, I've never met another guy who was so good at Latin dancing.

"I would have never pegged you as a dancer." My breath is still heavy from the activity.

"Why?"

"You're bulky," I say, trying to think of the right word.

"What?" He pulls back as if I've insulted him.

"Sorry. I just meant you're bulkier than the partners I'm used to," I explain. "I've always danced with tall, slim dudes. None of them were as muscular as you."

Pasha's lips slide into an easy smile. Instead of responding in words, he places his hand on my waist and guides me into another step. This time, it's a merengue to match the sultry music, which is much easier to follow in the tight proximity he likes to hold me in. In fact, it's the perfect dance for the way he likes to hold me.

He takes another step closer, placing his leg between mine. He releases my grip and slides his hand against the back of my neck, pulling me close as we rock and step in time with the music. I swallow back the desire pulsing through me.

Dancing with this sexy stranger makes me feel like Cinderella. And, like the fairy tale, when the clock strikes midnight, I'll lose it all.

Chapter Nine

PASHA

KRISTEN STIFFENS IN MY ARMS, SO I STEP BACK TO GIVE HER SPACE. As soon as I release her, she begins coughing.

I watch with concern as she turns her head and hacks into her elbow. A tear trickles from the corner of her eyes, which sends me into action.

"Everything okay?" I ask, putting my hand on her shoulder when it appears the coughing fit subsides.

"Yeah." She nods, briefly closing her eyes and wiping sweat beads from her forehead. "I just need some water."

Without hesitation, I place a hand on her back and guide her to the bar. Relief rushes through me when I feel her breathing steady as we walk.

I order a double shot of vodka and a bottled water from the bartender. When he brings the water, I loosen the cap and hand it to Kristen.

"Thank you." She accepts the bottle and immediately takes a long sip. Then she places her hand on her chest and says, "Sorry about that."

"You sure you're okay?"

"Yeah." She nods and wipes the wetness away from the outer

corners of her eyes. "My allergies are kicking in on this boat. Must be the tiny rooms with no windows, eh?"

"Your room has no windows?" I ask.

When we booked the cruise, both Blake and I opted for suites. Mine has a balcony, which doesn't seem very safe, but the extra space makes me more comfortable. Being too confined reminds me of the one-bedroom flat I grew up in with my *babushka*, my parents, my sister, and Svetlana, who moved in with us when her parents died.

"Yours does?" Kristen asks, eyes wide with envy.

"You should come and see," I offer.

She tilts her head and puts a hand on her hip as if I'd asked something inappropriate. I hadn't meant it that way, but I wouldn't send her away if that's where her mind went.

"How do you know how to dance like that?" she asks, changing the subject.

"Years of lessons," I say, a bit wistfully. I haven't danced like I had tonight in years. Not since I was a teenager. Dark memories flood my head.

"You took dance lessons?" she blurts out.

I like how she says what she thinks without filtering herself. It makes me feel better because I do the same thing.

"My parents were competitive dancers," I explain. "Well, my mother was."

"Really?"

I tilt my head and smile. "You are surprised by this?"

"I am," she says. "It's not very common."

"Maybe not where you're from, but for me this is very common. Is a way of life for many people."

"Were *you* a competitive dancer?"

"No," I scoff. "I played sports. Which made my father angry."

"He wanted you to dance?" Her question encourages me to continue, so I do.

I hadn't planned on mentioning my father's disapproval of my decisions, but it slipped out because I feel comfortable talking to her.

Fuck it.

"He always pissed because I do not want to dance. He think I waste my talent." I sip my vodka, then smirk. "But I have other talents."

"More talents?" she asks. "Do tell."

I lean closer, placing my lips next to her ear, and whisper, "Come to my room. I will show you these talents." This time, I meant for the comment to come out exactly as inappropriate as it does.

"Really?" she asks. Her lips, plump and shiny with gloss, morph into a scowl. "You just ruined anything we had going."

"Ruined?" I ask. "You are angry with me for asking? I do not stop thinking about you since you knock me down on track."

She smiles, then catches her bottom lip in her teeth as if she shouldn't be happy about the compliment. In a sweet, shy voice, she asks, "You've been thinking about me?"

Holding the rest of her fingers down, I take her hand and raise her pinky. "I am wrapped."

Kristen laughs and snatches her hand back. "You're crazy."

"For you."

"You just met me. What's the attraction?"

"How can you ask me this?" I ask, stunned by her question.

She rolls her eyes. "Other than physical?"

Maybe I haven't been clear enough in showing her how much I like her. It's been years since I cared about someone. Years since I wanted to go caveman—toss a girl over my shoulder and take her back to my place to provide for her and keep her safe. Years since I said something more meaningful to a woman than telling her she was using too much teeth on my dick.

I reach out and skim the back of my fingers against her cheek while keeping eye contact. "You are beautiful," I say, sliding my fingertips to her temple. "And smart and funny." I let my fingers trail down her soft, warm skin to the middle of her chest and tap her collarbone gently. "But you have darkness underneath. Is intriguing."

She shivers under my touch. "Why would darkness intrigue you? Seems kinda messed up."

"Life is not rainbows and vodka." As soon as I speak, I regret the words. Why would I try to bring such a beautiful person with so much energy and light down to my level?

But Kristen isn't fazed by the melancholic direction in which I've turned the conversation. She sets her water bottle on the table and grabs my hand. "Nope. It's cruises and salsa dancing. So, let's go."

Her soft touch and enthusiastic spirit lure me back to the dance floor. The blood warms under my skin, and my head hums.

I don't deserve Kristen. She has too much integrity and too much life to be taken on the emotional roller coaster being with me would provide. Tonight, I'll enjoy her graceful body in my arms and the steady beat of her warm heart against my chest.

Before I cut her out of my life tomorrow.

Chapter Ten

KRISTEN

THE BLOOD DOESN'T COME OUT, THOUGH MY HUSBAND SCRUBS AND *scrubs. Everyday, he has to step over my body. He grabs a boy running toward me, pulling him into his arms before he tramples me.*

"Watch out for Mom," he says, hugging the tiny child to his chest, stroking our son's soft sable hair. He weeps silently, shaking as the boy squirms and wriggles free from his grasp.

"I have no mom. And you have no wife. She's not really there. And neither am I."

I'm on the floor, dying in a pool of blood, gasping for the air I'll never have again. There's my son, inside my womb in a sea of life-giving fluid, choking for air he'll never know.

I WAKE UP SWEATY, clammy, and terrified. Turning onto my side, I bring my knees to my chest and wrap my arms around them. The only light in my cold, dark interior room comes from the clock on the bedside table, which tells me I've only been asleep for an hour.

A version of the same dream has been waking me up sporadically for the last five years, ever since I realized I'd probably never get married or have kids. Sometimes, it comes out of the blue, but usually, it happens right around the time I meet someone I really like.

Even my subconscious reminds me to keep it light.

Keep it fun. Don't get real.

Instead of attempting to go back to sleep and chance going straight back into the dream, I climb out of bed and pull a blue and white striped sundress over my head.

The temperature in the boat's hallways is comfortably cool, but the trembling in my limbs doesn't fade when I step out of the elevator and into the warm, humid air on the pool deck. The dream's recurring theme spooks me because I always interpret it as a twisted glimpse into my future.

Lights and music blare from a bar still going strong, so I keep walking. I want to lie under the stars and relax, calm down, and challenge my brain so it will stop obsessing over fictional boys or babies.

Though the pool has closed for the night, I continue walking across the deck until I find the perfect lounge chair to sit on. I lean back, stretch my legs in front of me, and gaze at the infinite sky.

Constellations have always mesmerized me. I don't know their names, but the hunt for their shapes relaxes me and takes my mind off my random nightmares and bouts of insomnia.

Stargazing is my version of cloud-gazing. Some people find shapes in the clouds and create stories about them. I do the same with stars when I don't know what constellation I'm looking at. I'm not the most creative person in the world, but mentally connecting the glowing dots keeps my mind busy, especially on nights like this, when I'm woken up by nightmares that send me spiraling toward depression.

I saw one of those demotivational posters on social media that said, "When you wish upon a star, you're actually a few million years too late. That star is dead. Just like your dreams."

I looked it up because I'm the person who looks up everything before I pass it on. It's not true. The dead star thing, I mean. Sure, some are dead, but millions of stars are still active and alive, waiting for our silly wishes.

But even if the dead star thing were true, imagine having a life span as long as a star that's already dead. It's been there for thousands of years, and people on Earth can still see it thousands of years later. A dead star "lives" longer than a human.

I don't want to live as long as a dead star. I just want to grow old.

Yes, I *want* to grow old.

I want wrinkles and hip replacements and bladder issues. At least, I want to live long enough to experience those things. When I was a kid, I dreamed of white weddings and happily-ever-afters. I dreamed I'd grow old with someone, just like all of my friends, because my parents never talked about the shortened life expectancy that goes with a cystic fibrosis diagnosis.

Nope. I didn't know about that until my high school boyfriend. Who broke up with me because we had no future. Scratch that. *I* had no future, and he couldn't pursue a serious relationship with someone who would knowingly—not willingly or purposely, but knowingly—die.

I don't need to live as long as a dead star. I want to be the light someone will remember long after I'm gone.

I touch the cotton fabric covering the scar on my stomach. The scar from a surgery I had when I was eleven months old. The scar kids used to tease me about when I was young. The scar that reminds me not to let anyone get close because I can't let someone love me. Not when I know we'd only have a few years together before I left him widowed and our children motherless. I don't even know if I can have kids because I never let myself research it.

We're all dying every day. But I'm still going to die first.

I squeeze my eyes shut, calling on all the inner strength I've built up over the last twenty-two years of my life. I could go months and months without letting my mind get carried away analyzing all the bad things about being born with CF, so why would I let it rattle me in the middle of paradise?

"Is this seat taken?" Pasha's voice cuts through the thick, sad silence.

My eyes flash open, and I swallow back a yelp of surprise. "Nope." I pat the chair next to me. We have our pick of poolside seating at this time of night. "What are you doing up?"

"Is vacation." He collapses next to me, clutching an empty plastic cup. "Party time."

I point to the cup. "You're empty."

Pasha leans back and lifts his butt, straightening his legs and digging a hand into a pocket of his gray cargo shorts. He pulls out a small bottle of vodka. "Always prepared."

"You're like an alcoholic Boy Scout," I quip, though the reference seems to be lost on him.

He offers me the bottle. I accept it and prop myself on an elbow before unscrewing the cap. There isn't a smell, but the bottle itself is warm, and the thought of drinking body-temperature vodka makes me want to puke.

Instead of taking a swig, I replace the cap and hand it back to him. "I can't drink warm vodka."

"Warm. Cold. Up. Down. Life. Death." Pasha shrugs and takes a sip. "Doesn't matter."

"Truth." I lay back and resume gazing at the stars. He adjusts his chair so it flattens into a lying position like mine.

We sit in silence, two sets of eyes fixed on the sparkling stars above.

"Do you believe there's life out there?" I ask. My words come out in a whisper.

"Life? Yes. Death? No."

The intensity of his answer stuns me into silence. I'm not sure what to say. I don't know if he wants me to say anything.

Pasha continues, "When people die, they die. They are not up in sky, in this happy place with other dead people. They are nowhere. They are gone."

"They're always with us. No matter where you think they end up."

"You believe this?"

"Yes. If someone who died helped shape who you are, then yes. I have my mom's cheekbones and eyes and my dad's nose and hair. They'll always be part of me, even when they aren't on earth anymore."

"Are they dead?" Pasha turns to face me, his fingers gripping his plastic cup until it's crushed in the middle, and the rim forms an infinity symbol.

"No."

He turns his head and focuses on the stars again.

"Are *your* parents dead?" I ask.

He releases his death grip on the cup, causing it to bounce off his stomach and onto the chair. "Yes."

Chapter Eleven

PASHA

"Oh. Oh my gosh. I'm so sorry," Kristen says quickly, averting her eyes.

I sit still, listening to my heartbeat thrum in the silence between us before I speak.

"We go through this life in a hurry. When we are young, we want to grow up fast. We hope for what comes next. Go, go, go. All the time, yes?" I sigh. "What if there is no next thing? What if—" I clap my hands, the sharp sound slicing through the monotone of our conversation. "*Boom!* Everything gone."

She wants to speak—I can tell by the way she squeezes her eyes shut and swallows. "Just say it," I urge her. "I like when you speak out."

She takes a breath and opens her eyes. "True. At some point, we're all going to die. And it's not up to us. You have to live the best you can while you're here."

"I think I die happy if I am in you tonight."

I'd like to blame my comment on all the vodka I'd downed when we parted ways after dancing, but it has little to do with alcohol and everything to do with self-sabotage.

Kristen should hate me. I want her to hate me without having to admit I didn't tell her the truth.

She bolts upright, just as I expected. "Excuse me?"

"I speak English," I slur, but set my gaze on the stars instead of her because deep down, I don't want to offend her. "You understand me."

She doesn't speak. And I shouldn't have, either. I should have gotten up and left. But I can't let my final words to her be something sexist and degrading. Even if she hates me, I don't want to treat her that way.

"I'm sorry," I whisper. "I am rude."

That's where I should stop. Apologize, drag myself back to my fucking room, drink more vodka, and pass out.

Instead, I give in to the thoughts bouncing around in my head like runaway ping-pong balls and continue, "My mother was the most important person in my life. She only want best things for me."

I pick up my cup and toss it toward the garbage cans a few feet from our chairs. It misses. It misses so badly that I realize there's only one can to shoot at. Someone who hadn't consumed the amount of alcohol I have tonight probably would have known that.

"Sounds like you and your mom were close," Kristen says softly as if consoling a child. "I'm really sorry."

I sigh and sit up. "I wish I switch with her."

"What?" she asks. "What do you mean you wish you could switch with her? Why?"

"Why do I deserve this cruise—to be in the sun, to be happy—when she's dead?"

Kristen swivels to face me, then reaches over and grabs my hands. "Why don't you?"

"Fucked up. Arrogant. Selfish. This is what people think." Because that's what I show them.

"Who gives a flying fuck what people think? They don't know you. They don't know what a good person you are on the inside."

How can she say that? Out of all people, she should know I'm not a good person. She would know I wasn't a good person if I told her the truth.

I squeeze my eyes shut and shake my head. Then I open them and look at her, ready to confess everything . . . until she lets go of my hands, puts a palm on my cheek, and rubs her thumb along the skin under my eyes, where dark circles regularly form.

"You know what I see? A speckled golden rim around your pupil that spreads into the chocolate brown of your iris. Light reaching into the dark." She smiles at me as warmth radiates from her eyes and her hand. "I see hope."

Fuck the consequences. I want to spend the entire week doing everything I possibly can to make this angel happy.

"You were sweet enough to recognize I didn't want to be around Spiros and saved me from him, though I have no clue why." She laces her fingers through mine. "You have a good heart."

"Who are you?" I say, but her penetrating gaze doesn't let up.

"Kristen," she says, drawing it out as if she doesn't think I remember her name.

"Kristen. Yes." I drop my eyes and squeeze her hands. "The beautiful Greek goddess planted on this ship to torture me."

"Torture?" she asks, irritation coating the word.

"I want what I cannot have."

"You want me?" She lifts her head and moves closer, so close to the edge of the chair that she'll fall off if she moves another inch.

But I'd never let that happen. I'd never let anything bad happen to her.

Instead of answering with words, I drop to my knees before her and run my tongue over my lips. She slides her fingers into my hair and parts her legs, allowing me to move closer. Then I slip my hands under her dress, skimming my palms up the outside of her thighs as the fabric of her sundress gathers around my forearms.

Kristen clenches her fists and tugs my head back before leaning down and pressing her lips on mine. Her initiating the kiss is the permission I need to deepen it and dip my tongue into her mouth.

I tighten my grip on her thighs but remove my mouth from hers.

I'm not a good person. How could she be so insistent that I'm a good person when the fact that I'm here, in between her legs, is proof that I'm not?

I drop my head into her neck and kiss her shoulder. After placing several soft kisses against her skin, I lower my head and press my cheek into her lap.

"How you know I am good person? Why you say this?" My voice wavers. What could she possibly see in me after one day?

The lull of concern replaces the carnal energy radiating from her a moment ago. She strokes my hair, transferring her peace to me and alleviating my inner turmoil.

"I haven't seen anything different." She pauses. "But I guess I only see what you allow me to see."

"There are people—they do not let go of the past. They hold things against me even if I change. If they always think of me as this person, why try to be anything else?" I ask.

By people, I mean everyone. Unfortunately, I'd gained a reputation as an arrogant punk, which is what some old-school hockey commentators call me because I'm knowledgeable about the game and play with a pride they don't appreciate. I'm supposed to be humble and dull, like a good Canadian boy. But I am Russian—a new Russian. I'm confident because I can back it up.

I save the stoicism for my personal life. Not many people know me outside of the rink. With the exception of my close friends, I keep to myself.

"If you've changed for the better, you can't worry about those people. There's nothing you can do to convince them. If they can't get over how you were in a snapshot of your life, then screw them. You know who you are, and you're the one who has to live with yourself," she said.

I lift my head from Kristen's lap and gaze at her, blinking multiple times to focus on her beautiful face. Her kind, soft eyes take me back to my childhood when my mother looked at me that way. With kindness—and hope.

"Why you taste salty?" I ask.

"What?"

"Your skin tastes salty. Why is this?"

Silence sits thick in the air. She doesn't answer right away.

"The truth," I command when she still hasn't answered the question after an exceptionally lengthy pause.

She curls her finger and beckons me closer. Then she whispers, "I'm an alien from Planet Pickle disguised as a human."

"Planet Pickle? I have something from this planet as well." I move the hand that had been resting on her lap to cup my crotch.

No wonder I have a reputation for being a dick.

But Kristen isn't fazed by the crude gesture. In fact, she bursts out laughing. "Oh my gosh!" She pauses to scrutinize me. "Did you think that would offend me?"

Her reaction makes me laugh. Everything she does surprises me. I'm not used to a woman who wants to understand me. The women I'm used to want to know how much money I have in the bank. They want to know if I can take them to expensive dinners and get them into exclusive nightclubs.

Kristen is challenging, intelligent, and compassionate.

"I should be offended by your lie," I counter.

She runs a hand through my hair again. This time, her fingers linger, tracing lazy circles on my neck. "I should get to bed," she says, but she doesn't stop her soothing strokes. "Will you walk me back to my room?"

Reluctantly, I nod and stand up. After helping her get up from the lounge chair, I offer her my arm.

Perspiration dots my forehead as we stroll silently through the thick, humid air. We move together, our bodies in sync and our arms intertwined.

I can't take my eyes off Kristen. Her tanned skin seems to glow in the moonlight. She has the cutest, most perfect nose and gorgeous cheekbones. And those lips, full and pink and slightly parted as if ready to—

Fuck me!

It's been a perfect night. I opened up to this woman more than I have anyone in my life, and I can't stop thinking about her mouth on my dick.

She turns to face me and catches me checking her out. I smile. No reason to pretend I haven't been staring when I've been busted in the act. She blushes and casts her eyes toward the floor.

I know she's smiling. I can tell by the way the skin creases around her eyes.

I'm so enthralled with Kristen that I don't take a moment to check the path in front of us—and I slam into a wall.

"Fuck!" Tears spring to my eyes involuntarily as pain shoots through my face. I bring both hands to my nose, which took the brunt of the hit.

"Oh, shit!" Kristen exclaims, though I hear her laugh. "Are you okay?" She reaches out and touches my cheek.

I catch her hand before she can connect. "You laugh at me and then have the nerve to try to be nice?"

"I—" she begins.

But I'm not angry; I just want to tease her. She tried to hide her wicked side, but I caught her laughing at my absentmindedness, which makes me respect her even more.

Who wouldn't crack up if their friend walked into a wall? It's the kind of stuff that makes people YouTube sensations.

I wink at her before taking her in my arms and spinning her around to press her back against the wall I'd just banged into. She gasps, a mix of excitement and surprise. Then I set a soft, sweet kiss on her lips. She closes her eyes and falls into my arms, sinking into my chest like butter melting across my *babushka*'s freshly baked black bread.

"Would you like to hang out with me in Barbados tomorrow?" I ask, standing so still I can feel her heartbeat against my ribcage.

"I'd love to," she says without pulling out of my arms.

I place a kiss on top of her head, inhaling the floral scent of her hair products. Then I take her hand again and walk her to her room.

Though Kristen seems confident and carefree, I sense a sadness in her. I decide to make it my mission to figure out why and try to fix it— or at least make her feel as safe and strong as I could in the days we have together.

She'll need it for when she finds out the truth.

Chapter Twelve

KRISTEN

Day 2

"WE DOCK IN PARADISE TODAY. Have you rethought the fake boyfriend thing?" Lena asks as she shuts the door behind her. Instead of sitting in the chair, she leans her hip against the desk. "Sia and I will help you ditch Spiros. Then we can lie on the beach, go shopping, and enjoy this beautiful island together."

We just finished a quick breakfast, and we're collecting our things before we leave the ship for a full day in Barbados, the first stop on the cruise.

"I'm excited to hang out with Pasha. I can't wait to get my lips on him again."

"Again?" she asks, straightening.

Damn, I meant to keep that part to myself. To avoid her eyes, I dig around in my suitcase for today's swimsuit.

"You've already kissed him?" she presses.

"I had a nightmare and couldn't sleep." I glance at her quickly. "I went to the pool deck to lie under the stars, and he showed up."

"He could be a serial killer."

There's the pessimism I expected, which is why I hadn't planned on telling her about my surreal meet-up with Pasha last night.

"You need to stop listening to so many true crime podcasts," I say, tucking a section of hair behind my ear.

"Someone has to be realistic."

"That's not realistic. That's paranoid."

"I'm just saying that you shouldn't be alone with him," Lena continues. "Not until you get to know him better. It's called being smart."

She has a good point. "You're right," I agree, softening my gruff tone. "But I never expected to be alone with him last night. I didn't know he'd be there. Sorry."

"I'm not trying to sound like your mom or anything. I don't want you to get hurt." Lena stops, and her face seems to pale as she thinks. "Every once in a while, I come across an article about that girl who disappeared from a cruise ship. Everyone knows the Dutch guy did it, but there's not enough evidence, and they never found her body. It's just so—"

"You're right," I say again, interrupting her before she has a panic attack. Hell, I'm about to have one just thinking about that horrible case. "Next time I can't sleep, I'll wake you up. I must've been temporarily blinded by the moonlight bouncing off his pecs."

Lena is fun to hang out with, but I know she has anxiety issues. It makes me see her cautiousness in a different light, and I appreciate that she called me out for being stupid.

I let my guard down last night, fascinated by Pasha's unexpected vulnerability. The multiple sides I've seen of him over the last two days intrigues me. That, coupled with the fact that he wants to be my fake boyfriend for a week, seems like a scary combination. Hiding the realities of my life from him for a week won't be easy if we continue on the intense path we set last night.

"Why don't we all hang out together?" I grab my oversized beach bag from the back of a chair and move around the room, looking for everything I'll need for an entire day.

"Really?"

"We just made plans to explore the island. His friend Blake is coming. You guys should, too. Safety in numbers, right?" I toss a makeup pouch and a bottle of digestive enzymes into the bag. "Are my sunglasses behind you?"

Lena twists around, searching the desk. "Why do you want to spend all your time with him? I mean, I get it when Spiros is around, but otherwise, it's kinda weird." She hands me my sunglasses, and I fix them on my head.

"He's fun. And—I don't know—I like him."

"But it's only for a few days."

"Maybe that's why I enjoy hanging out with him. He's hot and fun, and I'll never see him after this week. Guys like Pasha aren't looking for commitment. I'm the perfect girl for a fling, and this is the perfect scenario."

"What does that mean?"

I toss my beach bag on the bed, slightly annoyed that I have to explain this to my cousin, who's seen me at my worst—many, many times. "No reason to fool some guy into a commitment with me when I'm just gonna die halfway into our life together. It's not like I can ever have anything long-term. Why mess up someone's life?"

Lena falls silent. And, not for the first time, I wish my best friend were on the cruise.

Auden wouldn't let me get away with any self-loathing bullshit. Not that I complain often, but between last night's nightmare and my cousin grilling me about my love life, I can't keep the anger of knowing I'll never have a happily-ever-after at bay.

You can't promise someone forever when you don't have forever to give.

"I thought you were the optimist of the group." Lena rises from the desk and puts her hand on the doorknob. "I'm going to go get my stuff ready and grab Sia. Can we still join you guys?"

"Of course."

After Lena closes the door behind her, I pause my packing.

I know I should apologize.

I know I should, but I won't. I don't understand why finding someone I like to hang out with on the cruise has her panties in such a twist. Why go on a singles cruise if you don't want to find someone to hook up with? Isn't that the point?

I close my eyes and take a deep breath before picking up my beach bag again and refocusing on the task at hand.

Because of my health issues, I always make sure to have my medicines and enzymes with me. I'd rather bring everything I might need because I want to enjoy Barbados for the short time we'll be on the island without having to run back to my room in the middle of the day. Thank goodness I have a huge beach bag.

Chapter Thirteen

PASHA

Barbados

"WHAT DO YOU LIKE TO DO?" I ask Kristen as we walk hand-in-hand toward the paradise of Barbados.

Instead of answering, she leans into me and laughs like whatever I said could've been used in an audition for *Comedy Club*, a TV show I used to watch in Russia. I play along with it because I figure Spiros must be lurking around, and I want to get that guy off her back—without introducing him to my fists, which are itching to meet his face.

Kristen brings out all these primal, instinctual urges in me. But there's only one primal urge on my mind at the moment, and it has nothing to do with Dough Boy.

"Adventure," she finally answers. "The more life-threatening, the better. But not like drugs. I don't do drugs."

"You are funny girl."

Kristen's body stiffens. She doesn't stop walking, but something is obviously bothering her. "Do you take drugs?" she asks.

"Yes."

She stops abruptly, which causes Spiros to run straight into us.

"Come on, Man," I snap. "Get off her back!"

Various ways to get rid of Kristen's tail race through my head. One quick, firm punch to the nose would probably take care of it. There's nothing intimidating about him.

"Sorry," he mumbles before shuffling into the large crowd.

I wrap an arm around Kristen, steering her away from him.

"I take medicine when I am sick," I explain, picking up our conversation before Dough Boy bumped us.

"Okay." A nervous laugh escapes her lips. "Well, if we're talking about medicines. I take a ton. I've probably got you beat."

"I raise you vodka. Lots of vodka." I wink.

"Another thing we have in common."

I squeeze her hand and pull her forward. "We find life-threatening, non-drug fun. Then we drink!"

"You only live once," she murmurs. Then she calls back to her friends, "Come on, girls. Pasha will lead us to the fun."

When I lead our group directly to the nearest bar, she says, "I thought we were drinking *after* the adventure."

"I must talk to someone to find adventure."

Once inside, I find an empty table and pull out a chair for Kristen. Then I kiss the top of her head and make my way to the bar.

In my extensive world travel, I've learned that the best way to find the most incredible places is to ask the locals. I slide between two barstools and ask the bartender if there's a place to go cliff diving.

Kristen asked for adventure, and I'm going to deliver.

He rubs the bar with a dingy towel, shaking his head in response to my question. Guess finding a place will be more difficult than I thought.

"Can I get three mimosas delivered to that table, please?" I turn around and point to Kristen and her friends' table. The bartender nods, and I hand him my credit card.

I glance at the friends whom she introduced earlier, Lena and Sia. Thankfully, they don't seem put off by stopping here first.

I survey the crowd before I choose who to approach next.

The thin, elderly black man sweeping under a table near the restrooms doesn't scream excitement, but most people in the bar are tourists from cruise ships, so I don't have many choices.

"Why would you want to jump off a cliff?" the skinny man asks after I state my request.

"Fun," I reply.

The man snorts and shakes his head. "There are better ways to die."

My shoulders inch toward my ears, and my hands tighten into fists for the second time that morning. I press my lips together to stop myself from spewing a disrespectful response at the stranger. His words are so insignificant, yet so grating.

"And there are much worse," I snap, annoyed at the old man.

He may think his trite comment is wisdom, an attempt to share years of experience with a young man. Some of us have already lived through lifetimes of experience.

The man scowls and backs away, muttering something in French. Though I know enough to get by in a few languages, my French is slim, so I can't even venture an educated guess at what he said.

Thankfully, just as I turn away from him, a waitress taps my shoulder and tells me the bartender sent her my way. She gives me the name of a hidden gem—a cliff few tourists know about. I thank her by slipping her cash before returning to the table.

"He's trying to find an adventure," Kristen explains as I approach the table.

"And I have," I announce. "We go cliff diving!"

"Cliff diving? Are you joking?" Sia's fingers tighten around her champagne flute.

I'd bet a mouse has more adventure in its tail than she has in her entire body.

"You don't have to dive. You can watch. Or sunbathe," Kristen suggests.

"Take video?" I offer.

"Fifty bucks says you won't even do it," Sia mumbles.

"Challenge accepted." Kristen holds out her hand and waits for her friend to shake it.

Instead of commenting on how fucking incredible this girl is, I nod to their glasses and say, "Drink up. Adventure awaits."

Chapter Fourteen

KRISTEN

DO NOT ADMIT YOUR FEAR, KRISTEN KATSAROS. FAKE IT UNTIL YOU *make it. It's not as bad as it seems.*

Oh my freakin' goodness. I cannot jump into that water.

An involuntary shiver racks my limbs, and adrenaline buzzes through my body, sending a tingle to every inch of skin as I peer over the cliff into the gorgeous greenish-blue water. It looks inviting and terrifying at the same time.

Maybe I talked too big a game when I told Pasha I was up for an adventure; the scarier, the better. In my boasting, I'd forgotten to mention my massive fear of water.

It took my parents more than fifteen years to convince me to go on a cruise. Even the lure of Mickey and Minnie and all the princesses in the universe couldn't get my seven-year-old ass onto a boat in the middle of the ocean when they'd tried to plan a Disney cruise.

But that was well before I realized I had a shorter life span than most of my peers. Before I started agreeing to anything, because—why not? I wasn't sick all the time. I wasn't bedridden. Nothing should keep me from experiencing everything life had to offer.

And I'm not about to admit my fear to the hot guy I'm trying to impress who asked me to go cliff diving. I'll close my eyes and hope for the best.

I unbutton my shorts and lower the zipper before shaking my hips and pulling them down my thighs. Then I twist around and toss the bottoms onto my bag, which lies at Lena's feet.

"Damn!" Pasha exclaims.

"Are you scared?" I ask, daring to peek over the cliff again. He can't back out. If he backs out, I back out.

"No. I watch you take these pants off."

"Funny." I slap his shoulder lightly, which makes him smile.

Pasha says what he thinks out loud for everyone to hear.

And that smile. That simple upward turn of his pink lips, sheepish and cocky at the same time, causes a flutter in my heart. It makes me want to jump him right here and now.

I've never had a boyfriend for longer than a month since the relationship disaster that ended an otherwise excellent high school career.

A week-long boyfriend is the perfect relationship for me. So why am I paying him so much attention and allowing emotions to get involved? I notice more than I should for this kind of experience.

My foot shakes as I take a tentative step toward the edge.

Pasha grabs my hand. "Together?"

It doesn't work when I close my eyes tight in an attempt to will the shiver away. My heart punches and kicks against my chest, trying its damnedest to let me know this is not a good idea.

Pasha lets go of me and places both hands on my face. I lift my lids and stare into his brown eyes. "Listen. We'll jump together. You will not let go until we hit water, yes?"

I nod. He releases my face and turns toward the water. Then he lifts his palm, offering it to me, and I take it.

"You guys ready?" Lena asks.

I turn my head and glance at her standing next to Sia, who has her phone raised, waiting for us to jump so she can videotape the madness.

"*Adin, dva*—" Pasha says.

I tap his hip with our joined hands. "Wait! What?"

"I count to three."

"Speak English!" My voice shakes. My heart jumps.

Pasha puts his forehead on mine and meets my gaze. "We do this together. We will be fine."

I nod and relax a little. He presses a quick kiss on my forehead before turning back to the water.

"On three. Ready?"

"Yep," I lie.

"One, two—three!"

We bend our knees and fling ourselves off the cliff with our hands locked together. I scream as my stomach drops like it does during the descent from the peak of a roller coaster.

We slam into the water, human bars of soap falling into a bath. The impact tears my hand from Pasha's. Instead of freaking out, I let the weight of my body take me down before getting my bearings and swimming to the surface.

When my head pops through, I push the heavy veil of hair out of my eyes and immediately scan the area for Pasha. He's treading water a few feet from me with wide, expectant eyes, waiting for my reaction.

"That was amazing!" I can't keep the smile off my face. I swim to him and wrap my arms around his neck. Without a second thought, I smash my lips on his. He can't stop treading since I'd affixed myself to his chest leech-style, but he doesn't seem to mind being the one who has to keep us afloat.

"We do this again?" he asks when I remove my lips from his.

"Yes!" I want to spend the rest of the day jumping off this cliff. With him.

He tilts his head, then claims my mouth. His tongue parts my lips and explores, tangling with mine. I tighten my arms around his neck, bringing his body closer, which is problematic since we're already inappropriately entwined.

"I thought you meant jump again." My lips brush his as I speak.

"I cannot think about nothing," Pasha says, his fingers skimming the swimsuit fabric against my hip, "but how I get this off." He pulls the elastic at the upper leg opening of my suit and lets it go.

An intense shiver sails through my body when the elastic smacks against the sensitive skin on my backside.

My loins scream, *Why couldn't we have been born in the time of free love? In the days when no one thought about protection or diseases or babies? Ugh!* But my brain screams, *At least pretend you're smarter than that! Idiot!*

Where the hell did 'loins' come from? Weirdo.

"Let's jump again." I let go of Pasha, treading on my own as I scan the water for the easiest place to climb out.

Chapter Fifteen

PASHA

I FOLLOW KRISTEN, PINCHING PLAYFULLY AT THE BACK OF HER KNEES as we swim. The closest place to exit the water is a massive patch of coral, but we would cut the hell out of our feet if we tried to climb it. When Kristen looks back at me for guidance, I gesture toward a sandy part of the shoreline. It would mean a longer walk back to the cliff, but it'd be well worth it.

"You did well," I say, taking her hand as we return to our friends.

"That was amazing. Absolutely amazing. I never thought I'd ever do something like that."

"You said you want life-threatening adventure. This is too much?"

She leans in and kisses my cheek quickly. "It was perfect. Thank you."

The desire that's been building up over the last two days comes to a head. I grab Kristen's waist and pull her down, landing first to give her a cushion to fall on. I hit the warm sand with a grunt, then laugh when her body weight falls onto my stomach.

"You are light. Like leaf," I tell her.

She splays her palms across my bare chest and lifts herself up. Her wet hair hangs around her face, the ends curling onto her fingers.

She pats my pecs. "Are all aviators this fit?"

"Most," I answer honestly. Though, she doesn't realize we aren't talking about the same kind of aviators.

My hands roam across her back, from her shoulder blades down to her butt, where I stop. Her bathing suit rode up in our fall, so I have a handful of soft skin. I clutch her firm cheeks and position her body so she can feel exactly how much I want her.

I don't move and don't try to push her into anything she isn't comfortable with. It's her decision to make. If she wants to continue, she'll make a move. If she doesn't, she won't. Simple as that.

I move my hands from her butt to her waist and seize her lips. She groans and grabs my hair with both hands, then grinds her torso into me. I lift my hips, pressing against her.

Innocent touches. Hungry kisses. Breathtaking friction.

Living life to the fullest.

Almost.

There's nothing in the world I want more than to fuck her. Right here, on a random beach in Barbados.

"We need a condom," she whispers between swift breaths. Then she takes my earlobe between her teeth and pulls.

We kick up shards of smashed seashells as we writhe around. I roll us over until she's on her back. Then I inch down and lower my head, pressing a kiss onto the fabric covering her belly button.

A million ideas race through my head, things I want to do to her, but all of that can wait for a more comfortable place. Instead, I slide my hands across her hips and down the outside of her thighs. Then I reach between us and slide two fingers into her bathing suit. Her stomach tightens, and she curls into me, so I add my thumb and circle on top of her suit.

"Pasha. Pasha. Pasha!" Kristen cries out, writhing next to me as I increase my speed, using my fingers and thumb to attack all of her senses at once.

I don't give a fuck if peeping tourists can see us. The only thing I care about is making her happy.

"WHAT TOOK YOU GUYS SO LONG?" Lena asks when we return to the top of the cliff.

No one else had jumped except Kristen and me. I figured that would be the case until we returned and gave a full report of the experience. But it ended up being a great thing because if someone had jumped in after us, we wouldn't have been able to enjoy a sexy, sandy hook-up. Not that we cared, I guess. It's not like we'd waited to see if anyone else had jumped.

"We didn't want to climb up the coral, so we walked all the way from the beach at the resort," Kristen said, reciting the answer she'd rehearsed on our walk back. I didn't rehearse anything because I wanted to tell everyone I'd made her come with my fingers in less than two minutes.

But I guess that's not something girls brag about.

"Yeah. That's it." Lena plucks at Kristen's head as we walk by.

She waves Lena's hand away. "What?"

"Must be seaweed," I say, grabbing her waist and pulling her into me. I slide my arms around her and kiss her neck.

"Dry, sandy seaweed? Looks more like beach grass," Lena teases.

"Who else is jumping?" Kristen asks.

Over the rest of the morning, Lena and Blake both jumped multiple times with Kristen and me while Sia caught everything on video.

"How much time do we have before we need to be back at the ship?" Kristen asks.

Sia glances at her cell phone. "About two hours."

"Let's find a place to get some drinks and appetizers," Blake suggests.

Because we hang out with our friends the rest of the day, Kristen and I never have another chance to be alone together. Lena has taken it upon herself to keep Kristen occupied so we can't slip away.

Despite her cousin's efforts to cool our connection, we can't keep our hands off each other, touching, hugging, and kissing at every chance.

Luckily, we're on the same page physically, and if we don't ditch the cock-blocks soon, the entire crew will be getting an eyeful.

Chapter Sixteen

PASHA

BY THE TIME WE GET BACK TO THE SHIP, THE SIMPLE ACT OF standing next to Kristen has me panting in anticipation for the moment we'll be alone again.

"Shower, change, and meet back here in an hour for dinner?" Lena asks her travel-agent mode in full swing.

"Sounds good," Sia answers, dropping her sunglasses in her bag.

Instead of letting Kristen answer, I grab her hand and tug her toward the elevators, away from our friends.

"I'm out," Blake says. "I'm gonna barf if I have to watch those two maul each other anymore today."

I should feel bad for leaving Blake because he's been counting on being my wingman on this cruise so he can find a girl.

Then I look at Kristen, and any thought of being a good friend completely slips my mind. As it should when a man is about to fuck a particularly hot girl. It's one of the first lessons in Bro Rules 101. Blake knows that.

"Where are you guys going?" Lena calls after us. "Are you going to meet us for dinner?"

Kristen turns around to respond but only has time to wave in reply, because I increase our speed. Once we reach the elevators, I grab her hips, slam her against the wall, and crush my lips on hers. The only time I let go is to press the up button.

Then my hands are on her again, slipping under the skirt thing she wrapped around her hips after cliff diving. When I squeeze her butt, her hips thrust toward me, making contact with the front of my shorts and everything underneath. She giggles softly, then bites her lip. I know she's holding back, so I don't press her, though I do like seeing her cheeks light up with excitement.

We only unhook ourselves long enough to get into the elevator, get off, and walk to my room. The simple journey takes longer than usual because I can't help but stop every three steps to press my lips on her neck or chest.

Once inside, Kristen surprises me by taking charge. She pushes the door shut and drops to her knees in front of me, hooking her fingertips under my waistband. My abs tighten from her touch.

Tons of girls I don't give a fuck about have had their mouths on my dick. I'm not proud of it, but that's what those girls were there for—a quick blow job that meant nothing.

Kristen is entirely different.

I grab her hair and jerk her head back. "Get off your knees."

But she doesn't.

Instead, she pushes the hair away from her face and lifts her eyes to me. Her lips curl into a seductive smile that makes my knees weak. When she takes my cock in her mouth, I let out a groan and loosen my grip on her hair. Her tongue presses against the bottom as she slides her mouth up and down, bringing me in as far as she can. Then she adds a hand, twisting and pulling with perfect pressure.

"Oh my god," I whisper, falling back against the door. As she continues, her pace gets frantic, and she starts with these sexy little moans. If she keeps this up, I'm going to come in her mouth, and I want to be inside her when I do that.

Reluctantly, I push her head back and take a few deep breaths. Our eyes are locked when she reaches up and wipes her mouth with the back of her hand.

"I need to be inside you," I say, helping her onto her feet. "Stay there," I command, leaving her just inside the entrance of my room.

I jog to the bathroom, flip on the light, and unzip my toiletry kit. I always have a condom or two with me.

I remove one and return to Kristen. She looks beautiful as the moonlight streaming through multiple windows in my suite gives her bronzed skin an angelic glow. Even after I turned out the bathroom light, I could see her standing near the doorway, her head held high, ready for whatever came next.

When I reach her, I don't touch her. Don't kiss her. I wait, holding the condom between us like a question.

"I don't believe in forever," I say.

It's a dickbag thing to tell her before I fuck her against the wall, but I like her too much to let her get attached.

She deserves better than forever with someone like me.

"Good. Because I don't have forever," she answers.

That's all it takes for me to shift from neutral to drive.

I claim her mouth, rattling the generic seascape print hanging beside our heads when I slam her back against the wall. She rises to her toes, lessening the difference between our heights and giving me easier access to her. Excitement fills me as I grab her waist and lift her up. She hitches both legs around my hips like a pro. I lower my head and press my mouth to her neck. Kissing, licking, biting.

When I flick my tongue against her neck, her eyes roll back, and her head drops to the side. Watching her enjoy the moment almost makes me blow my load. I work feverishly, tearing open the condom as she squeezes my hips to hang on. She pants, desperate with need, spurring me on.

But before I push into her, I have to know that she's sober and understands precisely what we're doing.

I look into her eyes. "Are you drunk?"

"I've had three drinks all day," she answers breathlessly.

Then she lowers her eyes to the space between our bodies, where I'm rolling the condom onto myself, and the sight of her watching me is so hot that I have to stop and squeeze my dick before I blow.

Once I secure the condom, I cup her chin with my free hand and lift her face to mine. Our eyes connect.

"Are you drunk?" I ask again, making sure my tone is sharp and serious.

Kristen doesn't blink. "No."

"Good. You will remember how I feel inside you."

That's when I reach between her legs and push her bathing suit aside before slamming into her. She buries her head in my neck and sinks her teeth into my shoulder.

Chapter Seventeen

KRISTEN

STILL SLICK AND SWEATY FROM A FANTASTIC ROUND OF WALL SEX, Pasha cups his hands under my butt and carries me to the bathroom. How the hell he still has the stamina and strength to walk, let alone hold my weight, is beyond me. I'm not even sure if I'll be able to stand when he puts me down, and my legs have been wrapped around him the entire time.

He lowers me to the floor carefully and twists the water on, allowing the shower to run until it's warm enough to step under. While we wait, Pasha yanks the tie at my waist, which holds up my sarong. Then he slides the straps of my bathing suit down my arms. He doesn't stop until the one-piece lays at my feet.

Pasha traces his index finger over the angry slash across my stomach. I wince and place my hand over his, though the pain isn't physical.

"Does it hurt?" he asks, concern flickering in his eyes.

"No."

After over twenty years, the scar has had plenty of time to heal. The act of showing it to someone is what's painful. I haven't been completely naked in front of a guy since my high school boyfriend, who knew where the scar came from. Since then, keeping clothes on was easier. Not having to explain the genetic disorder wreaking havoc on my body gave me enough reason not to take intimate situations too far.

Being naked in front of someone means much more than trusting him enough to have sex. Standing completely nude in the stark bathroom highlights everything I've worked so hard to keep hidden. My scar glows, and my bones show through my skin, side effects of a disease that barely lets me gain weight.

I try to make it a positive by keeping my body healthy. Yet, the first time I ever wore a bikini, I heard the hushed hateful comments from random girls about starving myself to be thin. I've worn a one-piece suit ever since.

Pasha lifts his hand and runs his palm over my hair and all the way to the middle of my back. My skin prickles with a mix of fear and embarrassment at his touch. He guides me into the shower and under the stream of hot water. Then he removes his swim trunks, steps in behind me, and closes the glass door.

My heart skips with the click. I want to flee. We stand toe-to-toe, snug in the limited space. Pasha puts his hands on my waist, and I freeze.

He's seen my scars. Touched my bones. The disgust of letting that happen swirls in my stomach, building up in my throat until I want to throw up. I try to turn away from him.

"What's wrong?" Pasha asks, holding my waist firmly.

"I don't want you to see—" I stop, light-headed from my fears and the steam filling up the small space. I wrap my arms around my abdomen, covering my scar. "I can't."

"You are beautiful, Kristen. Every inch."

Instead of continuing my escape, I burrow into him, pressing my forehead into his chest. The stream of water pelts my shoulders. Pasha removes his hands from my waist. The next time I feel them, they're in my hair, rubbing shampoo through soothingly. When he massages the top of my head and behind my ears like a pro at a salon, I look up. Creamy lather runs down his arms, but he doesn't stop working the shampoo into my hair.

Our eyes meet, and Pasha's lips turn up, flashing me a sexy smile. I close my eyes and wrap my arms around his waist. With our bodies meshed together, I feel every inch of him against every inch of me. He spins us slowly, so I'm standing under the stream. He tilts my head back and rinses the shampoo from my hair. Then he reaches over me and grabs another bottle from the shelf in the corner.

I can't help the giggle that escapes as he squeezes a dollop of high-end conditioner into his palm.

"You use better products than I do," I tease.

He sets the bottle back on the shelf and runs a hand over the patch of hair on top of his head, slicked back from the pounding stream of water. "This deserve the best."

Relaxation sets in as Pasha works the conditioner into my hair with soft, even strokes. Instead of rinsing me right away, he lets it sit while he washes and conditions his hair.

Showering with a European dude is a fantastic experience for my split ends.

After he finishes, I grab the red bottle of body wash off the shelf and squeeze some into my hands. I rub his chest, then turn him around and rub his back with long sweeping strokes like the masseuse I wanted to be when I started college. That was before I'd taken Anatomy and Physiology and withdrawn because I realized I'd never be able to remember the names of all the bones and muscles.

Rubbing Pasha's body makes me want to screw him again.

Pasha arches, informing me I've hit a spot where he needs a particular kink worked out. After he relaxes completely, I change my focus to his shoulders. He arches again when I reach around to "clean" his front. But I continue, the body wash acting as a lubricant as I slide my hand over him.

Pasha turns his head and growls, "I try to make this sweet."

I don't let up, increasing the pace of my hand instead. "You don't bring out my sweet side."

Pasha tenses and grabs my hand, bringing it to a complete halt while holding his breath. The water streams over his body, rinsing away most of the soap. As he exhales, he shuts off the water and guides me out of the shower.

He retrieves a towel from the rack next to the shower and hands it to me, then smacks my ass and commands, "Bed. Now."

When I hear the familiar zip of wherever he'd gotten that first condom, I grin and gather the towel around myself. I've barely made it to the bed before he tackles me onto the soft mattress.

Chapter Eighteen

KRISTEN

LATER THAT NIGHT, I ALLOW MYSELF A FEW MINUTES TO BASK IN THE calming sound of Pasha's deep, even breaths before I remove his arm from my waist and carefully inch out of the bed so I don't wake him.

If my ultimate goal is to live the most adventurous and fun life I can, my emphasis has to be on the "living" part. I refuse to veer from my very specific health routine—even on vacation. I can play off the enzymes I have to take with every meal as a digestion aid because that's exactly what they are, but I don't feel like explaining the rest of my regimen to a week-long boyfriend.

I hate leaving, though, because I feel safe and comfortable in Pasha's arms. Sure, the attraction had been purely physical at first, but after talking with him and being around him, it feels like we've known each other for years. Making friends and having conversations has never been a problem for me, but something about Pasha makes me want to spill all my secrets. He may have been intrigued by the sadness I was hiding, but I'm interested in the thrum of kindness he hides with his cocky demeanor.

I search his cabin for any items I brought that I haven't tucked into my beach bag already. Though still small, his room puts my interior shoebox to shame. He has an ocean view and space to move—or at least space to screw me against a wall. Maybe I'd have more space if I hadn't used one of the two twin beds as a suitcase rack.

After shoving my swimsuit and sarong in my bag, I slip on the shorts and tank top I'd worn the day before. I've almost finished when Pasha begins moving. I hold my breath and stand as still as a statue while he turns onto his back from his previous position on his side.

When he stills again, I tiptoe toward the door.

"You are good at leaving quietly." His voice thunders in the silent room.

"Thank you," I whisper.

Pasha sits up. A rectangle of light bounces on his bare chest as moonlight streams through the window. "You can stay."

"I have things to do."

I have things to do. I sound like a freaking gambling addict sneaking out to the twenty-four-hour casino.

"You need help?" He squints, tilting his head to the side as if trying to make out my reaction in the dark. His mouth isn't curved in the sexy, seductive smile he normally flashes me.

The concern on his face, mirrored by the rigidity in his entire body, makes me want to rip my heart in half and give him one side. But I can't explain why I have to leave, because I'm already looking forward to sharing another exciting experience with him at our next destination and don't want to scare him off.

"I'm okay."

"Are you?"

Why can't he treat me like a real fake boyfriend would and let me walk out?

"I thought you'd be relieved that I left on my own instead of making you do the awkward morning wake-up thing."

I know the reality of my future. I'm doing guys a solid by not allowing them to get too close. Bringing someone else in just to lose me doesn't make sense. I'd rather sacrifice my happiness than someone else's.

So, what the hell am I doing with Pasha? Leading him on. Letting him in. Sharing secrets.

"Morning sex is not awkward," he says.

His answer catches me off guard. He wants to sleep with me again? I thought for sure he'd bail after sex.

The chase is over.

"I have a—" How do I explain chest wall oscillation therapy at two in the morning? "I'm kind of a health freak. I have this weird routine I need to stick to."

"Men believe this?" he asks.

"Believe what?"

"When you sneak out in middle of night. They believe this is because you are health nut?"

"No one's ever woken up."

It's not a lie. I've never snuck out on a guy before. I've never stayed at a guy's place before. All of my previous dates have had specific end times. If sex was involved, it was "bang and bow out."

Pasha tosses the covers off and gets out of bed. He moves toward me, totally naked, like it's no big deal. "I am health nut, too. We run, yes?"

"It's not that kind of health thing." I lift my hand from the door-knob and rub the snarled hair at the back of my head, wondering if I should be flattered or scared by his concern.

"Did you take the drugs?" he asks.

"Excuse me?" I tighten the grip on my bag.

"You take drugs at lunch. And now you act sneaky at night."

"They aren't illegal drugs." I lift my chin, indignant at his accusa-tion. "And I can leave if I want."

He lifts one hand to my face and brushes the other through my hair. "You can do this, yes. I want to be sure you are okay."

I can't help the embarrassment—and desire—burning my cheeks. I've never hung out with a guy who walks around naked. And Pasha's body is magnificent in its nakedness.

"What makes you think I'm not?" I ask.

A fake boyfriend shouldn't be concerned. He should roll over and let me sneak out of his room with a shred of dignity.

He places his hands on each side of my jaw and tilts my face to his. "There is something."

I sigh. "Hang around me long enough, and you'll find out."

"This is my plan," Pasha says. Then he presses a soft kiss on my lips.

My fake boyfriend's legitimate concern hits me like Cupid's arrow through the heart.

"Go back to sleep. I'm fine. I don't take illegal drugs. I like to wake up in my own bed." I kiss his cheek.

"Because you are health nut?" he asks, humoring me.

"Yes."

I lower my eyes to his bare chest. Pasha has an athlete's physique, built and ripped without being massive. More like a soccer player than a football player. His arms are jacked and covered with ink.

A huge tiger tattoo shaded with bright, bold colors begins on his right shoulder, wraps around his entire bicep, and spans all the way to his elbow. Below that, his forearm holds more vibrant artwork. A candle with an extinguished flame catches my eye. Smoke billows from the wick and morphs into intricate black numerals just above his wrist —a date.

"If I ask about these health things, you will tell me the truth?" Pasha whispers.

I slide my palm over the gorgeous artwork across his forearm before stopping on the numbers. "Yes." I brush my fingertips over the date.

"Go to your bed. I will see you soon."

Without another word, I slip out the door. My heart thrashes against my chest as I shuffle to the elevator. I rub my face with both hands and take a few deep breaths. I've averted the immediate crisis, but I don't want to think about how close he's getting.

Pasha has me breaking all my self-imposed rules.

Chapter Nineteen

KRISTEN

*T*RAPPED.

Trapped in Pasha's arms. Trapped in these growing feelings for him. Trapped in a lie.

My alarm goes off, jolting me out of another anxious dream. My heart betrays my head when I glance down, hoping to find his body in bed beside me. I bite back disappointment, rubbing my eyes, as the harsh realization sets in. It's just me in the tiny twin bed in my cabin. Alone.

Suddenly, I'm hit by the reality of everything I have to do before getting off the boat when it docks at our day's destination at seven this morning.

I'd returned to my room after two, then tossed and turned for three hours, fretting over how to behave around a phony boyfriend I might be falling for, until the alarm sounded at five. I'm restless and exhausted, but I still have to fit in a twenty-minute compression session, my morning run, and breakfast.

In a sleepy haze, I lean over and blindly search my beach bag for my inhaler. Once I find it, I stumble out of bed and unlock the door on the off chance that Lena and Sia come by while I'm hooked up to my compressor.

As I begin my treatment, my thoughts wander to Pasha. I haven't been able to think of anything or anyone else since I met him.

I'd gone into this cruise feeling trapped because my parents wouldn't stop pushing me toward Spiros. Trapped because I felt overwhelmed after starting a new job with responsibilities I hadn't scratched the surface of before leaving.

But Pasha had trapped me in a different way. He consumes every conscious thought—awake and asleep. With him, I've all but forgotten about my stifling fear of being stuck on a boat in a large body of water. And I haven't thought about the new job or the increased pressure my parents put on me to be with Spiros.

All I can think about is how amazing it feels to have a sweet, adventurous, sexy man who's full of surprises and wants to be with me even after he'd seen my scars.

Oh, shit. He'd seen my scars. He touched them as he ran his hands along my bony rib cage and sunken stomach. A guy as fit and buff as he is couldn't possibly think I'm attractive after seeing that. He'll think I'm sick.

I punch the compressor's power button, taking out my anger on the poor machine. Time to stop wallowing. If he doesn't want to hang out with me anymore, he won't. There are a ton of guys on this cruise. Meeting them is the point, not settling down with the first one.

Ten minutes into my session, there's a loud knock on my door.

"Cooooommmmme iiiiiinnnnnnn," I call, having some fun with the help of the vest shaking my chest. And, I hope, freaking Sia out at the same time. It's the little things that amuse me.

The door opens, and Pasha's head pokes through. "You okay?" He slips into the room and closes the door behind him.

"What? Yes!" I reach over, fumbling to flip off the compressor while trying to unhook the latches at my stomach and chest. In my haste, I begin coughing, as a good girl using her vest should be doing because that's the whole purpose. But I don't want to hack up disgusting mucus with Pasha standing there staring at me like—

Like nothing.

Nothing in his expression shows surprise or repulsion or . . . anything.

After one particularly disgusting—but productive—hack, I lean over and spit into the garbage can at my feet.

"What are you doing here?" I ask. The heat of embarrassment sweeps through me, warming my cheeks.

"We run today, yes?"

I look at the clock on the nightstand next to my bed: 5:17 a.m.

Nightmare? Dream? Awake? Asleep?

What kind of warped universe has me trapped?

I should have realized that neither Lena nor Sia would ever be up this early, even if we planned to be off the ship by seven.

Since Pasha still doesn't look fazed, I nod to my machine. "I have ten minutes left."

"Cool." He bends at his waist and reaches toward his toes, bouncing slightly as he stretches.

Pasha might not be affected, but I sure am. Not only by him walking in on the part of my health routine I wanted to keep hidden but also by the horror of my current appearance. Hair tangled and twisted from hopping straight into bed after showering with him and a night of fitful sleep. I'm still dressed in my usual PJs, a hot pink tank top, and black boy-short underwear—though my tank top isn't visible with my vest strapped on.

To add to the horror of the embarrassing situation, Pasha walks over to the bed and stops directly in front of my oscillator. His eyes dart around as if trying to figure out how it works or what it does.

Here we go. Question time:

What is that?

What's wrong with you?

Shouldn't you disclose the fact that you're a sick freak before you screw a guy?

I'm *not* a sick freak, but I'm sure it looks that way to someone unfamiliar with oscillation treatments.

Instead of looking at him and facing the reality that the relationship hoax has come to an end, I lower my eyes, inspecting my sparkly pink manicure as I fumble to refasten the straps of my vest. There's no reason to stop my treatment now that I've been outed.

The mattress dips when Pasha sits next to me. I look at him out of the corner of my wide eyes as he laces his fingers with mine and sets our joined hands on his upper thigh. The vibration and noise aren't scary for me, like they might be for a child, but his grasp comforts me all the same.

And there are no words to explain the comfort of acceptance.

Ten minutes later, I stop the machine and spit into the trash can. I unstrap my vest and place it over my compressor.

"Run. Shower. Breakfast?" Pasha asks.

I nod, still in shock that he can see me as I am instead of a sick girl with a crazy shaking vest. I stand up to change into my running clothes but pause before heading to the bathroom because even if he doesn't have any questions, I do.

"You don't want to know about any of it? The machine? The medicine?" My pulse races, waiting for his response.

"Yes. But I wait until you are ready to tell me."

"Okay," I say, exhaling a breath of relief.

"I am better at the spitting than you," he says with a straight face, as if that's an obvious way to transition the conversation.

"Really?" I ask, both disgusted and indignant. "Because twenty-some years of spitting out junk kinda puts me in the professional rankings."

"I show you after we run."

"You're gross."

One of Pasha's eyebrows lifts, and his gaze flicks to the compressor, then back to me. A silent reminder that I'm the gross one.

"These look nice." He reaches out and grazes the black Lycra hugging my backside. His roving thumb skims the inside of my thigh and dips under the bottom hem of the fabric. His touch sends shivers through me. "They look better on floor."

I hook my thumbs inside the waistband at my hips and take a breath before lowering my underwear. Though he's already seen my scars, getting naked in front of him still makes me slightly self-conscious.

His eyes are wide, which means I've surprised him. Without speaking, I climb onto his lap. When I move to pull down the front of his shorts, he places his hand on mine, stopping me.

"Condom?" he asks.

Damn!

I shake my head, disappointed in myself for not thinking about something so important before trying to be a seductress. But I don't have much time to dwell on it because he grabs my waist, stands up, and then drops me onto the bed I sleep on. Then, he falls to his knees and pulls me to his mouth. When his tongue flicks against me, I arch up, grinding into him. He works faster, pushing one finger into me, then a second, as he sucks and bites. The sensations are so mind-blowing I can't keep still.

"Stop! Pasha! I can't!" I pant, grabbing his hair while writhing against his mouth.

He lifts his head and looks up at me. "Stop?"

"No." I shake my head.

He smiles, then kisses the inside of my thigh before descending again.

I'd never describe myself as sex-crazed before I met Pasha. I usually keep my dating life easy and casual, except for one guy I dated for about a month during my first year of college.

Though I'd had to explain a little about my life, I never went into much detail or let him see any of the maintenance. Kind of like a woman who puts on makeup before her husband gets out of bed so he never sees her without. I've always kept my disorder a secret from guys. It was easy because I'd never been with someone who wanted to screw 24/7.

Thankfully, my cruise-ship-boyfriend is all about being adventurous. He doesn't seem skeeved out at all when I want to get intimate after my treatment.

Is it a cultural difference? Are American guys that superficial? Okay, that's a horrible generalization of an entire country of men. Maybe it's just the guys I've dated. Then again, after Evan, I'd never given anyone the chance to accept everything that goes with being with me.

No one needs the stress of getting serious with a dying girl.

Chapter Twenty

KRISTEN

St. Lucia

"Zipline," Pasha says.

"Excuse me?"

"This is what we do today. Zipline."

I've been zip-lining multiple times, so the thought of doing it again doesn't scare me. And, hell, we've already jumped off a cliff into a random body of water I knew nothing about, so doing something that involves being harnessed and strapped seems like child's play at this point.

We sign up for the full tour, which consists of twelve runs, each starting at different heights. After we complete a training program, a short, bumpy bus ride takes us and the other zip-liners, mostly people in their retirement years, to the initial location. We'll walk to the rest.

Not to sound too cocky, but the combination of mostly older people on the tour and getting through the first run easily has me feeling fairly confident about my zip-lining skills.

"Completely safe, right?" I ask the instructor as he buckles me into the harness before the second run. It's surprisingly comfortable like a toddler's bucket seat on a swing set attached to a line hundreds of feet above the ground.

"Completely." He tugs a few cords to check the connection and pats my back. "Just watch out for trees."

"Zip-line instructors shouldn't be allowed to have a sense of humor," I mutter, grabbing the metal bar above my head with both hands.

Evidently, my previous zip-line experience, including the first run, had only been on baby lines. Because when I make the mistake of looking down into the lush green forests of tangled trees below, I almost lose my breakfast. My stomach drops. My heartbeat spikes. I remove one hand from the bar and place my palm on my forehead where warm, clammy skin greets me.

"Do you have water?" I ask. "I think I need water. Icy water."

"We have no water. Take a deep breath. You will be fine," the instructor assures me.

Next to me on the deck, a creaky laugh mixes with a deep guttural one, and I know instantly Pasha has charmed another zip-liner. A pang of silly jealousy hits me, not because I think he'll run away with the cute old lady, but because I want him to pay attention to me and my fear. Maybe grab my hand the way he had when he sat next to me during my treatment.

But before I can ask, the instructor pulls a cord and releases me into the air thirteen hundred feet above the ground.

The initial drop isn't as bad as I imagined, and as I sail along, the ride gets better and better. And it gets fan-fucking-tastic when I glimpse the ocean and the beach over the tree line. The sight is nothing short of magnificent. Despite my fears and worries, an intense warmth rushes through me.

My shortened life span always sits in the back of my mind, like the batter on deck in a baseball game. That's why participating in as many adrenaline-inducing situations as possible has been a personal goal throughout my life.

I need to figure out why Pasha does it, though. Wasn't flying a plane for a living, and the corresponding fear that goes with air travel, enough of a rush for him?

Then again, he chose to be a pilot, so the thought of the plane crashing to the ground in an explosion of fiery flames might not even run through his mind.

As I fly through the air, I push thoughts of dying out of my mind. This is the vacation of my lifetime, and I've met a gorgeous guy who enjoys the same things I do. I want to appreciate every minute we have together.

"You did very well," Pasha tells me as we trek hand-in-hand across a worn path through the woods to the next run.

The gorgeous glimpse of the ocean over the trees comes back to me. "That run was particularly amazing."

"But you were afraid, yes?"

"Who wouldn't be afraid?"

"Me."

"Bullshit." I kick a large rock to the side and watch it tumble down a tree-speckled hill.

"Why I need to be afraid?" he asks.

"Falling? Crashing?"

Pasha waves his hand, dismissing my comment. "You have straps. You will not fall."

"Frayed wires."

"You are not really adventurous girl, are you?" he asks.

"I am. I like to try new things. I've just never tried so many life-threatening things in such a short period of time."

"You drive car?"

"Of course."

"I am scared of being in car. More accidents happen there."

"That's true. I guess I never really thought about it."

"'Pasha die when he run into tree while he zip-line on beautiful island, with his beautiful girl.' Is good way, yes?"

His beautiful girl. He could've said "a beautiful girl" or just "beautiful girl." Instead, he claimed me as his, and it seeped straight into my heart.

"More glamorous than being killed in a car accident," I say.

Pasha immediately tenses and drops my hand. I glance at him, wondering what chord I've struck.

"You okay?" I ask.

"I tell you about my mother, yes? How she die?" His voice, which had a teasing tone before, is flat and dry.

"You told me she died, but you never said how."

Pasha raises his arm and lifts a sprawling tree branch out of the way before it smacks us in the face. "Car accident."

My stomach drops. Why did I make that stupid comment? I just took his car example and ran with it.

To say I don't know how to talk to people about tragedy is an understatement. It's not that I don't have sympathy; I do. It's one of those awkward situations where I don't know what to say. I have a significant knack for keeping it real and telling people how it is. No reason to beat about the bush. But death doesn't fall into that territory. A lot of people talk about death with finesse, a skill I don't have.

"Zip by trees is safer than road," Pasha supplies in my silence.

"I'm sorry." I grab his hand and squeeze it.

"She is my favorite person. She care about me. Not like anyone else." The pain in his heart flows through his words.

"What about your dad?" I ask.

"My father hate me," Pasha whispers. He clears his throat with a slight cough and adds, "This feeling is mine, too."

"Tell me about them."

Pasha stops and stares at me as if I've asked him to bite the head off a bird.

"I want to know you," I explain. "I want to understand you."

"I'm sorry. This is surprise. Not many people ask to know me." A soft, empty laugh escapes his lips. "I communicate better with my dick."

I roll my eyes and tug his hand, leading him forward so we don't fall behind the rest of the group. I don't press him to tell me about his parents. My direct question might have offended him.

"My father, he want me to dance, but I am not good dancer." Pasha must notice when I open my mouth to call bullshit because he continues. "I mean, I am *good*, but not good enough. He want me to compete. He point out everything I do wrong. He never stop telling me how bad I am. Never stop pounding this into my head." Pasha taps his head with a closed fist. "I do not joke about pounding."

I swallow back my disgust. Who could hit a kid? How was that a viable way to teach?

"All the time. Over and over," Pasha continues. "I try to make him happy, but is impossible. He make me hate dancing."

"That's horrible."

"Biggest asshole." Pasha spits onto the dirt path. "I am better at hockey. But he do not support. He tell me I hurt my mother's heart because I do not dance. So, I play hockey. I ignore him. And he keep telling me how bad I am."

I squeeze Pasha's hand again—a lame gesture of comfort, but it's all I have to give. I can't empathize. For as much as I complain about my overbearing parents, I've never had a bad relationship with them. Any disagreements or anger between us was brought on by what I considered typical teen angst.

"They die in car accident years ago. A bus turn the wrong way on busy road and smash into the car. No chance." Pasha doesn't take his eyes off the path ahead of us. "I tell you what is fucked up, yes?"

"Yes." I want him to open up with me. To share his secrets with me.

"I do not miss him. I do not care. My life is better without him." The wavering rasp in his low voice tells me he's trying to convince himself more than me.

Time to show my fake boyfriend my true colors. "You don't feel that way."

Pasha stops abruptly. "You do not know me. How you know what I feel?"

"You're angry. And grieving. We all say things we don't mean when we're grieving. It makes sense. You didn't have a chance to tell him how you feel, to make it right."

"You do not understand." Pasha dismisses me with a shake of his head. He begins walking at a much faster pace, and I have to jog to keep up.

"Then help me understand," I call. "Don't run away."

He stops and turns around. "No. You help *me* understand. Why you want all the crazy adventures?"

"You really want to know?" I ask. I take a deep breath before speaking again. "I want to go on all these adventures and enjoy every minute of my life because my body can barely fight off something as simple as a common cold, and it will probably kill me."

Chapter Twenty-One

PASHA

WHAT THE FUCK?

It only takes Kristen a few strides to catch up to me, but on that last step, her foot hits a dip in the path, and she falls forward.

Adrenaline shoots through me, and I'm desperate to catch her before she goes down. I reach out and grab her upper arms firmly. Though I've succeeded in saving her from a face full of gravel, her head smacks my chest, causing her neck to whip back.

"Jesus!"

I cradle her neck in my hand and pull her closer with my other arm. She closes her eyes, takes a deep breath, then opens them again.

I reach down and lift her chin, holding her eyes with an intense gaze. "Why you say this? That you will die of cold?"

"I thought we were getting super deep in the jungles of St. Lucia." Her attempted quip falls as flat as her voice is when she delivers it.

How can she even joke about something like that?

"This is the reason for the medicine? The shaking machine?" I ask.

She nods. "Look, I'm sorry. I wasn't trying to be a buzzkill or anything."

I slip my fingers into her hair and brush my thumb across her cheek. "A cold?"

"A cold," she confirms. "I have a genetic disorder called cystic fibrosis. I was born with it, and I've been managing it all my life. You can't catch it," she adds quickly, as if reassuring me. "Colds are hard for me to fight off. A simple cold usually turns into a lung infection, which is even harder to eliminate. I've been in the hospital so many times, my favorite nurse keeps one of my blankets in her locker so it will always be there for me."

The luster that's been present in her deep brown eyes since the moment we met disappears, extinguished as she shares the shocking reality of her future.

Every word she delivers cuts like a knife to the abdomen.

My life hasn't been easy. As a child, I saw my father beat my mother until her face was nearly unrecognizable. As a teenager, I'd seen people murdered in the streets of Moscow. I identified my parents' bodies after the gruesome car crash that took their lives.

Even more recently, I volunteered in the children's ward of St. Christopher Hospital four days a week, every week that I've lived in Detroit. I spent the most time with the kids who were the worst off because I thought I could have the most significant effect on them.

I knew tragedy. I knew pain.

Or I *thought* I knew pain until this beautiful, bright being in front of me told me that a fucking cold could take her out of this world. It's not fair.

"You have been close to death?" I can't stop the morbid question. I need to know exactly what she's dealing with. I need to know how I can help ease her pain, her fear.

"Have I been close to death?" she repeats. "Probably. I don't think my parents tell me how bad it is when I'm in the hospital. They have a habit of sheltering me from the worst news. And I let them do it because I don't want to know. I never want to wake up in a hospital and find them standing over my bed sobbing because they know it's the end. They've always focused on the fact that I'm alive."

I open my mouth but can't speak, choosing instead to continue the soft caress of my thumb against her cheek.

"Your turn." Kristen covers my hand with hers. "What's your story? Your *real* story?"

Real? Interesting word choice.

"I wish him dead," I say after a pause. "I wish him dead many times. My own father."

She bites her lip but doesn't speak, so I continue.

"He yell at Mama all the time. Always mean. She not thin enough, her steps are not fast enough or good enough. No one good enough for *the great Artem*." I deliver my father's name as if introducing the leading performer at a carnival, the way Irina and I always did as kids to mock him. Out of earshot, of course, or we'd also get beaten. I shake my head at the memories.

I drop my hand from her face and step back, chastising myself for touching her while talking about him.

I'm not like him. I'll never be like him. If I say it enough, maybe I'll convince myself someday.

But what if I am?

"He hit her. Break her nose. Strangle her. Push her down on icy roads. But not in front of people he know. Never." I pause, trying to remember the words in English to explain. "My father manipulate. He know he have image to show people. He fake love and passion when they dance, but after competitions he tell Mama she ruin him. We are afraid of this man. He is different person after competition.

"But one day, I am eleven, he hit her so hard she fall and hit her head on kitchen table. Mama lay on the floor with blood coming out of her head. I am so angry and scared. All this rage in me, it comes out, and I hit him." My chest tightens as I conjure memories of that first fight with my father. I run a hand across the stubble on my cheek and chin. "He punch me back—so hard. He break my jaw, but I do not care. From this moment, when he raise his voice to Mama or my sister, Irina, I challenge him."

"Oh my god," Kristen says through an exhale. Her lips twist, and I know what she wants to ask before she opens her mouth.

"How could your mom stay with him?" she asks. "How could she keep you and your sister in that environment?"

"Is different in my country, Kristen," I say. How do I even begin to explain such a completely different culture to her? Nothing I say will make her understand that world. "When I fight my father—this is not common. Mama is angry at me. She do not want me to do this for her, because my father will not change. He is more angry. Everything I do make him angry."

Every decision I made. Every word out of my mouth. Hell, my presence alone provoked him. And after his career ended, my father took his disappointment and misery out on the people closest to him.

"I'm sorry." Kristen reaches out and takes my hand. I don't pull away from her, just look at our joined hands with sadness.

"My mother, she is good person. She love us. She send me to Canada to live with my aunt and uncle. I stay one year, learn better English. But I go back, because I must protect her. What son let his mother be alone with this man? These fights, they are normal. He will not touch Mama when I am there." I lift my eyes to Kristen's. "Better me than her."

She squeezes my hand, though I know by her silence and wide eyes that I've horrified her with my story.

"I wish him dead, but I do not wish for her to die with him." Tears cloud my vision, but I'll never let them fall. "I lose everything when I lose her. My mind. My heart. I lose my ability to give a fuck about anyone. Why bring more pain?"

"You have your entire life ahead of you," she pleads, squeezing my hands. "Your past doesn't define you."

I've never opened up to anyone about my past. Not a teammate. Not a girlfriend. The only people I spoke to were the women in my family who experienced my father's wrath: my *babushka*, Mama, Irina, and Svetlana. Only those women for whom I would give my life have seen me this vulnerable, this broken.

And now Kristen.

I shake out of her grip and place my hands on her cheeks, holding her face an inch from mine, imploring her to understand. She blinks once, but her gaze holds firm. She doesn't look away.

"I will not be him," I whisper. "I do not hurt people I love most. I *will* not. So, I choose no love."

Tears spring to her eyes. "You—"

"Come along, lovebirds!" Our zip line guide interrupts Kristin's response by calling out to us from a distance.

With the trance broken, I release her face and step back to regain my composure. Then I grab her hand again and lead her back to the group gathered at the start of our next run.

OUR ZIP-LINING experience was definitely more refreshing and exhilarating than death-defying. At the last run, two lines were set up side-by-side. Kristen and I sailed over the trees together. I couldn't hold her hand for safety reasons, but sharing the last leg of the journey together felt like we sealed an invisible bond.

I can't believe I shared the most intense details of my life after just a few days of knowing her. We've allowed each other access to the deepest, darkest secrets we've kept locked away.

Except one. Because I still haven't admitted who I am.

During the bumpy bus ride back, Kristen lays her head on my shoulder and snuggles close. I wrap my arm around her and rest my cheek on her head. Every dip and pothole brings us closer, literally. I can't stand the thought of her being jostled around in her fragile state, so I tighten my grip—a human seatbelt, pulling her deeper into me. Into my body. Into my soul.

If I can prove to her that I'm a good person, maybe she'll be able to look past the part where I didn't reveal my identity up front.

Instead of worrying about what will happen when we part ways— when she finds out the truth—I think about Kristen's motto: Allow yourself to slip into the moment and just enjoy.

I nuzzle her hair again, soaking up the warmth of her body . . . and her heart.

Chapter Twenty-Two

KRISTEN

"I'M STARVING," I TELL PASHA, PLACING A HAND ON MY GRUMBLING stomach as we shuffle single file through the aisle of the tour bus.

"Let's get food." He takes my hand, assisting me as I jump to the ground.

My throat itches, irritated by the dust and dirt the passengers kick up when they get off the bus. "Need to find my girls first. Lena has my bag," I explain.

Lena took my bag to the beach while Pasha and I went zip-lining. Though I *want* to find our friends and have lunch with them, in this case, I need to find them because I can't eat without the pancreatic enzymes I keep in my bag.

Though the beach is crowded, Lena and Sia are easy to locate because Blake is standing on one leg, toes digging into the sand, with his other leg lifted and curled at the knee. He holds the foot behind his back with his hand in what looks like a yoga pose.

It must be a great story because the animation in his voice has his body wavering, though he still keeps his balance. Then Lena says something I can't hear, and Blake bursts out laughing and falls out of his pose.

"You look like drunk bird," Pasha says when we reach them.

"Oh, good, because I was telling the drunk bird story," Blake quips. He drops onto a resort-issued blue and white striped towel and picks up a plastic cup.

"How was zip-lining?" Lena asks.

"So amazing." I kneel next to her, sinking into the warm sand. "Seriously. It felt like we were flying."

"How close was it to flying?" Lena asks Pasha.

"Why are you asking him? I'm the bird here," Blake says with a laugh.

Lena lifts the brim of the floppy straw hat covering her eyes to look at Blake. "I'm asking the pro."

"You're a pro at zip-lining?" Blake asks Pasha. "I didn't know." He tips back his beer.

"At flying," Lena explains. "I thought you two knew each other from work."

"We do," Pasha says quickly. "But Blake is not pilot. He is more, how you say it? Flight waitress?"

"Fuck you." The muscles in Blake's upper arms tighten as he crushes his plastic cup with one hand and throws it at Pasha, who bats it away with a laugh. "Don't you call yourself a Monarch now?"

Monarch? I wonder if that's a type of plane. I make a mental note to ask him later.

Pasha scowls at him and addresses Lena. "Being pilot is like being anywhere in plane. Is not like we walk on wings with wind in the hair."

"You don't have the wind in your hair because you don't have flow." Blake rubs his dark, shaggy hair.

Pasha whips his head around and shoots Blake another sharp look.

Are hair jokes off-limits?

Maybe Pasha recently had a hair catastrophe that forced him to get an unwanted cut. He hadn't been snippy with me during our joint shower when I mentioned how he used better hair products than I did. But then again, I followed it up with a hand job, so maybe he let the teasing roll off his shoulders. He seems like a guy who'd be super-intense about his perfectly coiffed hair.

"You guys better be ready to eat, because I'm about to gnaw my own arm off," Blake says.

"Yep. Let's go." I grab my beach bag from behind Lena's chair and sling the straps over my shoulder.

Pasha slides an arm around my waist, pulling me close as we wait for our friends to pack their things. I place my hands on his chest and rise on my toes to kiss his lips softly. He smiles and wraps his arms around me like we've been doing this for years.

Chapter Twenty-Three

PASHA

"It always amazes me that you can eat so much and still look like you do," Sia says to Kristen, her face filled with utter disgust.

Instead of reacting, Kristen shrugs and takes a gigantic bite of a double bacon cheeseburger that's bigger than her head. "All the fresh air from zip-lining made me hungry."

Sia opens her mouth to say something, but I prevent her from making another ignorant comment by launching into the story of our exhilarating experience. My timing isn't perfect, but it shut Sia up and got her off Kristen's back.

Suddenly, Kristen drops her burger and reaches around for her bag. She digs around in it, frantically searching for something.

"Shit," she mumbles.

"You okay?" I ask, placing a hand on her knee and leaning closer.

"Yeah." She shoots me a quick, appreciative smile. "Just can't find my medicine."

Lena, seated on Kristen's other side, peers into her bag. "Did you pack it?"

"I always pack it," she answers without looking up.

Panic flashes in her eyes as she begins removing things from her bag. She's removed a scarf, a wallet, and a bottle of sunscreen from her bottomless beach bag but still doesn't seem to have found the item she needs.

"Shit," she says again.

I squeeze her knee. "What's wrong?"

"I forgot my enzymes," she says, though she seems lost in thought.

"What can I do?"

She smiles, lifts her hand, and touches my cheek. "Nothing. I'm good."

"Is everything okay?" Blake's eyes shift from me to Kristen. His puzzled expression reminds me of someone looking at a monster with three heads coming out of one body. Which annoys the fuck out of me, but I cut him some slack because he doesn't know what Kristen has to deal with.

"Yeah," she assures him. "Don't worry about it, guys. It'll be fine."

Kristen rises from her seat and takes her beach bag off the back of the chair. "Excuse me, but I'm gonna return to the ship and get my medicine. Relax in the air-conditioning for a bit."

When she opens a small purse, I stand quickly and put my hand over hers. Then I pull out my wallet, and hand Blake a few bills, saying, "For our lunch."

Blake nods.

"What are you doing?" Kristen asks me. "Stay and finish eating."

I dismiss her with a shake of my head. "I'll go with you."

"No!" she exclaims, her eyes wide as she shakes her head.

I step back, confused at her vehement refusal to let me help.

"Thank you," she says, squeezing my hand. "I'll be fine, I promise." Then, she addresses the rest of our friends. "See you guys back on the ship."

Lena whispers something to Blake about stomach issues. He doesn't know Kristen has cystic fibrosis, nor do I think he would know what that meant even if he did. I appreciate that Lena respects Kristen's privacy by not telling a stranger about her personal business.

"What are you doing?" Kristen asks without turning around.

"I go with you," I say, quickly matching her strides to catch up.

"Seriously, Pasha, I'm fine. This has happened a ton of times. It's part of my life."

Instead of responding, I take her hand and lace my fingers through hers as we head toward the ship together. I made myself a part of her life for this week, and if she's in distress, I'll be at her side.

A few seconds later, Kristen grabs her stomach and doubles over.

Panic tears through me, but I rein it in because I'm here to help her with whatever she needs. I place a hand on her back. "What can I do?"

"Nothing. I—"

She tries to look at me, but something stops her, and instead, she winces. She grabs my shoulder, trying to use me to bring herself into a standing position.

I can't bear to see her in so much pain, so I scoop her up and secure her in my arms, crossing-the-threshold style. I pick up her beach bag which fell to the ground when she doubled over. After swinging it over my shoulder, I carry her until we reach the ship.

I dig into Kristen's bag for her cruise card, which we use to identify ourselves as passengers, and flash it as we board. I bring her to her room, unlock the door, and carry her to the bed.

"Can I get you anything?" I ask, leaning over her. Concern tears my insides apart. I don't know how to help, only that I will.

"Can you check the counter for a pink pill bottle?" She points toward the bathroom.

I do as she asks immediately, grabbing the bright pink bottle off the counter and returning to her side. "These?" I hold it up for confirmation.

Her cheeks, usually so bright, have a pale green tinge, but she nods and reaches out. "Thank you."

"I will stay? This is okay, yes?" I ask.

The last thing I want to do is leave her in pain, but the decision is hers. I understand stubborn independence better than anyone.

No." She shakes her head, confirming the answer I knew she'd give. "But I truly appreciate you helping me. I feel bad that you had to leave the group."

I watch with an equal mix of concern and interest as she empties a few pills into her hand and tosses them into her mouth, washing them down with a swig of water from the bottle on her bedside table.

"Enzymes," she explains before I ask. "They help my body digest food. I'm supposed to take them before I eat, but—" She takes a deep breath and clutches her stomach with one hand. Then she sits up and tries to get off the bed. "I forgot."

I put my hand on her shoulder, gently letting her know I'm here to help. I hate seeing her in pain. I have to do something. "What do you need? I will get this."

"I need antacids. I have some in the sparkly pink bag on the bathroom counter."

"Lie down," I command before leaving her side to retrieve the bag. I set it next to her on the bed. "Is not my place to look in this."

"Thank you." She quickly finds the antacids and pops a few.

Curious, I pick up the pink bottle filled with enzymes and inspect it. "You must take this when you eat?"

"Yep." Her halfhearted smile tells me she's tired. If I had to do everything she needs to do to be healthy, I'd be exhausted, too.

"Every time?"

"Even snacks," she confirms.

"Is bullshit." I set the bottle back on the nightstand.

Why should someone as amazing as her have to suffer that kind of pain just for eating a meal? Why should someone who made everyone around her happy have to go through so many things just to stay alive for who knows how many more years? How did she deserve that kind of life?

Kristen laughs. "Complete bullshit," she agrees. "But they're a necessity so that I don't end up like this every time I eat something." She rubs her stomach as if that will help the medicine kick in sooner.

She's too nice to say it, but she wants me to stop asking questions —and leave. I can tell by the way she keeps shooting glances at the door. Color has crept back into her cheeks, bringing them back to life.

"Thank you so much for all your help, but you don't have to stay with me," she finally says.

"You are sure?"

"Yes. I'll be fine. I swear, this is common." She pauses. "And if you stay much longer, I'll be mortified. Can you please spare me some dignity?"

I brush the hair off her forehead and feel the thin line of sweat at her hairline. "It does not feel right to leave you."

"Please?" she asks. This time, it's a plea.

"I am room six-forty-two. You will call, yes?"

"Thank you. I'll call you as soon as I feel better."

"You will," I tell her. "Or I will pound this door until we dock."

"I promise." Her tight smile morphs into a grimace, and I know the pain has come on again. "Please?" she croaks.

Every instinct tells me I must stay and help, but I respect her enough to heed her request. I back away slowly and close the door softly behind me.

It kills me to walk away because whatever is happening has her in so much pain. I have to trust that she'd let me help if there was anything I could do.

Instead of going to my room, I slide down the wall next to her door and plant myself there. If I hear anything—a scream, moan, any sign of distress—I'll pound on that door until I bust through. I refuse to leave her.

She'll just have to deal with it.

"Sir! *Señor!*"

When I open my eyes, a short, dark-haired man is standing over me, shaking my shoulder, waking me from the unexpected nap I'd taken.

I pull my phone out of my pocket and check the time: 4:57 a.m.

"Is this your room, Sir? You forget key?"

Lying crosses my mind, but I realize Kristen might not appreciate me barging into her room. So, I chose to respect her wishes.

"No." I shake my head. The man gives me a curious look, so I add, "It's a friend. She was sick, so I . . ." *Fuck it.*

I get up and stretch my arms over my head. Then I press my ear to Kristen's door, listening for signs she's awake.

"She okay?" the man asks.

"I hope so," I tell him. "You have paper? Pen?" I mimic writing on my palm in case he doesn't understand.

He holds his thumb to his ear and extends his pinky to his mouth —a makeshift telephone. "You call, okay? You call her?"

I nod. She'll be getting up to run soon, but it's not quite time, and I don't want to wake her.

The man, who I realize now is an employee of the ship because he's wearing a uniform, still hasn't left my side. It occurs to me that he probably thinks I'm some crazy piece of shit waiting to attack a woman when she opens her door, so I salute him and head toward the elevator. The last thing I need is some alert on my head, warning women about me.

I pop the elevator button with my thumb. I should have brought Kristen to *my* room last night. She'd have been more comfortable lying in my bed than in that shitty twin bed in her cabin. She could have looked out onto the ocean and gotten fresh air on the balcony.

And I would've been there to watch over her.

Chapter Twenty-Four

PASHA

I DON'T WANT TO MISS KRISTEN WHEN SHE SHOWS UP TO RUN, SO I get to the track at 5:15 a.m. As I wait, I jog two laps to warm up and do three sets of push-ups. I'm halfway through my first lap of walking lunges when a bright pink top catches my eye.

I jump to my feet, excited to see her. To hold her. To make sure she felt better this morning.

She waves animatedly and her face lights up, her smile visible even in the distance between us, which I close quickly by running to her.

"Morning!" She greets me with her arms open, ready to accept a hug.

I wrap my arms around her, lifting her off her feet and spinning her around once before kissing her.

Her lips curl into a smile underneath mine, so I pull back. "Good morning."

"I'm so happy to see you," she says. "I thought about you all night."

"You thought about me?" I ask, floored I even crossed her mind given the pain she was in. I lower her feet but keep my hands at her waist.

"I was so grateful for your help last night," she says. Then she looks down. "I don't know if I could have walked back to the ship without you."

I place my fingers under her chin and tilt her face to mine. I don't want her to feel embarrassed. "I would've carried you to the next island."

"That would've been challenging considering the depth of the water," she teases.

"You underestimate my strength and stamina."

"I could never underestimate your stamina, Pasha. The last few days with you have completely exhausted me."

Her sexy smile tells me she's joking again, but the words still concern me. After everything she's told me about cystic fibrosis, I realized we'll have to take it easy moving forward. And I have to be the one to spearhead that effort because I'm pretty sure she'll do anything to keep up with me.

"We relax today. And when you are exhausted, I carry you on my back like pig."

Kristen laughs—an eyes-closed, body-shaking kind of laugh.

I let go of her and take a step back. "What?"

"Piggyback?" she asks.

"Yes, piggyback. This is what I say, yes?" I still have no clue what made her laugh so hard.

"Actually, you said you'd carry me like a pig. Which sounds mean, not heroic as you intended."

"Ah, yes! Laugh at Russian man for getting term wrong. Why you say 'piggyback'? Where you get this phrase?"

Kristen shakes her head. Her laugh subsides, but her smile remains as bright as ever. She holds my head in her hands and brushes the close-cropped hair on the sides. "I don't know. All I know is that you make me laugh. You make me feel special. And I really like hanging out with you."

Before Kristen, I'd never had a woman look at me with admiration and kindness. It feels good to finally have someone get to know Pasha, the real person. Not Pavel Gribov, star center for the Detroit Aviators, or rather, the Charlotte Monarchs. In October, I'll start the season on an NHL roster for the first time in my career.

For a brief moment, sharing the information I've withheld about knowing Auden and Aleksandr crosses my mind. This is my chance to come clean. Maybe she wouldn't even remember the deplorable incident I'd orchestrated.

But I'm too selfish to confess.

Which is my problem in the first place, according to the media—and a few coaches and teammates.

Selfish—though I've led every team I've ever been on in assists each year.

Arrogant—because I celebrate the goals I work my ass off to score in professional hockey.

Flippant—because I have a sense of humor and don't let things bother me.

Everyone needs a villain, a person they love to hate. I'll be the villain because the things they call me out for are my defense mechanisms. I build my walls with brick to keep people away for good reason.

I don't want to be an angry, abusive asshole like my father. I don't want to waste my life pretending to be something I'm not for people I don't give a fuck about.

Let the media hate me.

Soon enough, Kristen will hate me, too.

But this is now. And right now, I can be Pasha, the man who will protect her, help her, and care for her until the moment we part ways.

I pat Kristen's backside, prodding her onto the track. "Let's get our run out of the way so we can get off this boat and find more island adventure."

THE FIRST PLACE I take Kristen is a colorful beach shop advertising swimsuits, towels, and cheap souvenirs. I need to get my girl out of those frumpy one-piece suits she wears. Sparkly or not, they do nothing to highlight how sexy she is—and I want to see more skin.

Plus, I owe her a new suit since I ruined her "tanning suit" the first day we met.

After flipping through multiple racks, I found a crimson two-piece that would look amazing against her tanned skin. I shove the hanger into her hand.

She holds it up, squinting at the tiny red bikini hanging off it. "I can't try this on."

"Why not?" I ask without looking up as I push through a rack of black bikinis.

"You saw my scar, Pasha," she says in a hushed tone, glancing around the small store to make sure she hasn't drawn any attention. "I don't wear two-piece suits."

I stop pushing hangers and gaze at her. "You serious?"

She nods and hangs the bikini back on the rack.

"You have one small scar. I have seen much, much worse." I pick up the hanger again and press the suit against her chest.

She scowls and slams it onto the rack again. "Way to make me feel like an asshole."

"What I do?" I ask.

Instead of answering, she shuffles away. I sigh and follow her, wondering how I could have offended her. I know she's insecure about it, but the scar isn't that noticeable.

"I know people have it worse than I do, Pasha. But I can't help but be self-conscious. I battle this alone every single day. The validation of a random guy telling me I have a nice body doesn't erase twenty years."

"I did not say this." I cup her shoulder and try to turn her toward me, but she won't budge. "Kristen, you are gorgeous. Every part of you. Even this scar you worry about. I do not know why you hide it. Is part of who you are. Is symbol of strength."

"It's disgusting," she whispers, wrapping her arms around her stomach as if the scar were visible through her cover-up.

I hate that she doesn't realize how strong she is, or if she does, she doesn't own it. Was her bubbly, positive outward persona just a front to the world?

"No. Is beautiful." I reach out and gently place her arms at her side. Then I move closer and put my hands on her waist. My thumbs skim the fabric at her stomach directly over the scar. Then I lift my eyes to hers before I speak. "Scars are battle wounds. They remind us we are alive."

"I don't want people to ask about it." She looks away. "I don't want people to stare and point."

"I will tell you this." I put my face directly in her line of sight and keep moving with her every time she bobs and weaves, trying to avoid my stare. Finally, she cocks her head and meets my eyes.

"If you wear bikini, people do not stare and point because of this scar," I assure her. "Is because you are fucking hot."

She laughs.

"Why you laugh? You know this."

My compliments only make her laugh even harder, though I don't understand why. There's no question that she's attractive.

Her laughter quickly turns into coughing. She turns her head and covers her mouth with her arm. I place my hand on her back.

"You okay?" I ask when the coughs finally subside. She nods.

"I spend much time at hospital," I say. "I talk to kids. They are sick and have injuries. Burns all over their bodies. Tubes everywhere." I motion across my face. "And these kids have beautiful outlook on life. Like you, when you do not worry about how others will think."

I grab Kristen's waist and pull her toward me. "I know about this sadness and darkness and insecurity, but you are light to everyone. You make people happy. Your friends love you. They are jealous."

She shakes her head and lowers her eyes.

"You have too much life to give a fuck what people think of this scar. You are strong and beautiful. You should be showing it off. Is proof of how much you kick ass on this illness."

"I'm not a fighter."

"Yes, you are. But you are also lover." I lower my hands, sliding them over her backside and squeezing. "A good one."

"Stop!" She laughs and bats my hands away.

I turn around and grab the red bikini off the rack for the third time. Then I pick up a black one. "You will try these on for me," I command, then add a "Yes?" to make it seem like a question.

"Fine!" She grabs the hangers from my hand and stomps toward the fitting room. "But I'm not buying them."

"Fine!" I match her haughty tone. "I will."

Twenty minutes later, we leave the store with four bikinis.

Chapter Twenty-Five

KRISTEN

St. Martin

"Come on, ladies." Blake drapes one arm across Lena's shoulders and the other over Sia's. Neither of my friends object as they stroll down the dock, away from the ship. "Our poolside cabana awaits."

Pasha and I stop and look at each other, dumbfounded, as Blake keeps walking without inviting us.

Blake yells as if he read our minds, "Cabana fits four. Come along, Kristen. You can bring your pool boy to fetch us drinks."

Pasha leans over and removes a flip-flop. He cocks his arm back and aims it at his friend's head.

I jump up and grab his arm. "Don't you dare!"

Pasha laughs and puts his flip-flop back on. He takes my hand, and we follow Blake to the beach cabana.

Once we've got everything set up, we order drinks and relax.

"I can't believe the cruise is almost over." Blake stretches out in his lounge chair. "I could stay in paradise forever."

"Being back home is gonna suck monkeys," Lena says, reaching over to grab the frozen strawberry margarita from the table next to her.

Enjoying the poolside cabana Blake rented ended up being the perfect way to spend our last day off the boat. I've had enough crazy and death-defying excursions for one week. I want to hang out, relax, and enjoy every minute I have left of Pasha's company.

Pasha and I sit together on a beach lounger. I'm straddling his torso, facing him while he lies sprawled out. My hair hangs down, shielding our faces from the crowd. I lean over and kiss him gently.

"We should fuck on this chair. Right now," Pasha whispers. He squeezes the outside of my thighs. Then his fingers crawl toward my butt, and he slides them under the fabric of my bikini bottoms.

I grin and gaze into his eyes. "You are so bad."

"Is bad to make you feel good? I think I am nice guy here."

"Can't you two stop for one minute?" Sia asks.

"Why you care?" Pasha asks her through the strands of my hair. He doesn't take his eyes off me, and I can't take my eyes off him. He has me completely mesmerized.

"It's annoying. You've been all over each other since you met. Can't you take a break? Or save it for your room?"

"Jealous," I mouth to Pasha behind our curtain.

His lips crack into a huge smile. "We swim?"

"Can we play in the water?" I whisper.

"Yes."

I straighten up and pat his hard stomach like a bongo drum. "Let's go!"

I've never had sex in water. Not in a pool or a hot tub, and certainly not in the ocean. How far would we have to walk out? What if the water is too clear? Can you even get a condom on in water? Would it be super obvious?

None of it matters. All I can think about is finding a semi-secluded space in the water and trying.

Pasha holds my hand as we wade into the aquatic paradise. I squeeze his fingers with every step until we settle on an area where the water hits our chests. My fear of the ocean melts away. I trust him. He wouldn't let anything happen to me.

"This is absolutely perfect." I scan the beach, where bodies fill every available patch of almond-colored sand as far as the eye can see.

"Almost perfect."

Pasha moves closer to me and softly brushes his lips against mine. I slide my arms around his neck as he grabs my hips, and we kiss again. The intensity stays soft and sensual, not aggressive or needy. He presses a little harder, and I lick his lips with my tongue, beckoning him to open his mouth. When he obliges, I slide inside. After letting me explore, I pull back, but he gently catches my bottom lip in his teeth. The surprising sensation makes me lose my footing, but Pasha squeezes my waist to keep me steady.

"I have a question," I say when he releases my lip. Though there isn't anyone even remotely close to where we're standing, I lean close to his ear. "How do you put a condom on in the water?"

He throws his head back and laughs. "We must be on beach for this."

"On the chair next to Sia, I hope. She would frickin' flip."

"Your mind turn me on."

"My mind?"

"Yes," he whispers into my ear as one hand moves from my waist to between my legs. He pushes aside my bathing suit and slides one finger into me. I take a breath and dig my nails into his shoulder. "You are smart and kind. Always think of others. Help others."

We're far enough out that the water hits Pasha just below his pecs, covering everything happening underwater. The exhilaration of standing in front of a beach full of people makes every touch much more intense.

He slides a second finger into me and rubs me with his thumb at the same time. My legs go slack. I hold myself up by cupping his shoulder with one hand and placing the other on his chest. His thumb moves faster and faster until I think I might collapse against him. I slide my hand down his chest and into the water. The elastic waistband to his swim trunks allows easy access to his hard length pressing against my stomach. He sucks in a sharp breath when I take hold of him.

"You want this? Right here?" His words come out in puffs of breath.

I nod, keeping my grip firm and moving faster to match his thumb's rhythm on me.

My hips kick, and my chest slams against his. It's difficult to hold myself back while being consumed by the sensations his thumb and fingers create. I hope that from the beach, people see a couple tangled in a lovers' embrace, not a girl bucking on a guy like a drunk on a mechanical bull.

But as the pace increases, so do our movements, which sends water splashing around us.

"Fuck, KK," Pasha whispers. He sinks his face into my neck and shoulder. His breath is hot against my sun-scorched skin.

Despite all the things that could take me out of the moment—the risk of getting caught, the sheer sense of embarrassment at trying to get Pasha off in the water, or the fact that I feel comfortable acting like this with a guy I met just a few days ago—none of them faze me.

But hearing the nickname my best friends back home use for me takes me out of the moment.

I pull away from him and ask, "Why did you call me that?"

"Don't stop. Can we . . ." His breath is rapid from what I've been doing to him. He pulls his fingers out of me to grab my hand and return it to him. "Please," he begs.

He pushes two fingers into me again, jolting me back to reality: here, getting Pasha off in the water. Exactly where I want to be.

Chapter Twenty-Six

PASHA

WITH KRISTEN'S ARMS WRAPPED AROUND MY NECK AND OUR BODIES molded like yin and yang, I finally understand true, unfiltered bliss simply from being content with another person.

Sure, I could chalk it up to the post-orgasm high, but I've never been so content to be with someone as I am with Kristen, so there has to be something more.

"I like spending time with you," I say, breaking the silence.

She opens her eyes and lifts her head from that comfy spot in the crook of my neck. "When did I tell you my last name?"

Fuck. Think, Pasha, think.

"You never tell me this," I say quickly. "I hear your short friend say it. She get mad at you very much, yes?"

"You don't even know." Kristen glances toward the shore, where our friends sprawl on lounge chairs. "She's not a bad person. But she gets annoyed when people do things she wouldn't do. And by *people*, I mean me."

"She need to get laid."

She bites back a grin and says, "I can't even imagine that. She's waiting for marriage to have sex, so it'll have to be a special guy for that to go down."

In Russia, marrying young is still common. I have friends who were married by the time they were twenty. I have no problem with how other people choose to live their lives. If I hadn't grown up with the father I had, maybe I would have wanted to be married that early, too. Perhaps I'd want to get married in general. Still, I couldn't imagine waiting to have sex.

Some people might say it's the man-whore talking, but I believe sex is essential to a relationship and especially to a marriage.

How much would it suck to marry someone and then find out you're completely incompatible in the bedroom? Or that she's a total bore—or a total freak? I like a mix of both: a girl open to being adventurous without taking it to the extreme.

Someone like Kristen.

I glance at the woman who made me think of sex on a whole different level over the past few days. Our compatibility in that department is off the charts. That's all I need for a week-long fling, but our emotional compatibility matches, too—and that part scares me.

"I'm hungry," I announce, grabbing her hand and leading her toward the shore. "We go eat."

Though we've spent sufficient time clutched in each other's arms, enjoying the post-orgasm bliss, when I let Kristen go, I want to grab her and hold her against me again.

"You're used to getting what you want, aren't you?" Kristen asks, a smirk tilting her lips.

"Is my life. I do what I want, when I want," I answer. "This is only way to live."

As we walk, the buzz of being with her still vibrates through my body, and I want to lead her somewhere I can actually get a condom on, like the beach chair I'd suggested earlier.

"You think about something, Yes?" I ask, squeezing her hand as we walk through the water toward shore.

Her eyes are wide when she looks at me as if I've caught her doing something inappropriate. "Nothing."

"You look guilty," I tease. Then I lean my shoulder into hers. "Tell me."

"I was thinking about fucking you on that chair." She points to the empty chair in the middle of her friends.

"Big talk." I laugh. "You are tease."

Kristen stops, which makes me swallow hard, and I plant my feet in the sand. We stand still as waves splash against our shins. She grabs my biceps to brace herself. Then she lifts onto her toes, leans in close, and whispers, "I'm not teasing."

Her breathy voice and flirty words make my stomach tighten. I lock eyes with hers, trying to figure out if I should believe her. She holds my gaze unblinkingly as she makes her intent clear.

This girl is going to dismantle me completely.

I bend down, grab her under her arms and behind her knees, and carry her through the water. When we reach the beach, I don't stop at the uncomfortable plastic lounge chairs our friends occupy. As we pass the chair we'd shared before going in the water, I reach out and grab her beach bag. She tightens her hold on my neck.

My heart thumps with every quick step I take through the sand. I swallow back the surge of lust that makes me want to drop to the ground and take her right on the beach in front of everyone.

Because as much as I want to be inside her, I need to figure her out first.

Chapter Twenty-Seven

KRISTEN

"ARE WE GETTING DRINKS?" I ASK, CONFUSED AND SLIGHTLY disappointed when Pasha sets my feet on the sand next to the Lazy Lizard Beach Bar. Over the past few days, I've figured out that Pasha is a man of his word—and a man of action.

Though my question was a joke, my stomach growls, reminding me that I need to eat.

He hands me my beach bag. "No. You don't need drink today."

"Excuse me?" I ask. The hair on the back of my neck bristles. He doesn't have the right to tell me when I can drink.

Pasha cups my face with his hand and sweeps his thumb across my jawline. "You cough too much yesterday. You do not need drink today. We will get water and eat huge plates of food. You bring the medicine, yes?"

The magnitude of Pasha's genuine concern hits me full force, and I stagger back, raking my wet hair out of my face with my fingers. "I . . . yeah, I have my medicine." I nod.

He tightens his grip on my hips and pulls me back toward him. "You will go easy today to be healthy. I want you healthy."

"You haven't seemed freaked by any of it."

"I tell you before, spitting and stomach things do not scare me."

Pasha's eyes lower to the scar on my belly, visible in the bikini I'm wearing, one of the many he bought me in St. Lucia. "I have seen much worse than stomach scars and shaky vests."

For some reason, his words have my mind grouping previous incidents, clicking them into place like puzzle pieces.

He wasn't fazed by my scars or my morning routine. He snapped at the old man in the Barbados bar who commented that there were better ways to die than cliff jumping. They'd affected him enough for a response but hadn't swayed him. Granted, he didn't see anything too horrible or embarrassing since I wouldn't let him nurse my stomachache. My daily routine is pretty simple, if not a little weird to an outsider.

He's never seen the brutal reality. He's never seen me lying in a hospital bed because something as simple as a cold turned into an infection my body couldn't fight off.

He's never seen my parents crying and praying and fighting while they tried to decide if they were doing the right thing when they secured the most cutting-edge treatments and medications for me despite not knowing the complete list of side effects they might have.

He's never seen the stack of bills from hospital stays and doctors' visits that forced my mom to get a second job because insurance didn't pay for everything.

I place my hands on his chest.

Suddenly, all of this is too much.

My heart pounds, and flight mode propels me back. I continue walking backward until I hit the rough surface of the Lazy Lizard's wall. Pasha reaches for my arm, but I bat his hand away.

"This was supposed to be fake and fun. Lots of sex. No emotion," I tell him, though the words ring in my ears, a reminder more for myself than for him.

He steps toward me. "If this is what you want, you should have sucked my dick and left my room, yes?"

His crass comment makes my skin prickle. "Excuse me?"

"This is not fake to me. *You* are not fake to me." With another step, he's closed the gap between us. "Am I fake to you?"

Pasha lifts his hands to my face and brushes my cheeks with his fingers. His lips are so close to mine, but he doesn't lean in. He stands before me with his head tilted as his warm breath hits my face.

"You've only known me for a few days," I protest.

"I do not know enough. I need more."

"I don't have more to give." I look away.

"You do," he commands.

His intense gaze makes me unsteady. He must feel my knees go slack because he grips my hips, presses me against the wall, and claims my mouth. Instead of pulling away when his fingers skim into my bikini bottoms, I swing a leg over his hip, opening myself to him without thinking about who might walk by or have a full view of us against a wall.

Screw the beach lounger. I want him to push into me right here against this wall. I can't give him forever. But I can give him this.

Right here. Right now.

In a few days, being with this man has sent all my previous feelings on relationships flying. He's expanded my thoughts on what living life to the fullest means. And he uncovered a sexually adventurous side of me I never knew existed—or hadn't ever felt comfortable enough to reveal to anyone before.

I reach into his swim trunks and try to pull him out, but instead of letting me, he presses his pelvis into mine. "Kristen," he hisses against my neck.

"Please, Pasha. Do it."

But he doesn't. He takes my face in his hands and tilts my head up. I can't avoid the pain, the hunger, the passion blazing in his eyes.

"Why are you scared to be with someone?" he asks. "Why you think you will not have happy life with a man?"

"I told you, I don't have forever."

"Who does?"

I shake my head, causing Pasha's hands to drop from my face. "You don't understand."

"Help me."

I slide across the wall, away from him, and step back to create some distance between us.

"You run from me?" Pasha asks, fumbling with the front of his trunks, making sure everything is safely tucked inside.

"No," I say, turning to face him. "I don't run from my problems. But I think this conversation has moved from fucking against a wall to sitting in a restaurant. Don't you?"

He looks from me to the entrance, then nods reluctantly. He places his hand in mine, and we walk into the Lazy Lizard.

"I'm going to wash my hands. I'll be right back," I say. We separate, each headed toward our respective restrooms before being seated.

I take those few minutes to calm my racing heart and figure out how much I'll share with him. I don't want to be the girl who brings up ex-boyfriends, but my breakup with Evan sent my dreams of having a future with a guy into the garbage disposal.

The worst part about being in this fake relationship is how real it feels.

I love being in a relationship—reveling in every kiss and tender touch and having someone to talk to or lay with.

I don't *need* it, but I love it.

When we've finished, Pasha and I meet at the hostess stand and follow her to our table.

"Can I have a bottled water, please?" I ask the waitress when she comes by our table for our drink order. To my surprise, Pasha orders water, too. I haven't seen him drink anything but vodka the entire trip.

I sit rigidly in my seat, scanning the menu for something to order when Pasha gently pushes it down.

"Spill your story," he says.

I set the menu down on the edge of the table. "What do you want to know?"

"Tell me why you do not get involved with someone."

"Evan, my high school boyfriend," I begin. "We dated for a couple of years. We'd made plans to go to the same college. As lame as it sounds for as young as we were, I was prepared for a future with him." I smile wryly at the realization of how stupid and naive I sound. "We weren't going to get married out of high school or anything, but we talked about staying together."

Pasha nods but doesn't say anything, allowing me to continue.

"In health class during my sophomore year of high school, my teacher had a lesson on disorders, and cystic fibrosis came up. He mentioned that the average life span of someone with cystic fibrosis in the United States was somewhere around thirty-five years."

"Shit," Pasha whispers, leaning back in his chair.

His reaction makes me pause—slightly. I'm used to it.

Thirty-five is tangible. Real. And not far away.

This conversation will be the end of everything with Pasha, just as it had been with Evan, which is why I have to be honest. Pasha deserves to know the truth—the reality I face every single day. I'm lucky to have had a fantastic, unforgettable week with him before having this conversation.

I nod. "My thoughts exactly. When I found out, I stood up so fast that I knocked over my chair on my way out of the room, sobbing—because no one ever told me about a shortened life span. My parents are wonderful people," I say quickly. Then I feel bad because it sounds horrible to say that in front of Pasha as if I'm rubbing my adoring family in his face when I know he didn't have the same. "But they never told me I wouldn't live as long as everyone else. They were honest but cautious with what they told me about CF. They wanted to make sure I had a positive outlook. We dealt with everything on a day-to-day basis. And I truly believed I could live a normal life if I took the necessary precautions."

"Being health nut?" Pasha asks with a small smile.

His gentle humor tells me that he wants me to be comfortable and continue to open up to him.

"And following my doctor's orders." I pause to allow the waitress time to set bottles of water and a bowl of tortilla chips on our table. "I don't know if my parents were in denial or if they were trying to shield me from thinking about it. Because once you know something like that, it consumes you. You start obsessing about it."

Pasha nods as if he understands.

"Before that moment, I honestly never thought about death. I'd thought about life—and the things I had to do to stay healthy. I was diagnosed as a baby, so managing CF is all I've ever known. Doctors were family friends. Hospital visits were commonplace. While we were dating, it seemed like Evan understood my routine, medicines, and treatments. When I spent two weeks in the hospital with a lung infection, he visited me every day. He brought me flowers and made sure my iPod was filled with songs. Even after the freak-out in health class, he calmed me down and helped me focus on life again. I think we were both young and optimistic."

"What make him change?" Pasha asks. "If he know and he is okay, what happened?"

Tears spring to my eyes, and I bite my lip, willing them not to spill out. I shrug. "I don't know. Senior year? Graduation looming? The pressure of deadlines and decisions we had to make about our future?

"Evan waited until the week before senior prom to deliver the bad news. He told me he couldn't go to prom with me, and he broke up with me at the same time. He spouted some bullshit about prom being a huge milestone in our lives. He wanted to look back on pictures and be happy."

"How this motherfucker say that? To girl he love?" Pasha's voice rises in anger.

"He said he couldn't invest any more in a relationship with someone he knew would die early. He couldn't risk getting married and having kids with me, knowing I'd die before I got to see them grow up."

"Jesus, Kristen." Pasha leans forward. His eyes are wide, and his usually full lips are a thin line of pity.

I keep talking because if I don't, I'll break down. Facts are facts. I can handle facts. "My looming death was the focus. It didn't matter that he could have a fatal allergic reaction to shellfish or overdose on his own douchiness," I joke to lighten the moment.

But the tears well in my eyes, ready to break free, while I recount the story. That moment with Evan Papandreou broke my heart and my spirit at the same time. He didn't want to deal with reality—that complications stemming from cystic fibrosis might shorten my life.

And I didn't blame him.

"He have no right to treat you this way. You are young. No one know what happens in future."

"He did me a favor," I disagree. "He made me realize that getting involved with someone is selfish."

"Bullshit." Pasha grabs a tortilla chip from the bowl and pops it into his mouth.

"Why?"

"Is bullshit. And he is fucking idiot. I meet many people in my life, Kristen. Out of all these people, *you* deserve to be happy. You deserve a man who love you with every piece of his soul. You can't worry about other people's feelings. Worry about what *you* want in life. Worry about you being happy."

I shake my head. "That's selfish."

"So?"

"How could I do that to someone?" My voice rises with my blood pressure. Why doesn't he understand? "How can I allow a man to invest time and energy into a relationship with me? How can I marry someone knowing that I can't give him forever? There is no forever with me. There's only right now."

"No one have forever," Pasha says.

"You know what I mean," I snap.

"And *you* know what *I* mean. Is stupid to allow this idiot to limit your happiness. Someone will love you, Kristen. Someone will beg for twenty years with you than none at all."

Pasha reaches out and brushes his thumb over the tears spilling onto my cheeks.

I close my eyes, sniffing back snot. Then I start coughing. And coughing. Pasha pushes a water bottle toward me, and I take a sip.

"I tell you I know many sick children, yes? These kids, they are told they will not live to be a certain age. Then they live past this age. Years past. Medicine change. Technology change. New treatments come. Is thirty-five still the age? Or is it more? Do you know people with this illness older than thirty-five?" Pasha fires questions at me. His passion catches me off guard.

"I, um—" I stumble for words. "Yes, I do know people older than thirty-five."

"You are very healthy. You are aware. If you keep this up, there is no reason you will not live long, happy life," Pasha says. He folds his arms across his chest as if he's won an argument.

"In theory, yes. But I can't help it if something simple turns into a major infection that my body can't defend against."

"And I cannot help if I choke on this chip." Pasha leans forward and lifts a tortilla chip from the bowl in the middle of our table.

"You're making it sound so simple." I shake my head. "Nothing is that simple."

"We are on same page, Kristen." Pasha drops the chip back into the bowl and reaches for my hand. "You want to live, and I want you to live. I want you to have best fucking life on earth. I prove this, yes?"

I nod.

"You will not think about thirty-five or twenty-five or one hundred and five. Fuck the future. You will think about now—about today." He lowers his voice. "Think about how good you will feel when I get you in my room, strip off this sandy, wet bikini, and—"

"Are you ready to order?" Our waitress interrupts his plans.

"Just the check, please," I tell her. Pasha's lips turn up in a knowing smile.

Chapter Twenty-Eight

KRISTEN

CRUISING

WAKING up next to Pasha on the last day on the ship is bittersweet. I feel so lucky to have met him and had this time, but I don't want to let him go. I don't want this to end.

But it will.

Everything ends.

Today, the ship docks in San Juan, and we'll go our separate ways.

During our joint shower after our morning run, Pasha said he had something special planned. Instead of questioning, I trust him enough to go along with anything he's scheduled since he hasn't disappointed me yet.

He leads me down the ship's hallway with his hand intertwined with mine.

"What are we doing?" I ask.

"We get massages."

I grab his hand with both of mine and stop as my pulse pounds with excitement. "Are you kidding?"

"No." His lips turn up in an amused grin.

"I haven't had a massage in years." I lift our joined hands above my head and twirl around underneath. "This is so awesome."

"Really?" he asks. "This is sad. I get massage every week. Sometimes more."

"Once a week or more?" I ask. That seems expensive—and excessive.

"Is necessary part of my job." Pasha pauses for a moment before adding, "Is stress reliever. I have much tension."

"I like your style." I press my palms against his chest and plant my lips on his.

I planned on just a peck, but Pasha wraps his strong arms around me and slides his tongue between my parted lips.

"Is hard to stop kissing you," he whispers against my lips. "I need to be closer."

His words send shivers through me, but I'm more interested in the thought of being absorbed in complete relaxation while getting a massage. "Give me an hour of bliss, and I'll get right back to you."

"I give you more than one hour last night." He dips his head and places his mouth on my neck.

"Are you *that* guy?" I tease.

He lifts his head. "What guy?"

"The bragger. The guy who has to let everyone know that you gave me multiple orgasms last night."

Pasha doesn't hesitate with his answer. "Yes. I am this guy."

Then he bends over, wraps his arms around my knees, lifts me, and tosses me over his shoulder. The head rush I get from being carried through the hallway upside down is nothing compared to the feeling I have being with Pasha.

AFTER GIVING instructions on which way to lie down on the table, the massage therapist leaves the room and I undress. I lay boobs-down, as directed, trying to get my face in a comfortable position on the weird little headrest.

When my therapist returns, she fumbles around momentarily.

Then I hear a door slide open. Confused, I lift my head and see Pasha lying on his stomach on a table a few feet away, smiling at me.

"Is couples massage." He winks before dropping his face into his headrest.

That's when my therapist flips on the calming music and goes to work.

At first, I can't relax. Not because Pasha lies naked just steps away. Not because I'd gotten a glimpse of his tiny, Swedish-model-looking therapist. I mean, sure, tiny darts of jealousy flew out of every pore at the thought of another woman's hands rubbing his body. But I don't blame him for that.

I can't relax because I have to say goodbye to him in a few hours, and I'm not ready.

The end has been on my mind since we started this charade, but this is our last day of sailing before we part ways forever. And I must admit, the thought of docking in San Juan and walking away from my fake boyfriend depresses me more than when my boyfriend of two years ditched me.

Last night, I dreamt of waking up wrapped in Pasha's arms with a huge down comforter and soft white sheets tangled and twisted around us. In the dream, when I rose from the bed, I stood in front of floor-to-ceiling windows, looking out onto the warm glow of city streets at night.

I racked my brain to figure out why the scene was so familiar. Then, I realized that it was the exact view from the photos Auden and Aleksandr had taken from the balcony of their high-rise condo in downtown Charlotte—the same condos Pasha said he lived in. It makes sense for my subconscious to connect the two.

Stop thinking. Just relax and enjoy because there's nothing you can do about it.

My brain knew our shenanigans were only for the week. My brain tossed aside everything Pasha had said about not being like this with any other girl. My brain knew the relationship was fake. So why doesn't my brain communicate with my heart?

Instead of letting me fall in love with a lie.

Chapter Twenty-Nine

PASHA

"Oh my gosh," Kristen moans as she lies satiated on the massage table. "My body has never felt so good."

She still hasn't opened her eyes, so she has no clue that I've dismissed our therapists and now stand next to her table.

"Never?" I ask.

I reach out and caress her face. I want to see her reaction when she opens her eyes and sees me standing over her—completely naked.

When her eyelids flicker open, she gasps.

"I need you now."

I grab her hands and pull her into a sitting position. The sheet slides down her chest and pools in her lap. I rip open the condom I brought with me and slide it on. Then I sweep the sheet off her legs and pull her hips toward me before pushing into her.

Kristen throws her arms around my neck, bringing me closer and deeper. Her knees rise as if curling into me is a natural reflex, and then she wraps her legs around my hips.

Instead of closing my eyes and enjoying how amazing she feels, I watch her. I want to remember how beautiful she looks with her eyes shut and lips parted slightly as her breath comes out in short quick puffs.

Suddenly, her eyes fly open, and she scans the room before staring at me with those gorgeous brown eyes. "Someone could walk in," she says.

I know no one will come in because I asked for extra time after our massages.

But she doesn't know that, and despite her concern, she hasn't stopped fucking me with every ounce of energy she has.

"You like this?" I whisper. "If someone come in?"

"Pasha," she moans, rubbing her clit on my public bone, creating a friction I know feels good for her.

"Fuck," I hiss as her moan sends a rush of adrenaline through me. I tighten my grip and dig my fingers into the flesh of her hips. Then I lean forward and crush my lips on hers. The intimacy of the kiss drowns me in emotion.

Being with Kristen fucks with my head. She's hijacked my thoughts and made me feel like I deserve to be happy. She makes me want to swing her over my shoulder and take her home—into my apartment, into my bed, into my life. Every time I wake up, my heart races at the thought of being near her.

And in a few short hours, it'll be over.

Chapter Thirty

KRISTEN

AFTER OUR MASSAGES, Pasha and I split up to finish packing since the ship is scheduled to dock in San Juan around ten p.m.

When I'm done, I head to Lena and Sia's room to tell them I won't be staying with them tonight, as we'd originally planned when booking the cruise. Since our flight home didn't leave until the following day, we had reserved a hotel room in San Juan for the night.

When I reach their room, I hear voices, so instead of knocking, I turn the knob and walk in.

"Hey guys!" I say to announce my arrival.

When I look up, the first thing I see is olive-toned butt cheeks. A man stands naked with his bare butt clenched and his hips pumping into someone bent over the desk.

"Spiros?" I gasp. "Oh God! Sia?" I can't tear my eyes away from the naked girl. She pushes away the hair hanging in her face to catch a glimpse of me, the person who'd interrupted their desk sex.

I shouldn't stare, but I can't believe it's Sia, the girl who's always said she was waiting for marriage to have sex, bent over taking it like a champ. And I never would have guessed that Snooze-Fest Spiros had such an exciting sex life.

I spin around. "I'm sorry! Oh my god. I'm so sorry, you guys!" I yell on my way out.

In the hallway, I close my eyes and bite my lip to keep from laughing. If I cared at all about Spiros, I might have been pissed. But I don't, and I'm happy he found someone.

"What are you doing?" Lena asks, walking toward me.

"You don't want to go in there right now." I shake my head and point my thumb at the door to her room.

"Well, I have to because I need to finish packing." My cousin edges by me and puts her hand on the knob.

"Trust me, you—"

Suddenly, the door swings open, and Spiros stands there with his shirt in his hands. Thankfully, he'd put his trousers on.

I glance at Lena, who doesn't seem surprised to see Spiros standing there half-naked. She should've shown up a minute earlier.

"Excuse me," he mumbles with his eyes at our feet. He inches between us and hurries down the hall.

"Hold your head up, Spiros!" I call after him. "That was some nice work!"

"Stop that!" Lena smacks my hand.

"Did you know?" I ask. The only time I saw Spiros and Sia together on the cruise was that first day at the pool when Spiros took Pasha's seat next to my friends. Then again, I haven't seen much of anyone except Pasha.

"Of course, I knew," Lena says before entering. "Well, I mean, I didn't know he was in there just now, but I knew they'd been hanging out."

She pauses and calls into the room, "Sia, are you decent?"

I guess the singles cruise worked.

"I'm not going to go back in there right now. I just wanted to let you know—"

"You're staying with him tonight, aren't you?" Lena asks.

"You're good! You should look into being one of those phone psychics," I tease her for reading my mind. Though, it's not like my choice to stay with Pasha is a surprise to anyone.

Chapter Thirty-One

KRISTEN

After we dock, Pasha and I give Lena, Sia, and Blake hugs before we flag down a cab to take us to Hotel El Convento, where Pasha booked a room for himself. We probably could've walked, but we have a lot of luggage—well, I do, with everything I had to bring.

The warm, bright yellow building beckons us inside, where we're met with gorgeous black and white checkered floors that span the entire lobby.

As Pasha checks in, I wander around, taking in everything from the grand piano to the marble stairs and golden gate at the entrance to one of the hotel's event spaces. The decor is gorgeous, old-world, and grandiose.

We go straight to our room, exhausted from everything we'd done that day.

"I'm so tired," I moan and fall back onto the huge bed.

"It was rough day of massages and sex." Pasha winks at me. "Is about to get longer."

"Are we talking about the day or . . . ?" I glance at his pants.

"Both." He lifts his T-shirt over his head, discards it, and tackles me.

LATER THAT NIGHT, after we settled into sleep, I lay content in Pasha's arms. Before I can stop it, a tear trickles down my cheek and onto his chest. Then another.

"What is this?" Pasha asks, wiping the wetness off my cheek.

"I'll miss you." As soon as I let the words slip, I feel stupid.

Missing someone after knowing him for only a week sounds so lame. And crying in his bed is just plain pathetic. But I'm not ashamed, because I *will* miss him.

I'll miss the closeness. I'll miss his smile and his kiss. I'll miss his unquestioning acceptance of my illness. I'll miss being the person he talks to about his conflicts with grief.

Pasha hugs me into his body. "When is your flight?"

"Um . . ." I lift my head to look at his face. "I think it's at noon."

"You will miss it."

"What?"

"We spend the day in San Juan. I read about, uh, I do not know how to say this. Glowing water."

"Glowing water?" I ask.

Pasha laughs. "I need translator."

"You speak English very well." I rub his back, sliding my hand across his shoulders and kneading his neck.

His tense muscles relax, and his eyelids flicker as I kneed. "Yes, until I talk about this beautiful water."

"I could call my best friend. She's a translator," I say flippantly. Not that we need one. We understand each other just fine.

Pasha's neck strains, and his eyes pop open. "I am joker about translator."

I chuckle at his reaction. "Yes, Pasha, I know. You are strong independent man," I say, mimicking his accent. "Glowing water sounds cool if that makes you feel better."

And glowing water does sound cool, even though he could be talking about the effects of nuclear waste for all I know.

"You will change your flight. We spend the day together in San Juan, and I take you to this water."

I sit up. "Wait. Are you serious?"

"Yes." He catches my eye. "You think I am joker?"

"Yeah." I lift my hand from his neck and slide it over my forehead. "I mean, I'd love to, but I don't have that kind of money."

Sure, I have a job, but it pays my bills and allows me to have somewhat of a social life, and that's about it. I'm pretty sure switching my flight at the last minute would be a major dent in my bank account.

"You say yes, and you do not worry."

Lena and Sia will have a conniption. I can totally envision my cousin hopping on my back and taking me down before she let me stay an extra day with Pasha. Being on a cruise around thousands of people is one thing, but staying in a foreign city alone with a guy I just met sounds like a front-page headline for the crime section waiting to be written.

What part of the brain loves adrenaline? The part that craves crazy, life-threatening situations? I guess it doesn't matter. I've already made up my mind because I trust Pasha. And I want to live life to the fullest while I'm still alive.

"Yes. We can check at the airport tomorrow to see if it will work out. If it does, I'll stay," I say, despite knowing the backlash I'll receive from Lena and Sia.

And my mom.

Oh, shit. Mom is gonna have a fit.

She's supposed to pick me up at the airport, but I don't have my phone to call her with flight change information.

"We check with your friends first, yes?"

"It's my decision," I say, my tone sharper than I'd intended since I'd been thinking the same thing.

Pasha weaves his fingers into my hair, raking it from my face. "Your friends care about you. They worry. No one will worry when you are with me."

"I'm not worried. You're my safe zone." I know I'm about to sound like the biggest dork, but I can't pass up my opportunity to tell him how much he's impacted me in such a short time.

"What does this mean?"

"It's never been easy for me to open up to people about my health.

Except you. You have this air about you that you don't give a fuck about anything or anyone, but you're easy to talk to."

"For you. I like the talk to you. You bring out different side of me. I like person I am with you."

I lower myself to his side, set my elbow on the bed, and hold my head up with my palm. My fingers slide across the ink on his forearm, drawing invisible swirls. "Why do I get a different side of you?"

"You challenge me. You see me. You do not—um—what is the word?" He pauses. "You do not judge me and my life. I have fresh start with you."

"Should I be worried about that?"

"No," he says quickly, "but like I tell you before, I am dick." Pasha laughs. "You have not seen this side of me. You hold nothing against me."

"Why have two faces? Why show me one side and other people another?"

"I do not want people to be close. It hurt too much when they leave."

"Why do you assume they'll leave?"

"You know this answer, Kristen," he says. "You have this same fear. I do not want pain when someone leaves. You do not want to cause this pain. I am selfish. You are kind."

"It's kind to get involved with someone like me, knowing from the beginning that I'll break your heart."

Pasha touches my face and brushes his thumb across my cheek. "Getting involved with you is most selfish thing I ever do."

"How so?"

"I should not have fallen for you. I should not have led you on knowing it will be over after this."

I wince. Though I know the truth, hearing him say the words aloud cuts like a razor.

"What if I want to keep in touch with you?" I ask softly. "What if I want to make this work after the cruise?"

"You will not like who I am after this cruise."

"Why?"

"I tell you. I am dick." He doesn't laugh this time.

But I'm not buying it. He shared too much of himself this week. I stare at him, willing him to continue.

He rubs the back of his neck. "I had issues. When I see people happy when I am not happy. I am not nice."

"We all have a past. That doesn't mean we can't change."

"Except this experience won't change me." Pasha takes my face in both of his hands. "I will be worse because when I am home, I will be even bigger bastard because I let you go."

I shake out of his hold. "And I just told you it doesn't have to end. So, you don't have to return to acting that way."

Pasha's face goes blank. He puts his hands behind his head and lays back on the pillow. "But I will."

I kinda wanted to slap him and knock the nonchalant expression off his smug face. "Why don't you want it to continue? Do you have a girlfriend back home?" I bolt up, gathering the sheet across my bare breasts. Goosebumps prickle my skin and my heart thumps.

"I have no girlfriend."

If he had acted like a cold jerk when we first met, I would believe that's how he usually acts. But the first thing he did when we met was help me with Spiros, so I know he's genuinely kind. Then, I got to know him—the real person under the arrogant façade. I can tell he's being a stubborn ass to save himself from heartbreak.

I could easily follow him down the emotionally unavailable path, but we've come too far and shared too much. Instead, I'll salvage the positive. "I know you have a good heart. I know you can be nice."

"Why you think this?" He keeps his eyes on the ceiling.

"Because you clam up when I compliment your character. You avoid my eyes. You turn away."

"This mean nothing."

"Whatever." I tickle his ribs. "I saw you chatting up the old ladies at the zip line. Dicks don't flirt with old ladies. They stand behind them and complain about how slow or annoying they are. You're sweet when you aren't pretending to be a hard-ass."

Pasha's eyes veer to my chest, and his eyebrows pull together, seemingly annoyed that I'd covered my breasts. "I do not flirt with old ladies."

He reaches out, slides his index finger into the gap between my breasts, and tries to tug the sheet. I inhale sharply and bat his hand away, holding firm, though his touch sends tingles up to my ears and down to my toes. "We're talking about how soft you can be."

"Is more fun to be hard." He winks.

"Should I be freaked out that you're getting excited talking about old ladies?"

Pasha reaches over and pulls me on top of him with one swift motion. "You get me excited. If you talk about fish guts, I get excited."

I tuck my hair behind my ear. "That's gross."

"Our first fight is over, yes?" he asks.

"Fight? You thought that was a fight? You obviously haven't spent time with me outside of paradise," I say.

"This feisty side turn me on." He bucks his hips, and I bounce onto his lap.

I laugh. "Everything turns you on."

"Everything about you," he corrects, pressing against me.

Pasha holds my head in his hands and brings my face down to his. He kisses my forehead, then my nose, before covering my mouth with his.

Chapter Thirty-Two

KRISTEN

"No!" Lena says when I tell her I'm staying an extra day to hang out with Pasha. "No. No. *No*."

How can she be so bent out of shape at eight in the morning after a week of relaxation and fun?

We stand nose to nose in the San Juan airport with the conversation playing out exactly as I knew it would. But I've already decided, and nothing she says will sway me.

"I'm not asking permission," I say. "I'm just letting you know."

"Do you understand how stupid this is?" she asks. "You'll be here with no phone. No friends."

I shrug and ignore her. "If you don't hurry, you're not going to make it through security in time to make your flight."

"Ugh! You're so stubborn!" Lena yells.

Sia is silent as she rolls her suitcases alongside us. When we reach the check-in line, Lena speaks again, this time in a hushed tone. "I would jump on your back and push you through the line if I didn't think I'd be arrested."

"Don't get arrested. Get on the plane and order a drink. I'll see you soon." I lean over and hug her.

Despite shooting me evil looks, she keeps moving toward the self-check-in kiosks. "Have fun telling your mom!" Lena yells back.

I give her two thumbs up and a fake smile before turning away.

My stomach drops as I walk over to the chairs where Pasha has been waiting for me.

"Can I borrow your phone to call my mom?" I ask. He nods and holds his phone out. I take it, gulping as I press each number. When the line starts ringing, I start sweating.

"Hello?" Mom asks tentatively.

Relief washes over me, happy she answered an unknown number.

"Hey, Mom! It's me."

"Kristen?" she asks. "What number is this?"

"I'm borrowing a friend's phone. I lost mine on the second day."

"What?" Mom asks. "How?"

"Sia dropped it in the ocean."

"You've got to be kidding me," Mom mumbles. "On purpose?"

"No! It was a total accident. We were taking a selfie against the rail." I shake my head with the mental flashback of my poor phone plunging to its watery death.

Better it than me.

"So, you didn't get any pictures?"

"No, but the girls will send me theirs."

"I'm sure Spiros got some, too."

"Well, I'm sure he got pictures, but he better not have any of me," I say. Then I close my eyes, waiting for the wrath of my matchmaker mother.

"What does that mean?" she asks.

"I barely saw him. He did his thing, and I did mine." Before Mom can chastise me for not hanging out with Spiros, I gush, "But I met an amazing guy."

"Really?" Her tone perks up. Then she sighs. "Well, good. I can't wait to hear about him when I pick you up. Are you at the airport?"

"Yeah, about that. I, uh, missed my flight."

"Excuse me?"

"I'm at the airport waiting, but the eleven o'clock flight out tonight is the only flight with any seats left."

"Are Lena and Sia with you?"

"No." I bite my lip. "They made our original flight."

"How did they make the flight, and you missed it? Aren't you all together?"

It's time to talk fast and hope for the best.

"I—I had a tough time saying goodbye to Pavlos, the guy I met." If I'm going to lie to Mom anyway, giving her his fake Greek name sounds like the best idea. She'd be on the next plane if I told her his name was Pasha. "I didn't realize what time it was, and I spaced. When I got to the gate, the doors were already locked. They wouldn't let me on the flight."

Mom sighs. "Who are you with?"

"Pavlos," I say, glancing at Pasha on the seat next to me. He reaches out and squeezes my free hand.

"Are you serious, Kristen?" Mom screeches. I pull the phone back, holding it away from my ear.

"Mom, it's fine, I swear. I'm not dumb. He's a good guy. I promise."

"You say you aren't dumb, but that's not the impression I'm getting from this conversation." Her voice rises with every word. "He's a complete *stranger*. You just met him. If I could come through this phone and—"

"Mom, please. It's okay. He's amazing. You'll meet him soon. I promise." Then I add, "Have Lena show you pictures."

"What does he do? What family is he from? Do they live close?"

"He's an avia—a pilot," I lower my voice, though Pasha can hear everything I'm saying. "His parents passed away." I bite my lip. "But he's got family all over."

"Greece?" she asks, her tone perking up at the thought.

"Not sure if any are in Greece. He has a sister in Chicago and an aunt in Canada." At least I'm not lying to her.

"I can't wait to talk to him when you get off the flight tonight."

"Well, um, he won't be on my flight, Mom. He lives in Charlotte. But we're going to meet up next time he's in town. Or he can jump on a flight to see me. It's all so romantic."

I play up the star-crossed lovers aspect, laying it on thick because

Mom is a romantic at heart. The more I hype Pasha, the better chance I have of calming her nerves.

"This is . . . I can't believe this is happening! Are you an idiot, Kristen Aurelia Katsaros?"

"Mom . . ."

"I understand that you don't like Spiros. Point taken. I will never talk about him again. But this is just insane, Kristen!"

"Mom, listen. Just listen."

Silence.

Either she wants to listen, or she hung up on me to call the police.

"I am a smart person. I keep a can of Mace in my bag. I know how to defend myself. You've gotta trust me."

More silence.

"Mom?" I ask.

"I trust you, Kristen," Mom says, her voice softer than it had been but still tense. "But I don't know where you are. I don't know this guy you're with. You don't have a phone. You realize all of this sounds like an episode of a crime show, right?"

I swallow back the fear that rises in my throat. "I know it sounds that way, but I'm on his phone right now, Mom. You can call it or text it at any time today. And I'll let you know when I'm back at the airport for my flight."

"What do you mean, back at the airport? You need to plant your butt in a chair and wait to see if standby seats open up on an earlier flight."

Silence seems like the best response. No reason to make Mom any angrier than she already is.

"You're going to do what you want, aren't you?" she asks, worry and defeat in her tone. "So what can I say?"

"Say you trust me," I plead.

"I do trust you," she spits. "I don't trust him."

"*I* trust him," I say firmly. And it's true. Sure, the situation sounds super shady, but Mom didn't spend the week with Pasha.

"Have you talked to him about CF? Do you have enough enzymes? How about your inhaler?"

"Yes. I'm good with everything. And he knows. He's totally cool."

Mom sighs. "I know you're an adult and can make your own decisions, but you can't stop me from worrying about you."

"I know, Mom. I appreciate that. I love you so much. You and Dad have taught me to be smart and strong. Just trust me. Why don't you send a text to his phone?" I suggest, hoping that if she knows she can contact me through calls or texts, it will make her feel better about the situation.

"Hold on," Mom commands.

Less than half a minute later, I hear a beep alerting me of a text coming into Pasha's phone. I look at the screen and see Mom's number. I press the message and read it:

This is Helena Katsaros, Kristen Katsaros's mother. If my daughter goes missing, it was the owner of this phone.

"Geez, Mom," I mumble.

"What? What did you expect me to say?" Mom counters.

"Are we good?" I ignore her rhetorical question. Despite being an adult who can make my own decisions about how I spend my vacation and my life, I don't want Mom to be angry with me—especially when she has a valid concern.

"You better send me hourly check-ins, Kristen. If even one hour goes by that I don't hear from you, I'm calling the police," Mom warns.

"I love you, Mom."

"I love you, Kristen."

Chapter Thirty-Three

PASHA

ONCE WE'VE GOTTEN THE CALL WITH KRISTEN'S MOTHER OUT OF the way, changing her flight is pretty simple—until the girl behind the counter asks for payment.

Kristen elbows me out of the way and thrusts her card toward the woman. I step in front of her, push her arm down, and place my credit card directly into the girl's hand.

Throughout the cruise, Kristen offered to pay for her share of everything—drinks, excursions—but I paid for everything. She'd protested and given me a few annoyed looks the first few times, but it didn't bother me. I will always pay for my girl. I don't know any other way, nor do I want to.

"Pasha!" she chastises. "You've helped me so much, I'll never be able to repay you. Please, let me get this."

"No," I say firmly as the woman takes my card. "I ask you to change this flight. I pay these fees." As we wait, I add, "I never ask to repay me. This offends me."

"Offend you? How can it offend you? I've never expected anyone to pay my way. I thought guys wanted independent women who can take care of themselves."

"I do not know these guys. Why you want man who make you pay for anything? This is not man. This is pussy."

For a moment, Kristen is speechless. When she opens her mouth to say something, I shut her down by simply raising an eyebrow.

"Thank you," she says.

I nod, sign the credit card receipt, and wait for the woman behind the counter to give Kristen her updated boarding pass. Then we walk out of the airport.

Once we're outside, she reaches up and brushes my temple with her fingers. "Why do you have a glint in your eye?"

"Glint? What does this mean?" I stop on the curb and raise my arm to hail a cab.

"A sparkle. It's like you're trying to keep a secret."

"I am happy to spend this day with you." I sweep her into my arms and plant my lips on hers.

When the driver asks where we're headed, I direct him to drop us off in Old San Juan.

"Do we need to sign up for the glowing water thing?" Kristen asks while securing her seatbelt.

I hold up my phone. "I book this morning."

"How did you find out about this glowing water tour?" she asks.

"I do much research before this cruise. I say, Pasha you will try something new each place."

"Do you do adventurous stuff all the time? Or just for this vacation?"

"I try adventure in every city. Maybe I have food. Maybe I climb mountain. It depend how much time." I reach out, pinch the clasp of her silver necklace, and slide it to the back of her neck. Then I nod at the charm. "Is very pretty. Why peacock?"

Kristen chuckles softly as she touches the silver charm resting on her collarbone. "It's a symbol of immortality." She pauses. "Ironic, right?"

I can't laugh, though I know she's trying to keep the conversation light.

"But it also reminds me to stay centered and have a lighthearted approach to life. To be grateful for what I have. And to laugh because it keeps me healthy."

Chapter Thirty-Four

KRISTEN

COLORFUL, SPANISH-COLONIAL-STYLE BUILDINGS LINE THE STREETS of Old San Juan, housing hundreds of shops and restaurants. After popping into a few stores, we're drawn to an electric orange door and slip in to grab a drink at the bar.

Music-theme artwork and multiple paintings of Bob Marley pop under stucco walls painted in bold reds, purples, and greens. The decor matches the pulsing beats of the reggae music pouring through the speakers.

"Why haven't you gotten anything for yourself?" I ask as Pasha places the bags of things he'd bought for me at our feet.

He slides onto the barstool next to me, mumbling something in another language, blowing his faux Greek image out of the water again.

"English, *Pavlos,*" I remind him.

"It translate to 'Silly girl.'" He grins before bringing our joined hands toward his mouth. "Because I have everything I need right here." His soft lips brush the sensitive skin on the inside of my wrist.

Every touch makes me tingle. "You know it makes me want to run away when you talk like that."

My thoughts drift to the intensity of our whirlwind romance over the last few days. A relationship that should have been flippant and fun by definition alone spiraled into a connection I can't deny—a connection I never allow myself to have with men.

"I find you easy," he says. "You are beautiful, fun, loud."

I interrupt him by cocking my head, silently questioning if he intended "loud" as a compliment.

"This is good thing. You are bold. No bullshit," he explains.

His description makes me smile. Not everyone appreciates—or understands—my loud, no-bullshit personality. Since he's bold and loud himself, we mesh well.

"You have good attitude of adventure. Of life. Too many people, they worry about tomorrow. Why is this?" Pasha asks.

"To plan the future?" I suggest.

"There is no guarantee."

Truer words have never been spoken. I've been living for the moment my entire life. I have to because I don't know when my body will finally give out. Out of anyone he could be talking to, I understand too well.

"Why do you say that?" I ask. I have a reason to think—and live—the way I do; now, I want to hear his.

"Life should be lived. Today. Now."

It's not the answer I want. It's too vague—a cop-out. Time to be bold and blunt, as he claims to appreciate from me. "Can I ask you something personal?"

"Of course," Pasha says.

I glance around the empty bar before asking, "Are you sick?"

Pasha leans back, his eyes wide with surprise. "Why you ask me this?"

"The only people I know who live like they're dying are actually dying."

"We are all dying," he responds.

"I know." I shake my head to sort out my thoughts. "I know we're all going to die someday. I'm not talking about basic biology. I'm talking about reality."

"What is difference?"

"People our age are supposed to think they're invincible."

Pasha laugh. "People who believe this are destined to die early."

"Some of us are destined to die early anyway."

Pasha's eyes narrow and he grabs my hand. "You act happy, but you fall into sadness quick. Is easy for you, yes?"

His use of the words "fall into sadness" is a sweet way to let me know I'm being a buzzkill, so I change the subject.

I nod to an arched doorframe along the back wall. "Wanna have sex in the bathroom?"

His response is quick and firm. "Yes."

I smile. "I'm kidding." My suggestion was meant to get his mind off how much of a downer I'd turned into.

"I am not," he says.

I scan the bar. Other than the bartender, there's no one else here. We've been the only ones in the place since we came in.

"I'm pretty sure we'd get caught."

Pasha places a hand on my thigh and slips his fingers under my shorts. "What will they do? Kick us out? We must leave anyway."

His nimble fingers brush between my legs, coaxing me into believing the logic in his reasoning, but the thought of being caught still makes me wary.

He leans in and whispers, "With you, I cannot get enough. You are warm and safe."

Without a second thought, I jump off the barstool and lace my fingers with his, leading him through the arched opening to the hallway for the restrooms. I drag him into the room labeled with a woman's silhouette, figuring that would be the cleaner of the two.

We're lucky because it's a room with one toilet and a sink rather than a large space with multiple stalls. Pasha locks the door behind us, then spins around and grabs my shorts, unsnapping the button with one swift tug. I pull down my zipper as he lowers the front of his shorts. He grabs my hips, lifts me up, and turns us so my back is against the door. I wrap my arms around his neck and dig my face into his shoulder as he guides himself into me.

"Oh my god!" I cry out with sheer ecstasy from the feel of his thick cock inside me.

At the same time, he whispers, "Fuck!" into my shoulder.

Now, I'm no expert, but having sex standing up with another

person attached has to be hard as hell. I know the guy is in shape, but Pasha doesn't seem fazed at all. He's stronger than any man I've ever dated. Not that I've ever tried any position other than missionary before him.

Our bathroom escapade is fast and intense. After one particularly exceptional thrust, I shift, but Pasha grabs my hips and holds us both completely still. He takes one hand off me and presses his palm against the door. I squeeze my eyes shut and tighten my arms around his neck as I try to control my breath against his shoulder.

"You are my home. My strength," Pasha whispers against my hair as he grinds against me.

His words send an initial pang of elation through me. The high turns to sadness just as quickly because I'll never be his home. I'll always be the vacation fling he'll tell his buddies about.

Despite our conversation just a few moments earlier, I can't help but think about the future. What about next week, when we're back home, living our everyday lives?

Can I go back to a mundane existence after meeting him? Will I dream about what could have been? What kind of fallout would I have from today?

A loud knock interrupts my thoughts.

"What are you doing in there?" a man yells. "Get out of there."

My body shakes as Pasha laughs, but I don't share his feelings about the lightness of the situation.

"*Un momento,*" he answers in Spanish as he lets me go.

As soon I'm on my feet, I fix my clothes into place so I can walk out looking somewhat respectable.

We both wash our hands quickly, then Pasha opens the door and sweeps his arm out with a flourish, allowing me to exit first. I duck my head so I don't have to see the disdain on the bartender's face and shuffle past quickly. Pasha follows close behind with his fingers on my back to let me know we're in this together.

Thankfully, we'd paid our bill when our drinks were delivered, or it would have been even more awkward. When we reach the fresh air, I take a deep breath.

Pasha bumps my hip with his and laughs. "I did not realize this would embarrass you, Miss Adventure."

"I've never been this"—I lower my voice—"*sexually* adventurous before."

He laughs again. "Good. This side of you is all mine."

Pasha knows how to bring out the best in me, from the fun and adventurous side to the self-conscious parts I keep to myself. I've never given myself this freely and openly to anyone before.

My chest tightens, wondering how I could ever give anyone else this much of myself after being with him.

Chapter Thirty-Five

PASHA

Kristen and I walk through the streets hand in hand, laughing and joking with a familiarity that shouldn't be there after less than a week of knowing each other. I can't get over how easy it is to be with her, as if we've known each other for years rather than days.

"This way," I say, pulling her toward a kiosk on the corner of the street.

Send a message in a bottle

Glass bottles in various sizes and colors litter the surface of the stand. Stacks of paper, torn and dyed to appear old and withered, sit on shelves above. I step away to speak to the cashier, leaving Kristen to check out the various assortment of bottles available. I see her reach out and touch a glittery pink bottle out of the corner of my eye.

No surprise there. Based on her wardrobe and nails, I know she loves pink and sparkles, which matches her personality.

Bright, happy, extroverted.

After I pay for two bottles, I shove my wallet into my back pocket and say, "You will choose bottle and paper, yes?"

Her eyes light up, and she immediately grabs the glittery pink one she'd touched.

"What are you gonna write?" she asks.

"I will tell this world how awesome I am." I wink at her.

"Don't even wink at me like you're joking," she says. "I have no doubt that's exactly what you plan to write."

I shrug because, on any other occasion, she'd be right. "What will you write?"

"I'm going to tell everyone how awesome you are, too," she teases.

"You are smart woman. I like this." I finish scribbling my message and start rolling the paper.

"You're not going to show me?" Kristen asks as I stuff the paper into the green bottle I chose.

"Nope." I press the tiny cork into the top and stuff it in the front pocket of my shorts. "You done?"

She scowls at me and taps her lips with the end of the pen as she contemplates what to write.

Writing a message in a bottle is more pressure than you'd think, especially when the cashier told me that he would retrieve the bottles from the water as soon as we were out of sight and mail them to me at the address I'd given him when Kristen was out of earshot.

"Got it!" she says.

I love how her entire face lights up when she thinks of something.

I lean toward her, peeking over her shoulder to catch a glimpse.

"Oh no!" She smiles coyly before turning her back to me. She hovers over the kiosk for increased privacy. She finishes the note quickly, rolls the paper, and shoves it into the bottle.

"Done," she announces as she pushes the cork in. "Now, what do we do?"

I nod goodbye to the cashier and grab Kristen's hand again. We walk down the crowded street to the bay.

I point to the water. "The man says we throw them here. He arrange this with city. Said this is only place."

"Cool."

As Kristen rolls the bottle between her palms, I watch the sunlight reflect off the glittery pink surface. At first, I don't know if she'll actually throw it because she loves that sparkly bottle. Then, to my surprise, she wraps her fingers around the thin neck and cocks her arm back.

"Ready?" she asks.

I smile and nod. Her bright eyes sparkle in the sunlight, like a human version of the bottle she's throwing away. My chest constricts. Even if I never get the bottle back, a silly gimmick can be replaced, but I'll never be able to replace her.

"*Adin, dva—*" I count.

"*En español, por favor,*" she says using the predominant language in Puerto Rico.

"*Sí,*" I agree with a smile. "*Uno, dos, tres!*"

On three, we both chuck our bottles as hard as we can. Mine sails far past hers, but she seems proud to have made it into the water, so I don't say anything.

We watch in silence as our messages float further out. I take a deep breath and squeeze her hand on the exhale, fixing my gaze on the water.

"How many languages do you know?" Kristen asks after letting me have a moment.

"A few. I am not the best. But I know words in quite a few," I say. "You speak Spanish, yes?"

"A little. Enough to say 'please' and 'thank you.' Order a beer. Ask for the bathroom." She shrugs. "The basics."

"We are both multilingual."

"What's your native language?" she asks. The question surprises me, though it shouldn't. I can't believe she hasn't asked before now.

"Slovakian?" The lies keep flowing.

"Are you asking me or telling me?"

I wink. "I'm making sure being Slovakian is acceptable to a beautiful Greek girl."

"It's about the person, not the nationality."

"You like the person?" I ask.

"Yes." Kristen stops in the middle of the sidewalk and turns to me. "You are a wonderful person. I can't believe I was lucky enough to have met you." She rises onto her toes and kisses me.

When she pulls away, I glance at my watch. "We need to get cab to next place."

I had to change the subject fast because I have zero knowledge of anything Slovakian except the names of a few hockey players. And I've avoided talking about hockey for a week just in case it sparked something in her memory.

"The glowing water?" she asks.

"Yes." I drag her toward a corner, then crane my neck, searching for a taxi. "You will love this. I promise."

Chapter Thirty-Six
KRISTEN

THE TOUR COMPANY FOR THE "GLOWING WATER" EXCURSION PASHA booked could make a killing if they sold foam mats to sit on during the van ride to the location where clients put kayaks in the water.

Potholes riddle the dirt road, rattling the dilapidated van and sending passengers sliding and bouncing into each other. Couple that with the lumpy seat with springs digging into my flesh, and by the time we finally file out, my butt feels like I sat on a mat of jagged rocks.

"You all brought your mosquito repellent, right?" our tour guide asks once we've all gotten out of the van. "Time to spray down."

Pasha pulls a can of bug spray out of the pocket of his shorts and points the nozzle at me.

"Close your eyes," Pasha warns before spraying me with a mist of chemicals.

I cough. Which was nothing new, of course, but with the fumes swirling from every direction, I literally can't stop coughing. I run toward the van to get away from the group of sprayers. Pasha follows me.

"Are you okay?"

"Yeah." I cough again. "Too much at once. I need to catch my breath."

"I'm sorry, I should have thought first." He shakes his head.

I touch his forearm to stop his apology. "It's okay."

He nods, but his shoulders drop as he walks away to spray himself.

I finish hacking and try to compose myself. Every time I cleared my throat in the van, people on the tour cringed and turned away as if my cough would bring on a zombie apocalypse. But they didn't know, and I didn't explain.

I let them keep their distance like I should have done with Pasha.

OH MY GOD. *Oh my God. Oh my God. Oh my God. Oh my God.*

As I hold the paddle with one hand and grip the edge of the vivid yellow kayak with the other, my stomach feels heavy, like I've just scarfed an entire pan of Aunt Dimitra's baklava.

Kayaks are narrow. And in these particular kayaks, we're sitting on a bench that's level with the sides of the boat, not safely tucked into the cup-like floor. The many reasons I've never noticed the various types of kayaks flood my mind. Because I'd never been around scary-ass kayaks before. Because I'm afraid of water. Especially at night when I can't see what's lurking under the surface.

"You okay?" Pavel asks.

I nod. Probably because if I open my mouth, I'll either barf or scream.

Pasha was so excited about taking me to see glowing water I just went along with it, assuming we'd be gazing at it from atop a bridge or something.

I didn't realize we'd have to kayak through the mangroves to get there. I didn't even know what a fucking mangrove was until this trip.

Mangroves, as the tour guide explained, are creepy clusters of trees at the water's edge.

Okay, our tour guide didn't call them creepy. That was all me. Because paddling through a river canopied by hundreds of giant trees with massive twisted roots along the sides when it's fucking dark as tar is fucking creepy.

At this particular moment, I kinda hate Pasha.

Screw him and his super-sweet extended trip to see glowing water in San Juan. Couldn't he have taken me on one of those small plane excursions to look at it from above?

Complaining makes me sound like a spoiled, ungrateful brat, but I'm okay with that. Because trekking through water we aren't familiar with in the pitch black is fucked up.

"You are okay, yes?" Pasha calls over his shoulder. "You are sure?"

I nod again, this time turning my head slightly.

"You gonna help paddle?" he asks.

I thought I might be falling in love with him. I'm an idiot.

With shaking hands, I release my grip on the side of the kayak, grab the paddle resting on my lap, and dig into the water.

"Don't dig," Pasha commands. "Just skim the top."

"I've never done this before," I snap.

"No shit?" Pasha teases.

"Please don't let us tip over. I beg you."

"We will not tip."

"I'm gonna barf."

"You are this scared, yes?" Pasha asks.

Though I believe he's sincere, his voice holds a lilt of laughter, and using my paddle to knock him out of the boat crosses my mind. Except that would tip us for sure, and I can't risk that.

"If we live through this, I will kill you for taking me here."

"You will forget your fear when you see glowing water."

This water better glow like a fucking candy kid at a rave because my insides are about to burst from my mouth.

And I assume we still have to kayak back to our starting point after seeing the "glowing water" in what the tour guide called a biolumines-cence bay. Knowing the correct terminology doesn't help since I still don't understand what causes the water to glow. Hopefully, we'll find out soon.

Once I get used to paddling, the act isn't so bad. In fact, it's excel-lent exercise. But my head won't let me forget that this wobbly kayak could tip at any time. Especially when a fucking tree almost clothes-lines me and knocks me out of the boat.

I duck and shift abruptly to the right to dodge a low-hanging cluster of tangled branches. I shriek and drop the paddle in the water to grab the sides of the boat.

"Pick it up," Pavel snaps.

Though flustered and frightened, I manage to bite back my fear and reach over the side, grabbing the paddle and sweeping it out of the water. "We almost tipped. We almost tipped."

"No, we didn't. I swear this to you," Pavel assures me. "But you must keep hold of the paddle."

"It felt like we were gonna tip." My voice shakes. I bite my lip to hold back tears.

"I'm having second thoughts about this trip, Kristen."

"Ya think?"

"I did not know you would be this afraid."

"Jumping off a cliff into water in the light of day, I can handle. Wading through a beautiful pool with a swim-up bar is totally my style. But paddling around in the dark looking for glowing water is not my idea of a good time."

Silence.

The silence isn't one of those "comfortable" silences people lie about, either.

Nope.

Totally uncomfortable since I just blasted the guy who wanted me to see this glowing water so much that he paid to extend my vacation.

"We will be there soon. And I will never scare you again."

Of course, he won't. We'll never see each other again. The thought makes me want to barf far more than this pitch-black, wobbly boat ride.

"I'm sorry. I didn't expect this."

Silence again. So, I shut my mouth and paddle, hoping I don't burst into tears. After navigating the channel through the scary-ass mangroves, we finally reach an opening.

"This is Mosquito Bay, the brightest of the three bioluminescent bays in Puerto Rico," the tour guide tells us.

The glowing stick hanging from the tour guide's neck is the only hint I have of where to look as she speaks. Thankfully, our boat is among the first to reach the bay because of Pasha's skills. When the rest of the kayaks catch up, we paddle out farther as the guide gives us the spiel.

"The bay is full of dinoflagellates, or dinos, which are single-celled organisms that are sort of half plant, half animal. When agitated, they emit a bluish-green light. You can put your hand in the water to agitate or use your paddle. Try it out."

I lock eyes with Pasha before I try it. The smile on his face reminds me of a kid excited to try a science experiment at school. He extends his hand to me, and I take hold. Then we dip our hands into the water together, lightly stirring the water.

A glowing, bluish-green zigzag streaks over the water when we wave our joined hands across the surface. It's slight but magical nonetheless.

"Whoa," I whisper, squeezing Pasha's fingers.

We catch eyes again, where his expression had morphed from childlike wonder to a smile of satisfaction.

This was what he wanted to show me, to experience with me.

So innocent. So primal. So stunning.

Life in its simplest form is amazing.

Emotion overwhelms me. I shut my eyes as I realize this is a once-in-a-lifetime bucket-list experience. But the rush of blood to my heart has little to do with the breathtaking simplicity of the single-cell organisms making the water glow and everything to do with the man whose hand I won't release until we have to start back toward shore.

Chapter Thirty-Seven
PASHA

THE ENTIRE TIME WE PADDLED BACK, KRISTEN COULDN'T STOP talking about how amazing the glowing water was and how touched she was that I encouraged her to experience it.

The compliments are a 180-degree change from her curt comments on the ride out. And because I'm a complete and total bastard, I'd misunderstood her complaining until it finally dawned on me that she was deathly afraid.

How could she still speak to me—still trust me—after I'd put her in a situation that frightened her so much? I hurt her without even realizing it.

I've been so mesmerized by her kindness and how she sees me that I completely forgot who I really am—the person who's been withholding information that would change her opinion of me.

Which solidifies that I'm a coward and a liar who deserves to be hated.

On the van ride back to where the excursion began, Kristen's skin is dotted with goose bumps from the chilly night air filtering through the open windows of the van. I wrap my arm around her and hug her to me. As I slide my hand up and down her arm, she snuggles into my side and sighs with exhaustion.

"I am asshole, taking you on this trip without checking. I did not know you are afraid of water," I say. "The cliff diving, I think—I just think anyone is afraid of cliff diving. I'm sorry."

Kristen peels herself away from my side. "Don't apologize, Pasha. That was amazing. I'm the one who should be sorry, acting like an ungrateful drama queen the entire time even though it wasn't so bad."

"'Not so bad' does not mean same as 'good.'"

"It was beautiful," she assures me. "I've been on more crazy experiences with you in a week than in my entire life before now. Things I would have been too afraid to try, even with all my big talk about life experiences."

"Is this compliment?" I ask.

"Yes. Thank you." She quickly kisses my cheek and snuggles into me again.

If there's one thing I've learned about Kristen over the last few days, it's that she doesn't lie. At least, not that I'm aware of.

She's a better person than I am.

It's going to kill me to let her go.

Chapter Thirty-Eight

KRISTEN

THE AIR IS SO THICK ON THE CAB RIDE TO THE AIRPORT THAT I think I might choke. As much as I want to blame the humidity, I know it's because it's almost time to say goodbye to Pasha.

He runs his hand across my thigh, along the soft fabric of the yoga pants I'd changed into for the flight home. It's not even a sexual touch, yet my stomach tightens, and there's a pulse between my legs as my body reacts to his touch like it has since the moment I met him.

"This was best week of my life. I do not deserve you, Kristen. You are too smart and beautiful and honest and good. So fucking good." He takes a deep breath and shakes his head. "You deserve better man."

"Stop saying things like that." I reach out and press my palms to his cheeks. "You are a wonderful person. And even if we never see each other again, I need you to remember that. To know that. You have so much good in your heart. You're sweet and kind and selfless."

Pasha tries to pull back when I speak, but I hold his head still. "Yes, you are selfless. You would have done anything to make me happy. To make me smile. I know that. I felt that. You can try to pretend whatever you want, but you are one of the most amazing people I've ever met. And I don't give that compliment very often."

"It was all you." He smiles. "You bring out protector in me. You make me want to be good man. You have light in you that I want in me." He winks. "This is why I fuck you so much."

"Oh no!" I shake my head. "You can't turn this into something less sentimental. If this is the last time I'll ever see you, I need to lay it all on the line." I take a deep breath. "In just over a week, you have set the highest standard for how a man should treat me. You've shown me that I shouldn't be afraid of loving someone and letting someone love me." A tear slides down my cheek. "You've shown me that there are people who will accept me for who I am and what I can offer. Even if I can't offer forever."

Pasha's eyes glisten. "I envy this man who lucky enough to get every single second you have to give."

"Jesus," I whisper. "Why are we doing this?"

"Because you deserve happiness."

"As do you," I counter. "It's okay to change. It's okay to forgive. The people who matter will accept you for who you are and what you have to give. Fuck the ones that don't."

When the cab comes to a halt, I realize we've arrived at the airport. We sit quietly and stare into each other's eyes.

Finally, I break the silence. "This feels like a funeral, doesn't it?"

Pasha leans back, and his body visibly relaxes. "Whose?"

I laugh. "Two sappy lovers saying goodbye. Seems so Shake-spearean."

"I love—" He stops. "That you say Shakespeare." Pasha holds my face in his hands and looks into my eyes. "You are the girl that I could marry." He closes his eyes and presses his forehead to mine. "I do not want to let you go. I do not want you to leave my life."

"It doesn't have to end. I'm open to trying a long-distance relation-ship," I plead.

Pasha shakes his head. "If we meet under other circumstances, this could go on. But not right now. Is complicated."

"It doesn't have to be." I feel the tear slide down my cheek before I can even try to stop it.

"Fuck!" Pasha curses, squeezing his eyes closed. "Saying goodbye to you is the hardest thing."

"Then don't."

I sound so pathetic. Pleading. Begging. What's wrong with me?

He glances at his watch. "You have thirty minutes for the check-in."

I shook my head as tears flowed freely down my cheeks. "Please don't do this."

He doesn't say anything.

I finally sat up and took a deep breath. "Better get going."

Our cab driver opens my door, and I get out. Pasha follows me, though his flight isn't until tomorrow morning.

"I've never been able to be so honest and free with any other guy. I never wanted to show that side of myself to anyone but my friends. I'm glad I opened up to you. I'm a better person for knowing you."

Pasha opens his mouth to speak, but I stop him.

"See you soon," I whisper. Then I square my shoulders and grab the handles of my suitcases in each hand, rolling them behind me. I refuse to say goodbye because I truly believe there will be life to our relationship after this.

"Goodbye," I hear Pasha say as I walk away.

I wince and bite my lip. It takes everything I have not to break down in tears as I walk into the airport alone.

Chapter Thirty-Nine

KRISTEN

Go go go, I silently will the cab driver. *I cannot be late for my best friend's wedding reception.*

I'd been so wrapped up in my first day back at work after the cruise that Auden's celebration completely slipped my mind. If I had been thinking correctly, I would've never stayed the entire day with Pasha.

I'd scheduled that early flight out of San Juan for a reason. I wanted time to rest after the trip because I knew a full day of work and then Auden's celebration would take a considerable toll. But that's how my schedule worked out. My parents had purchased the cruise before Auden and Aleksandr had picked a date to hold the party—and well before I'd gotten a job.

"Thank you so much." I pay the driver and scramble out of the cab.

My dress rode up while sitting, so I stop to compose myself before entering. I shimmy my hips while tugging at the hem, but the black, body-hugging skirt pops back up to mid-thigh.

Was it this short when I wore it on the cruise? No wonder Pasha couldn't keep his hands off me.

My heart hurts at the thought of Pasha. Yesterday morning, he texted Mom's phone to make sure my flight landed safely. His thoughtful text made me giddy and gave me a glimmer of hope.

No more messages came through after that, so it didn't seem like he'd reconsidered the idea of a long-distance relationship. It sucks knowing the instant attraction and close bond we'd formed was over. But there's no reason to spend more time obsessing over a guy I'd never see again.

You can't fall in love with someone in a week, especially not during the fairy-tale scenario we had on the cruise. Pasha and I were two free spirits who found each other in the bubble of a perfect vacation.

The whirlwind relationship served a purpose. It taught me not to settle, no matter how much my parents pressured me. After a week with Pasha, the thought of dating someone like Spiros sounds like hell on earth.

Instead of dwelling on lost love, I pull Mom's phone out of the glittery silver clutch I'd bought to match my glittery silver pumps and shoot off a text to my friend, Lacy. I knew she'd be there since she was me and Auden's roommate for two years at college.

Lacy: Who is this?

Me: It's KK. I have my mom's phone. Lost mine on the cruise. :(

Lacy: Oh! Get your ass in here! Auden has been asking about you every five seconds for the last half hour.

Me: I'm walking in now.

I'm the worst best friend ever.

I dash through the doors of the Roostertail, a swanky restaurant on the Detroit River, and quickly find the Marine Room. In my twenty-two years as a metro Detroit resident, I'd heard of the Roostertail on multiple occasions, but I've never been here.

It takes me a minute to find my bearings once I enter the magnificent room. The space has Auden written all over it, from the gorgeous blood-red sashes tied around the back of each chair to the floor-to-ceiling windows showcasing a striking view of the Windsor skyline across the river.

Aleksandr did an exceptional job prompting the decorators. He had taken the reins in planning the party because Auden said she didn't want to make a big fuss about getting married.

She said she wanted a huge celebration like this after she and Aleksandr had been married fifty years. But relationships are about compromise, and since he agreed to a courthouse wedding, she agreed to this big-ass party.

After the childhood trauma she had, she deserves the celebration. And she deserves the wonderful man who put this perfect party together for her.

I bask in the warm glow of sphere pendant fixtures wrapped in white lights dropping from the ceiling and candles flickering on each table as I scan the room for Lacy—or anyone else I know.

I finally see Landon Taylor, Aleksandr's best friend, standing in a group of hockey players. They used to pay together on the Aviators, Detroit's minor league hockey team. Landon was traded but ended up staying in Detroit and playing for the NHL team here.

We hooked up once right when Auden and Aleksandr first got together, but it was nothing serious, and we're totally cool with each other.

I hurry over to the group and drape an arm across Landon's shoulders. "Hey, guys!"

"Geez, KK! You scared me." After the surprise subsides, Landon's lips morph into a smile.

I think the girl next to him smiles too, but her head is tilted down, her face barely visible under the veil of dark hair. I can tell without even being introduced to her that it's Landon's new girlfriend. Auden told me about sweet, shy Gaby, the sister of Drew Bertucci, Auden's best friend growing up.

Instead of waiting two seconds for Landon to introduce me to her, I extend my hand. "Hi! I'm Kristen, but you can call me KK. Everyone does."

When she lifts her head, her eyes are wide with surprise. "Hi," she croaks. Then she clears her throat. "Hi. I'm Gaby."

"Gaby!" I throw my arms around her. "I've heard so much about you."

Her smile falters, and she looks a bit panicked.

"Don't worry. It's all good stuff," I assure her. Then I look over Gaby's head and scan the room. "Is your brother here, too?"

It probably seems like I'm interested in him, but I just want to see what he looks like. I've never met him in all the years I've known Auden. Probably because he had a shit fit when she started dating Aleksandr.

Aleks thought it was jealousy, but I didn't. I knew they had more of a brother-sister relationship, and Drew thought he was saving Auden from getting her heart broken by a young, arrogant hockey player.

Good thing Aleksandr is the furthest thing from a ladies' man. The guy is hot and slightly cocky, but he's not a player.

"He's around here somewhere," Landon answers. "I saw him a few minutes ago."

I lower my voice and lean in toward Landon and Gaby. "Who are all of these perfect male specimens?"

"Most of them are guys on the Aviators. Do you want me to introduce you?"

"No, not yet. I'm headed to the bar to grab a drink first."

"Want me to get you one?" Landon asks, raising his pint glass. "Gaby and I are both running low."

"No thanks. I'll go up there. I need to see what they have."

"It's a full bar," he assures me, always going out of his way to be helpful—even if the help is dismissed. It was one of the reasons I wasn't attracted after our hookup.

Golden Retriever guys aren't my type.

"Oh my gosh, Landon! I want to stroll around and check out the eye candy. Did you have to make me say it?"

The joke comes easily since my friends expect flirty and fun KK. Plus, it's hard to ignore all the sexiness in the room. As a hot hockey player himself, Aleksandr's main group of friends consists of buff athletes.

Too bad I can't stop thinking about Pasha. But it's over, and there's no reason to be a buzzkill at my best friend's wedding reception. I'll spill the entire cruise story and whirlwind romance to her another time.

At the bar, I stand in line behind a platinum blonde with dark roots wearing a skintight red dress more appropriate for a club than a wedding reception. Then again, I shouldn't be so judgmental since the dress I'm wearing is equally tight and short.

Usually, I'd make friendly small talk, commenting on her gorgeous strappy black stiletto heels to break the ice. But she's busy tapping away on her cell phone, so I refrain.

Instead, I scan the room again, taking in the crowd. Before the cruise, the sheer number of hot men to flirt with would've been an exciting thought. I'd be working this room like the social butterfly I am. But flirting isn't on my mind after Pasha.

Where is he? What is he doing? *Who* is he doing?

Ugh.

It was only a week. How could he have had this much of an effect on me in a week?

It feels like he ruined me for other men. I can't imagine having as much fun with anyone else. I can't imagine having a connection like we have with anyone else. I can't imagine—

"Miss? What can I get you, Miss?" The bartender's voice brings me back to the moment.

"Sor—" I start. When I look up, I realize his question was for the blonde in front of me, who's still tapping on her phone.

"Vodka," she demands without looking up.

The bartender nods and grabs a bottle from the shelf behind him. He pours straight vodka into a glass and pushes it across the bar. The girl looks up to grab the glass, then walks away.

"What can I get you?" He sounds tired, though the party has barely started.

I catch a flash in my peripheral vision and shriek.

Hastily, I apologize to the bartender while digging into my purse. I throw a five onto the bar. It's an open bar, but I feel bad for screaming in his face. "I'll be back."

Neither my five-inch heels nor the slippery wood floor would stop me from sprinting to hug my best friend.

"You're here!" Auden throws her arms around me. I squeeze her tight, holding back the tears that spring to my eyes. I've never seen her look so radiant.

"You are gorgeous!" I say when I pull back and take in the sight of my friend in a traditional wedding dress.

Auden looks stunning in a strapless, ruched gown the color of champagne, dotted with crystal bling resembling tiny bubbles. The fabric hugs the curves of her hips and upper thighs before it flows into three asymmetrical tiers and a final lacy tier at the bottom that brushes her spectacular glittery heels—the same heels she'd worn for her wedding at the courthouse. The dress' mermaid silhouette fits in with a reception on the water.

"Is it lame?" Auden asks, brushing her palms across the fabric at her hips.

"Lame?" I repeat. "You are absolutely stunning! And I've never seen you so happy."

My best friend pulls me into another hug.

"Don't you dare cry," I warn her. I don't want her to mess up her perfect makeup. Also, I don't want to cry. If I cry, I won't be able to stop, and my night would be over. The tears would start with happiness for Auden and continue in sadness over Pasha.

"Where the hell have you been? Why haven't you returned my calls or texts?" Auden asks when we pull away.

"Sia sent my phone over the rail on the first night of our trip."

"No!" Auden's eyes are wide.

"Yeah, it sucked. I was phoneless. But I'll get pics from Lena and Sia and post them soon."

"You have a lot of explaining to do," Auden says.

It's an odd way to ask about my trip, but I brush it off because this party is about celebrating Auden and Aleksandr's marriage.

"I'll tell you all about it. But not tonight." I take her hand and tug her toward the dance floor. "Tonight we party."

AFTER MORE THAN two hours of dancing, drinking, and chatting with friends and Auden's family, I excuse myself to use the restroom.

Being among my people is exactly what I needed to keep my mind off my broken heart. It's exactly the return to reality I needed after the cruise. Plus, now that Auden lives in Charlotte with Aleksandr, I want to enjoy every second with her.

When I entered the bathroom, the blonde in the red dress who'd been in front of me at the bar stood at the sink, inhaling a cigarette. Scratch that—from the pungent odor, it has to be weed.

"Hey." She meets my eyes in the mirror and offers me the joint.

"No thanks," I say, shaking my head and hightailing it to a stall.

When I return to the party, Auden and Aleksandr are snuggling in a corner. I can't help the jealous pang in my heart at seeing them so happy and content. They have an amazing relationship. They help each other. They make each other better.

I've only ever felt that with Pasha. He made me better. And he said I made him better, too—at least for a short time.

I wish I were snuggling in a corner with him right now.

I glance at the happily married couple once more before swinging by the bar. Then, I carry my drink to the patio, still thinking about Pasha.

I can't figure out why he wasn't open to pursuing a long-distance relationship. Why throw away something so special when we both felt the connection?

I pull Mom's phone out of my purse and send him a quick text. I know trying to keep in contact is stupid, but I do it anyway.

The worst that can happen is that he doesn't respond, right?

Multiple phones ding and buzz amid the crowd enjoying the fresh air on the patio. I toss the phone back in my purse and spin around to go back inside. As I grab the door handle, I catch a familiar face out of the corner of my eye.

Confusion and surprise hold me captive, stopping me from moving forward.

What the. . .

Though his head is tilted down with his eyes locked on his phone screen, there's no doubt who the perfectly gelled dark hair belongs to.

Chapter Forty

PASHA

"PASHA?" KRISTEN'S VOICE CUTS THROUGH THE THICK, HUMID AIR.

Here we go.

I lift my head immediately, needing to see her one last time before the bottom drops out. I am ready to face her wrath because I deserve it.

Hell, I crave it.

She stands before me in a tight black dress that hugs every curve.

I remember the dress. It's the same one she wore on the first night of the cruise—the night we danced, our bodies intertwined and in sync for hours. I can't help but scan her from her tanned legs all the way up to her face. Her lips twist in confusion and disbelief as her eyebrows veer together, creating an angry wrinkle between them.

"What are you doing here?" she asks. Her eyes darken as they flick between me and Svetlana, who sits beside me with her arm slung across the back of my chair.

To Kristen, I'm sure it looks like Svetlana and I are together. Ironically enough, I'd just been telling her about Kristen, though I left out the part about knowing she'd be here tonight.

"I know the groom," is the only thing I can say.

"I'm . . ." she begins, then shakes her head. A thick chunk of her silky brown waves falls into her eyes. She tucks it behind her ear before speaking again. "I'm really confused right now. We just spent a week together. You knew I was from Detroit, and you didn't tell me you'd be here for a wedding reception?"

Her eyes shift to Svetlana again. And I watch as pain and anger replace the previous look of confusion and disbelief as if I've silently plunged the knife of betrayal deeper into her heart and twisted it.

"That's her, isn't it?" Svetlana asks me in Russian. She leans closer and whispers angrily. "Did you know she'd be here?"

I wave her away with my hand and stood. "This is what I cannot tell you," I tell Kristin. "This is how I know you will be angry with me."

"Well, yeah! It doesn't take a genius to know I'd be pissed to find out that you had a girlfriend the entire time you played me on the cruise."

Svetlana bolts to her feet. "What are you doing, Pasha? What did you tell her?" she yells at me, still speaking Russian.

I shrug her off again. In English I snap, "Give me a minute."

"No. You will explain this to me—to us—right now," she demands, also in English.

"I will explain nothing." I slam my hand on the table.

"Fuck that! You'll explain everything!" Kristen yells. "Who are you? Who the fuck are you, for real?" Her hands curl into fists at her side.

I close my eyes. "You know who I am."

"No, I don't. I know who you pretended to be: Pasha, a sweet, adventurous, fictional man from a cruise. I don't know who you really are."

Suddenly, Auden bursts onto the patio with Aleksandr on her heels. "What's going on?"

"I have no fucking clue," Kristen mumbles, still glaring at me.

"Pasha, what's going on?" Aleksandr repeats.

"Who *is* this guy?" Kristen asks. She tears her eyes away from me, silently pleading with Auden for an answer.

"Shit," Auden whispers, closing her eyes briefly and pinching the bridge of her nose with her thumb and middle finger as if comprehending something. "That's Pavel Gribov. He's one of Aleksandr's teammates."

Kristen turns to me again, her eyes widening as the recognition of how she knows my name sets in. She staggers backward.

I lurch forward, reaching out, but knowing I can't go to her.

"Did you know who I was when we met?" she asks quietly. It's just like her to get straight to the point.

"Not on the track," I answer. "But when you say Varenkov at the pool, I realize who you are."

"Why didn't you tell me who *you* were?" she snaps.

"Because you would never give me chance if you know." I drop my gaze to the ground, too ashamed to look at her.

We both knew the truth. I'm not proud of how she found out because I know not only have I hurt her, but I've embarrassed her, as well. I should have been a better man.

But this situation proves that I'm not.

I stand behind my decision. I don't deserve an amazing person like her, and she doesn't deserve a lying bastard like me.

Chapter Forty-One

KRISTEN

Pavel Gribov.

Pavel fucking Gribov.

My fingernails dig into my palms as I squeeze my fists tighter. My blood boils with anger, and I can't speak.

He's not wrong. If he would have told me his real name when we first met, I would have told him to fuck off.

I'd never met Pavel Gribov—or even seen him. I'd only heard about him from Auden.

He's the jerk who set up Aleksandr to make it seem like he cheated on Auden in a vicious attempt to break them up when they first started dating.

He's the jerk Auden had described as "a freaking horrible prick who runs his mouth and makes everyone around him miserable."

And I fell for him.

"I am right, yes?" Pavel asks when I don't answer.

I press my lips together and nod.

As ironic and idiotic as it sounds, I can't believe everything we'd discussed and shared over the last week was completely fake.

Questions barrage my brain, but I don't know which one to ask first. Especially since all I want to do is cuss the bastard out. Or run home and cry.

"I barely lie to you," he continues. "My name is Pasha. I was Aviator. I live in Charlotte."

"But . . . you . . . I—" I can't finish the sentence; hell, I can't begin the sentence since, technically, those things are the truth. Though he wasn't an aviator in the sense I believed.

It's still considered lying when you intentionally omit integral information, right?

Okay, maybe it wasn't lying, but it's definitely deceitful. And I don't need someone who could pull off that kind of deceit so easily in my life.

"A lie is a lie. There is no 'barely.'" I run a hand through my hair and tug at the roots before lifting my eyes to him. "I don't care who you are. I don't care what you do or where you live. I never want to see you again. I never want to speak to you again."

"If you would understand why I—"

"Understand? Understand what?" I interrupt him. "That you're a sick fuck who gets off on making other people miserable?"

After a short silence, Pasha says, "I'm sorry I hurt you. But . . ." He stops momentarily, then keeps going, "I warn you. I tell you what will happen after the cruise. I tell you that you deserve someone better."

His nonchalant attitude stuns me into silence. How can he be so cold after knowingly inflicting so much pain? His voice is void of any emotion—no anger, no sadness. His tone holds nothing but complete indifference.

At least anger is fueled by some kind of emotion. Anger is passion. Anger would mean he felt something.

I should hold my head high, turn my back, and walk away after being pulverized and embarrassed in public, but I can't. I want to see him react, to show some emotion. I want him to understand how much he hurt me.

But his detached responses take away the satisfaction.

"Pavel." Auden steps between us. "You need to leave."

He nods and turns around. The girl follows him, though she doesn't look happy or smug. No, she looks pissed. Evidently, I'm not the only one he played.

Though every limb in my body feels numb, I reach into my purse and fumble for my phone. I need to get out of here. It's one thing to cause drama. It's totally different to cause it at your best friend's wedding reception. It should have been the second-best day of Auden's life, and I ruined it.

"KK." Auden's warm hand cups my bare shoulder. "Are you okay?"

Her hand stays a constant comfort even with each heaving breath I take. I shake my head furiously. "I'm— fuck! Where's my phone?"

When I finally feel it, I pull it out, but it slips from my grasp and crashes to the ground. Mom's phone. The one I borrowed tonight because I'd been reckless and irresponsible with my own.

I watch it fall. Watch it smash.

Hundreds of glass shards bounce across the concrete. There's a pain in my chest that feels like someone shattered my heart with a sledgehammer, sending it flying into a million different pieces, a mirror of the broken screen.

Broken phones can be repaired. I'm not convinced my heart can.

"I have to go," I whisper, shaking Auden's hand from my shoulder and rushing to the door.

"Kristen!" Auden calls out.

I can't turn around. I can't stop walking until I reached the curb outside the restaurant. If I stop, I'll fall apart.

The last time I'd broken down like this was with Evan, the boyfriend who opened my naive, optimistic eyes to the dismal future of my relationships.

Before Evan, I never realized guys wouldn't want to commit to me. I never realized guys thought about being widowed or about children who would be left motherless.

But the pain that pierced my heart when Evan dumped me was nothing compared to the agony of Pasha's indifference. I thought I'd grown and learned since that moment in high school. I let my guard down and suffered the ultimate heartbreak.

Now that I know every minute with Pasha was utterly fake, why would I be surprised that he'd walk away with his tail between his legs?

The image fit with the words Auden had always used to describe him: heartless and miserable.

And to think I felt bad for him. I understood his pain came from a place of heartbreak and grief.

He tried to warn me about this exact situation. He knew who I was the entire time. But he didn't stay away. He let me into his life—let me fall head over heels for him. He knew he would break me, and he continued anyway.

Despite the irony of it now, I silently repeat the mantra I shared with Pasha on the cruise: *Don't waste your precious time on earth with someone who makes you miserable.*

Chapter Forty-Two

PASHA

"WHAT THE FUCK WAS THAT?" SVETLANA YELLS AT ME WHEN WE reach the Roostertail's parking lot.

Though we hadn't come to the party together, she made sure to leave with me because, like the sister-figure she's been my entire life, she had to rail me for what just went down inside.

"I don't want to talk about it."

"What do you mean you don't want to talk about it? You wouldn't shut up about this girl you met on your cruise and then she is here? And why was she so surprised to find out your name?" Svetlana fumbles in her purse, looking for something in the darkness. Then she pulls a joint out. "Why wouldn't you tell her you'd be here? It sounds perfect and romantic. But you fucked it up."

I slap her hand, and the joint falls into her bag. "Put that away until you get home."

"You killed my buzz, Pasha." She glowers at me. "I'm so pissed. I need to call Irina."

"Don't call Irina." I roll my eyes. I don't need both of my sisters railing me for something I already feel horrible about.

How does she not realize I did what I did because I don't deserve someone as good as Kristen? I deserve the girls who want to blow my cash on coke and suck my dick.

"You bring home every skank in the city, yet when you find a good woman, you fuck her over. I don't get it. What's your problem, Pasha?"

The cab I had the hostess call for us before we left pulls up in front of the restaurant. I open the door, allowing Svetlana to get in first. Her dress hikes up her thighs as she climbs in.

"Pull your skirt down, or I'll take a picture and post it on social media," I say. "Wonder what Arkady would say if he saw that." Of course, I'd never really do either—take a picture or blast it on social media for her fiancé, Arkady Zukarov, to see—and Svetlana knows it.

"Fuck you, Pasha," she spits, tugging at her dress as she settles into the backseat of the cab. "Be miserable. That's your business, but don't bring everyone else down with you."

I slide into the cab behind her and give the driver the address of Svetlana's house in Royal Oak. Even though the hotel I'm staying at is closer, I'll make sure she gets home safely first.

I take a breath and stare out the window.

"Explain." Svetlana pats my knee, but I don't turn toward her.

"I don't deserve her," I say.

We pass parts of Detroit that look like they've been destroyed by war. The desolation and despair seep through the window and mingle with my foul mood. I can't wait to get out of this shit hole of a city.

Soon, everything becomes a blur—traffic lights, street signs, houses. I'd driven a route like this multiple times in the years I lived in Detroit and went downtown for work, but I still can't tell exactly where we are. My mind is on Kristen and how I hurt her, not the route to Svetlana's house.

"You knew my father, Sveta," I say, using her diminutive. Everyone has a diminutive in Russia—hence the name Pasha, the diminutive of Pavel.

"Yes. So?"

"What do you mean, 'so'?" I ask, finally turning my gaze to her.

"I want to know what *you* mean. What does your father have to do with this?"

She inches closer to me and tries to put her arm around my shoulder, but I shrug her off. I don't want to be consoled or touched.

"Kristen said something on the cruise that stuck with me." I pause. "She said, 'If someone who died helped shape who you are, they'll always be part of you.'" I glance at her. "He's part of me, Sveta. I learned how to be a man from him."

Svetlana grabs my chin and holds my face still. "No. You didn't."

I shake my head, trying to free my face from her grip, but she holds me firm. Then she squeezes my jaw and makes me look at her.

"Pasha, you are not like him. You are a good man. A successful man. You could never be like him."

"But what if I get hurt and lose my career? What if I get angry and jealous like he did?" I close my eyes since she won't let go of my face. "I don't want to hurt her."

"You could never do that, Pasha. It's not you." She releases me. "Stop thinking like that."

"I can't." I drop my head into my hands. "I never gave a shit about anyone until her. She's loud and fun and has a quick mind. She gives shit back to me, ya know? But I care too much, and she's sick."

"What do you mean, sick?"

"She has this medical disorder. She may not live much past forty."

"What?" She draws back.

I nod. "I can't bear to lose her, Sveta. Losing Mama killed me. I can't get involved with Kristen and lose her, too." I turn to the window, feeling the desolation and despair that riddles this city creeping into my chest.

I'm ashamed as I repeat the exact thought I chastised Kristen for having. Especially since I know it's a lie—a stupid defense mechanism.

"You've already gotten involved. You already love her."

I glance back at her. "I don't love her."

Svetlana's palm connects with the back of my head and sends me forward. "You do. Maybe you haven't admitted it to her, but you do. I can tell these things. You're too protective and sappy."

"Please don't tell me I am too nice," I plead.

"Too nice? Who would ever tell you this? You're an asshole."

I nod. She's right. I've only been called nice by one person in my life: Kristen.

"You say you don't want to be like your father, but I want to remind you that you don't have to hit someone to be mean," Svetlana says. "Destroying a person's soul is just as bad."

Chapter Forty-Three

KRISTEN

THE FOLLOWING DAY, I WAKE UP FACE DOWN ON MY BED STILL wearing last night's dress, minus my shoes. I try to open my eyes but feel a slight tug from the glue I used to apply fake eyelashes holding my lids together. Gently, I peel the lashes away and blink a few times.

From across the room, I notice a rectangular package on top of my dresser. If it was there last night, I didn't notice. I get up and hit my inhaler before retrieving the box—a new phone. A pink Post-it note flutters to the ground.

Didn't want to wake you. Hope you had fun at Auden's party. Call me when you get up. Love, Mom.

Looking at the box reminds me of how I trashed Mom's phone last night.

Ugh. Last night.

Pasha. His girlfriend. Ruining my best friend's wedding reception.

I set the box on the bed for a moment while I strap on my vest for my morning therapy. Since I have time to kill, I use the session to set up the new phone. As soon as I do, a hundred dings alert me to social media notifications, emails, and text messages.

Though my heart hits the hardwood floor as I slide the bar on my phone, my lips immediately turn up in a smile as I read through the initial messages Auden texted me while I was on the cruise.

> Hope you're having fun on your cruise! I miss you.

> Not knowing what you're doing is killing me! Love you! Miss you! <3

> I just filled up for $2.09 a gallon. Go to the Circle K on Graham.

> Shit. That last text was for Sasha! Sorry, KK! Love you! <3

> Find a hottie yet?

> Sasha just made me try caviar. It's so gross!!! Who eats fish eggs?!?!

> I need to hear your voice. Call me as soon as you step off the boat.

Auden's texts continue, with random silly messages we always send each other and questions about my trip. Then they change.

> OMG. OMG. Why am I seeing pictures of you all hugged up on Pavel Gribov?

> You're on his Twitter feed so much it's like wallpaper.

> And Instagram.

> And Snapchat.

> You look super-hot, btw. Do you ever take a bad picture?

> OMG! You're kissing him!!!!!! Why are you kissing Gribov???

> What is going on? Turn on your phone! CALL ME! WTF!

> Dude! Your cruise is over! Why have you not called me?

> Are you alive?!!??

> Srsly. Are you okay? What's going on? I'm calling your parents! P.S. I love you! <3

Despite texts from others, I stop reading after that one and press the power button to turn the phone off completely. Then I take off my vest and pull the covers over my head.

Auden knew about Pasha. She tried to tell me in the only way she could while I was on the cruise. If Sia hadn't dropped my freaking phone, I would've known before I made a fool of myself at Auden's reception.

Fuck my life.

Chapter Forty-Four

PASHA

CHARLOTTE, NC

LANDING IN CHARLOTTE TO start training camp for the Monarchs should have been my proudest moment. I've worked my ass off my entire life to get to this point—beginning the season with an NHL team.

Hockey has been the only constant in my life. Playing got me through my childhood. It gave me something concrete to focus on: being stronger, faster, more skilled—all the things I wasn't as a dancer, according to my father.

When I chose to play hockey, it enhanced his wrath—and saved me from it simultaneously. Hockey took away the pain because it removed me from him and the ridicule and embarrassment that came with being around him.

In a way, hockey took my mother and father away from me as well since they were on their way to one of my games when they died.

Back then, I thought *that* had been my lowest point.

Shame and self-hatred emanate from my pores and coat my throat.

I'm surprised the person seated next to me during the two-hour flight from Detroit to Charlotte can't smell it.

How will I face my teammates after I ruined Aleksandr and Auden's wedding reception? Though I left a few messages, I haven't had a chance to apologize to him face to face. How could I do that to him after spending the last year trying to get our friendship back on track?

How could I embarrass Kristen in front of her friends by letting her discover who I was at that party? Only a sociopath would do that. I knew the reception would be the first time we saw each other after the cruise.

I didn't plan on hurting her. I didn't say to myself, "I'm going to let her find out who I am in front of all these people to inflict the most pain and embarrassment possible."

But I might as well have because that's precisely what happened.

Fuck!

I had hundreds of opportunities to come clean.

I could have said something about it on the cab ride to the San Juan airport. I told her she wouldn't like the person I was when we got back. Why didn't I explain? She would have had time to be angry and recover before seeing me again. Why did I choose to do it on what was supposed to be our friends' happiest day?

Because everything my father had ever said about me was true.

Horrible. Selfish. Stupid. Thoughtless. Coward.

I guess if you hear something enough, you start to believe it. And if you're really lucky, like me, you may even start to become it. I'm a walking, talking, breathing prophecy.

But I don't want to be like that. I don't want him to be right.

I want to be the man Kristen saw me as. And to do that, I have to make changes.

Aleksandr and Auden won't be home for a few more days, but I know what I must do as soon as they return to town.

Apologies have never been easy for me, but admitting my mistakes and asking for forgiveness are necessary if I ever hope to forgive myself.

Chapter Forty-Five
KRISTEN

Royal Oak, MI

> I know you don't have a phone, but when you do, please just call me and let me know you're okay.

GETTING Auden's text makes me realize that we have a true friendship, even after I ruined her wedding reception with my stupid drama. It feels even worse knowing she probably spent the rest of the night worrying about me.

It takes me a moment to respond. Finally, I type:

> I'm fine. I swear. I just need some time. I'll talk to you soon. <3

> You have a phone??

> Mom replaced mine. I'll call you later.

> I love you, KK.

Despite what I told her, I'm not fine. I haven't stopped crying since I got home. Hadn't stopped punching my pillow, wishing it were Pavel Gribov's face.

But I'm not ready to talk to anyone, especially my best friend, whose reception I ruined. The best friend who relies on me to be the drama-free voice of reason in her life.

It's just after noon when I wake up again. I hear someone rustling around in my kitchen, which is alarming since I live alone.

I open my bedroom door slowly and peek out. A familiar figure wearing his trademark worn-out Detroit Lions ball cap stands at the counter.

Dad.

My family has this weird habit of letting themselves into each other's homes. Growing up, I never thought anything of entering my grandparents' house without knocking or having my aunts and uncles do the same at our house. If we were home, our doors were always unlocked.

I didn't find it weird at all. Maybe because it's all I knew. It wasn't until high school that I realized it might not be the norm.

It doesn't help matters that I live in the studio apartment above the Royal Oak location of the Olive Tap, Uncle George's chain of specialty olive oil stores.

I'm willing to bet everyone in my family has a key to the store—and, subsequently, my apartment. But Uncle George only charges me three hundred dollars a month for rent, and I'll take the chance of family members barging in randomly for that deal.

Instead of rushing out, I close the door quietly and shuffle to the bathroom attached to my bedroom. After washing my face and brushing my teeth quickly, I change into comfy joggers and a long-sleeved T-shirt before leaving my room to face Dad.

"Hey, sweetheart," he greets me when I enter the kitchen.

"Hi, Dad," I reply, stopping next to his chair and giving him a flimsy hug before continuing to the fridge. I jerk the door open, hoping I left a can of pop or something in there before my trip. The shelves are stocked with fresh produce and other staples.

I look at Dad over the refrigerator door. "Did you buy me groceries?"

"You've been gone for a week. I couldn't let you come home to an empty fridge."

The simple gesture of kindness shocks my dead heart back to life. "Thanks, Dad."

He smiles. "How was the party?" he asks before taking a bite of his sub.

"A complete and utter mess."

"What happened?" he asks, mouth still full of food.

"I found out *Pavlos* is a lying jerk." I remove a carton of orange juice and set it on the counter. Then I open the cabinet above the sink and pluck a tumbler off the shelf.

"I thought you were in love with this boy," Dad says.

"I wasn't in love, Dad," I mumble as I pour juice into my cup.

"Not in love, eh?" He gestures at my face with his sandwich. "Then why are your eyes all red and puffy?"

"I had a bad night."

"Because of him?"

I nod and take another sip of OJ.

"Do I need to kick his ass?" Dad asks.

I know he's joking, but I nod again anyway.

"Want to talk about it?"

"Yes, I do," I admit.

Talking about relationships with their father might be uncomfortable for most people, but I enjoy talking to my dad—without going into too much detail. He gives me the elusive male perspective I can't get talking to my girlfriends.

He pulls out the chair next to him at the table. "Tell me what's going on, *kukla*."

"Pavlos was at the party. He lied about a bunch of stuff he told me on the cruise. He's not an aviator. He's a hockey player."

"The Red Wings?" he asks, his voice perking up. I never got into sports, but Dad is a huge fan.

"No, the minor league team here."

"So he *is* an Aviator?" Dad confirms.

"Well, yeah, I guess," I huff. "But that's not the point, Dad. He said he was an aviator, like a person who flies planes."

"Did he ever say he flew planes?"

I pause to think about it. "No."

"Then why did you assume he flew planes?"

"Because he said he was an Aviator!" I raise my voice as frustration takes over.

He puts his hand over mine to calm me. "I'm just trying to make you see something, Kristen. He said he was an Aviator, and he is. He never said he flew planes?"

"No, but he said he loved traveling to different cities and—"

"Hockey players travel to different cities," he interjects.

I pull my hand out from under his. "Whose side are you on, Dad?"

"Sorry." He lifts his hands in the air. "Continue. What else did he lie about?"

I contemplate my next move. I get my bluntness from my dad, the master. He tells it like it is—or at least like he sees it. In this case, his "honest" perspective ticks me off. In trying to help, he's enhancing my frustration. Why can't he just let me vent?

"I want to talk to Mom."

"Oh no! Your mother will agree with everything you say, and you two will blow this out of proportion." Dad's voice softens. "Auden called us last night saying you left the reception extremely upset. Your mom and I were worried, especially since we hadn't seen you in a week, and last we heard, you were staying in San Juan with a stranger you fell in love with."

I lean back in my chair and fold my arms across my chest.

Dad mimics my posture.

"Ugh. Fine!"

"What else did he lie about?" Dad asks again.

"His name isn't Pavlos. He's not Greek at all. He's Russian."

He raises an eyebrow. "You couldn't tell he wasn't Greek on the cruise?"

"I knew he wasn't Greek, Dad. But he didn't tell me exactly who he was. He's the guy who was a huge jerk to Auden and tried to break up her and Aleksandr and—" The words spill out of my mouth in a jumble.

"Whoa! Whoa! Back up."

"I knew he wasn't Greek. I called him out right away," I begin again. "I didn't care about that. I know Mom will care, but I didn't."

"Okay. So why did he lie about being Greek?"

"He was on the cruise with his Greek friend. He lied to be part of our Greek singles group."

When Dad laughs, I glare at him.

"What?" he asks. "I would've done the same thing if I hadn't been lucky enough to be born Greek. We have the most beautiful women in the world."

I let up on the glare to throw in an eye roll. "Why do I talk to you?"

He smiles but stays silent. It's funny how talking to Dad makes me feel better, even when he's honest and blunt and trying to help me see things from a different perspective.

"He said he lived in Charlotte, so I mentioned Auden and Aleksandr. He was weird about it but said he didn't know them. Total lie. Straight to my face."

"Let me recap to make sure I'm following. He didn't tell a beautiful Greek girl he was trying to impress that he knew the friends he'd tried to break up. Most likely because he knew this girl would automatically hate him and not give him a chance. Got it."

I stare at my dad, shaking my head in mock disgust. "I hate you sometimes."

He pulls me into his side and kisses the top of my head. "You could never. You're the biggest daddy's girl."

I snuggle under his arm. He's totally right. I could never hate him. He's my rock—my soft, snuggly rock.

Burrowed in the warmth of his embrace, I realize that Dad reminds me a little of Pasha. Or Pasha reminds me a little of Dad. Both men are blunt, honest, and unapologetic.

"Can't you just see it from my perspective, Dad?" I ask.

"I know you're upset, *kukla*. And maybe you have the right to be. But that's not why you talk to me, is it?" He rubs my hair. "What drew you to him?"

I pull out of his arms. "He's really sweet and smart and fun. We did so many amazing things together. Zip-lining and cliff-jumping—" I stop there. Dad doesn't need to know *all* the fun things.

"Excuse me?" Dad's eyes widen. I got his attention by telling him Pasha put his little girl's life in danger.

I continue. "And he wasn't even fazed by all my CF stuff. He sat by me and held my hand during my oscillation treatments. When I forget my enzymes and got awful stomach cramps, he carried me onto the ship. He opened up to me about his past." I pause and look down as everything Pasha told me runs through my head. "Which was pretty horrible."

"He sounds like someone very special."

"Yeah," I whisper as a tear slips down my cheek.

"I know it hurts to be betrayed." Dad reaches out and wipes my face. "I'm not dismissing your feelings or condoning his lies." He tilts my chin up so we were eye to eye. "But people make questionable choices when they're trying to survive. It sounds like this guy may be trying to survive right now."

I nod again. "He is."

"He allowed you to break through a pretty thick wall."

"Yes! I honestly don't think he's ever let anyone through before. His feelings were so raw, so painful."

"What made you tell him about your CF? You were only on the cruise for a week."

"I don't know," I admit, shrugging. "We started talking as a way for me to get away from Spiros." I look up to judge Dad's reaction to that admission. His lips curl into a small smile. "Sorry."

"You really don't like Spiros, do you?" he chuckles.

"Nope." I laugh, too. "The more time Pasha and I spent together, the more we talked. And it wasn't stuff like 'What's your favorite movie?' It was deep. I think I opened up to him because I knew it was only for a week. He was a safe place with a built-in expiration date."

Dad leans back, interested in my response. Maybe I should mention that Dad is a mediator—the guy people go to for a fair, logical perspective in heated battles. He spends his days asking the hard questions that people don't usually ask themselves, especially during exceptionally emotional times.

Which explains our bluntness and honesty, eh?

"Maybe he felt the same about you?"

"I think he did." I take a deep breath. "But I'm still so angry. I wish he'd told me. After the cruise. On the phone. In a text. Why didn't he come clean before making a fool of me at the reception?"

"I don't know, sweetie. Sounds like he's a little immature in how he handles things. Give it some time. Let the hurt settle. See how you feel in a few days." Dad taps the crust of his sandwich against his plate. He seems to be contemplating his next question, so I know it'll be good. "Did who he could be ever cross your mind? Maybe when you talked about Auden and Aleksandr?"

"Honestly, Dad? No. I don't know if I had blinders on or if I was so caught up because I found someone as cool as him on the cruise. But it never did. I feel like an idiot, ya know? But I'd never met him before, so I didn't know what he looked like. And I don't follow hockey at all. How would I know who a freaking minor league player is?"

Dad nods as he chews, which makes me paranoid, so I continue, "Does that sound dumb? Do you think I knew subconsciously and let myself go with it?"

"No. I don't think that at all. I just wondered. You two have a minimal degree of separation. He knew you'd be at the reception."

"Here we go." I pull my chair closer to the table and lean in. "Dad's gonna kick some ass."

"I'm not kicking anyone's anything, Kristen."

"Oh." I sit back in my chair and down my orange juice. He brought up a good point. How stupid am I that I didn't put two and two together?

"It sounds like he wanted the chance for you to judge him for who he really is, not the preconceived notion you had from his past actions."

I think about that for a minute. "He did say something about that —about people judging him for his past without giving him a chance to prove he'd changed."

"What did you say?"

"Well, I didn't know he was talking about me. I thought he meant his family or something."

"So, what did you say when you didn't realize you fit into that group?"

"I told him to fuck those people's opinions."

Dad doesn't even flinch. "What would you say now?"

I shrug and pick up the juice glass, bending my wrist and moving the remaining liquid at the bottom swishing from side to side.

My father's silence persists. I know from experience he'll be able to hold out much longer than I will.

"I don't know, Dad." Instead of answering, I reach out and pluck a banana pepper from his plate.

Dad doesn't react; he just watches as I chew.

Finally, I give in. "Now, I would tell him that if he doesn't want to be judged by the things he's done, don't do shitty things. Be a better man."

"Can he be forgiven?" Dad asks.

"Anyone can be forgiven. It doesn't mean I want to open myself up again."

"You're in for a long and lonely road if you don't want to open your heart, Kristen."

Tears blur my vision. Before I met Pasha, I never felt lonely when I didn't have a boyfriend. I skated through college, keeping everything about my life easy and positive. I like being a ray of sunshine on a cloudy day. I like being the one who makes enthusiastic, positive suggestions when negativity begins.

Once, I overheard Auden describe me to a guy she wanted me to hook up with. She said I was "smart, strong, independent, and fun." Then, in a low, wistful tone, she added, "Everything I wish I could be." I've never been given a kinder compliment.

"I'm not ready to open up again at this moment. Everything just happened. It's not like I'm swearing off men forever."

"Good. Because there are a lot of Greek boys out there who would be honored to marry such an intelligent, gorgeous woman."

"It all comes back to marrying Greek boys. Typical Greek father!" I tease. When I smile, it pushes the tears onto my cheeks. I brush them away. "I love you, Dad."

"And I love you, *kukla.*" He squeezes me. "Love is hard. It's crazy and unexplainable and amazing. Take time to heal, but don't let it make you shut down. You have too much fire inside. Too much life to live."

The entire discussion made me realize that I'd fallen in love with my father.

Not literally, of course, but the similarities between the two men are scary. It came out in the respectful way Pasha had treated me, the compassionate way he'd cared for me, and the introspective, honest way he made me see things differently.

From the start, I felt comfortable being myself around Pasha. His powerful presence wrapped me in a blanket of safety, security, and serenity.

Which makes the loss even more difficult.

Chapter Forty-Six

PASHA

"Pack your shit, Gribov."

Charlotte's coach, Mike Kingston, sits behind his desk, still sporting the black Monarchs pullover he wore during practice.

"Excuse me?" I ask, leaning forward in my chair. I heard him, but I need clarification because I'm pretty sure he said to pack up my shit.

"What the fuck is going on with you?" He squints, peering at me with concern rather than anger.

I swallow and slump back. Drops of water from my sweat-soaked hair drip down my neck and into my shirt. "Having rough time finding the groove."

"Do you want to play in the NHL?" Kingston leans forward.

"Yes, sir. Why you ask me this?"

"You don't look like you do. We drafted you because you're smart and fast. You have a sixth sense of what will happen before it happens. You know where to be. You make your teammates look good." He leans back and slaps a cup off his desk. Water sprays across my T-shirt. "But I haven't seen any of that over the last two weeks. You're slow, *at least* a second or two behind everyone else on the ice. And you couldn't score on an empty net from five feet away."

"I know. I'm—"

Coach interrupts me. "When was the last time you fought, son?"

"I don't know. Juniors, maybe." I shake my head. Every night, I get into verbal fights because I chirp at guys, but I can't recall the last time I'd gotten into one with my fists.

"And you probably didn't even win that one because you're not a fighter, Gribov!"

His words slice through me, and I wince, though Coach Kingston couldn't have known how I would interpret them, nor how much they affect me.

I'm not a fighter.

If I were, I would have kicked the shit out of the guy who came at me in last night's game, like my father had done to me and my mother.

I'm not a fighter.

If I were, I would have fought for Kristen.

I'm a coward.

"I like you, Gribov, I really do," Kingston continues when I remain silent. "I know you have the skill to be here. I'm just worried about your desire." He leans back in his chair and fold his hands.

It takes every ounce of self-control not to put my fist through his desk.

For the last month and a half, I've woken up in a haze and gone through the motions of the same basic routine I've had for more than fifteen years: Rink. Skate. Practice. Game. Workout. Home. Travel. Rink. Skate. Practice. Game. Workout.

I've worked my ass off for years so I wouldn't be labeled by people based on an anti-Russian mindset that still persists despite the fact that Russians have been in the NHL for over three decades.

I've been doing this for fifteen years. This is the first time a coach has ever accused me of being lazy and uninspired, traits that fit the North American stereotype of a Russian player.

What's worse? I agree with him.

"I'm gonna be honest with you, kid. Jimmy's offering you in the deals when he's talking to other teams."

Jim Miller is the Monarchs' general manager. Though it's always in the back of my head, this is the first time anyone has come right out and said they're actively trying to trade me.

"So, I'm done?" I ask as if my confidence could be screwed anymore.

"You're going to Detroit. I'd like to see you back, kid. But if I do, I better see the player we drafted. I guess we'll see what happens."

And by "see what happens," he means I need to get my shit together, or I'll be traded faster than I can say *dasvidaniya*—goodbye.

I lift myself off the chair and slink out of his office like a dog with my tail between my legs.

Two months ago, I'd been flying high after getting the call that the Monarchs wanted me to start the season with them. I broke the lease to get out of my apartment in Detroit early, confident I'd spent my last stint in the minors.

I'd finally achieved my goal of starting the season on an NHL roster. But getting sent down within the first two weeks of the season completely diminishes the accomplishment.

Maybe it would have been different if I could keep my brain on hockey instead of on how royally I'd fucked up with Kristen. If I'd kept my head down and focused, I wouldn't be on my way to the Monarchs locker room to collect my shit.

"What's up, Drago?" Luke Daniels asks, using the nickname I picked up last night after getting my ass handed to me in the fight.

It doesn't bother me that my teammates chose to use the surname of the Russian boxer Rocky knocked out at the end of the fourth movie in the series. They did their best with what they had to choose from about Russians in North American pop culture.

The part that bothered me was how the fight itself had come about. I took the bait from the guy, who'd chirped something ignorant and generic about my mother. Usually, shit like that doesn't bother me. It gives me an excuse to respond with one of the clever comebacks I'm known for. But this time, I couldn't think of one, and that's what set me off.

"Clearing out," I say.

"Aw, shit, man." Luke's jovial tone takes a downturn. "Sorry, Gribsy."

"Do not worry, Lukey," I tease, ignoring his sympathy. "I go back to Detroit and put up numbers. I will be back."

Luke swings his bag over his shoulder and walks over to me. He holds out his fist, and I bump it. "Work it out, man. And get your ass back here, where you belong."

I nod.

Luke was captain of the Aviators when I first came to the team. We'd played two seasons together, off and on, as we both got called up to Charlotte and sent back down. He's a strong leader. Someone I admire. Someone who sees me as the player I am and doesn't try to change me into something else.

I think about telling him how much I always appreciated that, but it seems too final like I'll never play with him again, so I keep my mouth shut.

When I finish gathering my stuff, only a few guys are left in the locker room. They come up to me one by one.

Fist bump from a teammate. "Good luck, Drago."

Another rubs my head. "We'll see you soon, man."

Then, a veteran player punches my shoulder. "Get your shit together, Gribsy."

It feels like they're making the rounds at a funeral, giving their condolences to the grieving widow. I can't wait to get to my car.

The Monarchs booked me a flight to Detroit for the following day, which gave me the evening to pack up the bedroom in the apartment I shared with Blake and figure out where I will live when I return.

I pull out my phone and open up my contacts. The very first one was *Angel moy*—"my angel." That's how I entered Kristen's number into my phone.

My thumb hovers over the number, but it's not even hers. It's her mom's.

Even if I did have her number, it's not like I can call after two months of silence.

I slide downward on the screen, scrolling until I reach Svetlana's name and pressing the phone icon.

"Hey, Sveta, mind if I live with you for a little while?"

Chapter Forty-Seven

KRISTEN

Royal Oak, MI

Life is too short to waste time crying over a man.

It's healthy to mourn a loss—of people, pets, or a relationship—but at the same time, I know I have to pick myself up and continue on with my life.

Before meeting Pasha, I'd gone years without caring if I had anyone special in my life. I like dating, kissing, and having a person to hang out with and snuggle up to.

But I don't *need* a man.

The best way to get over a loss is to prove to everyone that I'm still a strong, independent woman. Something as simple and silly as a heart-break over a week-long fake boyfriend won't take me down.

I jump back into work—and life—with more determination than ever. Before the cruise, I'd only been at my job for two months, and I'd made it a point to learn as much as I could quickly. Once I got back, I was in overdrive.

Mike Rollins, my boss at Motor City Bar Management (MCBM), is neck deep in responsibilities. He's overseeing the renovation of one bar, hiring staff for a brand-new place, and dealing with all the headaches that go into keeping tabs on the rest of the thirteen bars MCBM owns.

I don't have enough experience or knowledge to find the talent, negotiate contracts, and sign off on checks, but I can manage schedules, coordinate staff, and create and cover every MCBM property with marketing flyers for upcoming events.

I'd been hired to take administrative and event coordination tasks off Mike's hands, but I want to learn everything—and make more money. So, I tack on extra hours and help at events that were planned before I started working here. If a bartender or server called in sick at one of the bars, I jumped in to take their shift.

At first, Mike was surprised at my willingness to help with all aspects of the bars, but after two months of taking as many things off his schedule as I could, I think he realized that taking charge is part of my personality.

My parents instilled the idea of working hard and striving to be the best since birth. I come from a long line of business owners who hire family members to do everything. I've done bookkeeping and appointment scheduling at Dad's counseling practice. I've been a server at my grandparents' diners, sold specialty olive oil at Uncle George's stores, and even hand-picked olives at my family's massive grove in Greece.

My job as a server and bartender at a steakhouse and brewery for four years in college gave me even more experience to be an asset to MCBM.

After being on my own for a few months, I realized how quickly paychecks go when you live alone and have no roommates to share the costs. I need every extra shift I can pick up and all the family discounts I can get.

But I'm making it work because taking the job isn't about the money. It's about getting experience, being independent, and accepting a job because I want to do it instead of taking something just to get by. Which means I have to watch every single penny of my spending. I'm thankful Uncle George charges such cheap rent.

"HEY!" I greet Auden, holding the phone against my ear with my shoulder as I carry a box of wristbands through the parking lot to my car. "I might lose you—I'm in the parking deck on my way to work."

"How's work going?" she asks.

"It's good. Crazy busy. But fun. I'm working the 1975 concert at Meadow Brook tonight."

"No way! Wait—MCBM doesn't own Meadow Brook, does it?" Auden asked.

"Nope. It's a side hustle. I'm working their merchandise stand."

"Why didn't you tell me? I would've flown up."

"Mike just asked me if I wanted to do it this morning." I set the box on the backseat floor behind the driver's seat and shut the door. "Maybe I'll hang out by the tour bus to see if I can hook up with Matty," I tease, referring to Matty Healy, The 1975's lead singer, whom Auden has a massive crush on.

"You suck! You know he's on my list."

After seeing the *Friends* episode with Isabella Rossellini, we each made a list of five celebrities we could hook up with without it being considered cheating.

"I'm telling Aleksandr," I tease.

"Aleksandr understands."

"Speaking of your *super-hot, perfect* husband," I say, stressing the adjectives. "How are you guys doing? Pregnant yet?"

"Oh my gosh! Don't even joke about that," Auden says. "It's not funny."

Startled by the strength of her protest, I jump, and the phone falls away from my ear. Luckily, I catch it before it hits the ground.

Had I broken a mirror in the last few months? There has to be an explanation for my recent bad luck with phones.

"What? Like that's a crazy question." I'm pretty sure she and Aleksandr are humping like bunnies all the time. No one can be that careful.

"It is a ridiculous question. We're not ready to have kids yet. Not for a long, long time."

"You're totally preggers!"

"Please stop. That's how rumors get started, and Sasha can't be worried about rumors like that during the season."

"Fine. But I better be the first to know if you are."

"The first?" she asks. "Shouldn't my husband be the first to know?"

"Nope," I reply. And I'm dead serious.

"You're such a freak," she says through a laugh. "All right, I just wanted to check-in. I'll let you go so you can get to the concert and become a Matty Healy groupie."

"Is that jealousy I hear?" I tease.

"Nope. I'm giving you my blessing. Tell me all about it."

"I will leave no detail untold."

"That's my girl," Auden says. "You sure you're doing okay?"

I sigh. "I am the best I have been in months. I promise."

"Good. Have fun at work, bitch ass. I love you."

"Love you back." I hang up the phone and drop it into the cup holder in my console.

Auden's calls have become more frequent than ever before. I know she's worried about me because of Pavel, but I told her a hundred times that I'm fine, and I am. I jumped back into an exciting job that keeps me busy and challenges me. Over the last month, I've finally been able to think about something other than Pavel Gribov.

Chapter Forty-Eight

PASHA

Royal Oak, MI

Fuck.

I jiggle the door handle to Svetlana's house in downtown Royal Oak for the tenth time. Still locked. I don't have a key, and when I call her phone, it sends me straight to voicemail.

When I spoke with her after my flight landed in Detroit, she told me she left the front door to her house unlocked when she left for work that morning. I had no problem getting in earlier when I first arrived. But when I left to walk to the bar on the corner, I twisted the inside lock on the doorknob before I shut the door out of habit. I didn't think anything of it until I got home.

I tried all the windows I could reach to see if she'd left one unlocked. She doesn't have a garage, so there aren't any tools available to pick the lock or bust something. Plus, I hesitate to break a window for fear a neighbor would think I'm breaking in and call the police—since, technically, I *am* breaking in.

After exhausting every option, I sit down on the top step of the front porch, shivering and clutching my hair, trying to figure out what to do. I text Blake:

> Who do I call if I am locked out of Svetlana's house?

Svetlana.

I hated when he gave me the same sarcastic answer I would have given him.

> She does not answer. Should I call 911?

Are you desperate to get into the house because someone is coming at you wielding an ax?

I roll my eyes.

> No.

Then don't call 911. Being locked out isn't an emergency, dickbag.

> I hate you.

Have fun sleeping on Svetlana's porch.

Shaking my head, I put my phone back in my pocket. Then I realize the house is only a few blocks from the fire station. The firefighters must have tools to get me in.

I stand up, shove my hands into the front pockets of my jeans, and start walking to get help.

Chapter Forty-Nine

KRISTEN

AUDEN WILL BE DISAPPOINTED WHEN I TELL HER I HADN'T EVEN gotten to meet Matty Healy, let alone hook up with him.

Turns out that when you work the merchandise table at a concert, you don't get to hang out with the band because you're there until every last tween has purchased what they want. By the time I finished, thin guys in the band were already cozied up on their tour bus, ready to depart for Chicago, where the band had a show the following night.

Not that I really would've hooked up with any of the guys. My immune system can't handle rock stars. And I have a feeling tour buses are a breeding ground for every kind of bacteria known to man.

It's probably not a bad thing to eliminate from my bucket list.

Panic interrupts my thoughts as I drive toward my apartment and see two Royal Oak firefighters standing in the yard of the cute pale blue house two doors down from the Olive Tap. I slow to a snail's pace and keep glancing at the old house Uncle George turned into a store.

Thankfully, I don't see smoke or flames coming from it—or any house near it—so I return my focus to the road and turn into a nearby parking spot.

I jump out of the car and run toward the store. Neither firefighter standing outside the blue house seems to be in a hurry. I sniff the air and scan the area again, relieved I don't detect any hint of a fire.

Then, I walk around the building to the side of the store, where a staircase leads straight to my apartment.

I've just unlocked the door when I hear gruff voices and laughs. I pause to listen to the conversation since the jovial tone verifies that there's no immediate danger.

"Don't you have any neighbor friends you can give a spare key to?" one of the men asks.

"I just move back. Have no friends around here." The voice is unmistakable.

Pasha.

I'm a smart girl. I know I should ignore the conversation and push through the door into the safety of my apartment.

But the tiny, masochistic devil on my shoulder tugs me back down the stairs and out to the street. I peer around the building in the direction the voices had come from.

Now, four men are standing on the lawn—Pavel and three firefighters.

What is he doing there?

"Are you okay?" the beautiful blonde girl who'd been with him at Auden's wedding asks from her car. She's parked in front of the neighbor's house—the one separating the blue house from the store. "Sorry, I just got your voicemail."

Everyone turns to look at her, which means they all look my way.

Though I'm 98 percent sure he can't see me, I jerk my head back and close my eyes as my heart hammers under my chest.

What if he did? He looked in this direction. Do I dare look again?

Yes.

I crane my neck slowly and see the firefighters speaking with the girl. But Pavel isn't looking at them. He's looking my way.

Shit!

I don't want to hang around to see if anyone spotted me creeping at one in the morning, so I back away, race up the stairs, and push through the door to my apartment.

Maybe he saw something, but there's no possible way he could have known it was me. I'd never mentioned living in Royal Oak or that my Uncle owned a store on the cruise.

I, on the other hand, learned a few interesting things from my snooping.

Pavel Gribov is back in Detroit.

And his girlfriend—who Auden claims isn't his girlfriend—lives two houses away from me.

Chapter Fifty

KRISTEN

THE EARSPLITTING "MUSIC" COMING FROM THE STAGE MAKES ME wish I hadn't picked up this bartending shift. I wonder if Mike booked this band because if he did, I need to have a talk with him about how much they suck. No melodies. No rhythm. Just screaming into a microphone on top of screeching guitars and thumping drums.

Late nights and early mornings took a significant toll on my health during the first month of my job until I got used to three to four hours of sleep at night and a mandatory afternoon nap.

Thankfully, I'm in the kind of work where I have the flexibility to do that. But I haven't been sleeping well since I found out that Pasha and his girlfriend live two houses away.

What horrible thing had I done recently for karma to screw me over like that?

The memory of seeing them together makes me think about all the intimate things Pasha and I did together.

Is he doing those things with her right now?

Everything makes me think about him. And about how much I loved hanging out with him. And about how strong he was. And how he understood me. Somehow, he understood me.

Pasha.

Ugh! Pavel freakin' Gribov.

Hockey star. Dickbag. Liar.

No reason to waste time thinking about that sorry sack of shit. No sadness. No anger. I refuse to let thoughts of him take my emotions hostage.

He deserves a firm smack across the—

"Can I get a double shot of vodka, please?"

Hearing Pasha's voice feels like my brain bashes into a brick wall.

I didn't expect to see him here. And judging from his wide eyes and scowl, he didn't expect to see me here either.

I stare at him. Unable to speak. Unable to breathe. Unable to look away. But my body betrays me, swaying toward him when I should be stepping back.

"What the fuck are you wearing?" he yells.

Suddenly, understanding washes over me, waking the anger inside. I'd mistaken his expression as a sign that he was unhappy to see me, but that wasn't it.

It's a scowl of jealousy. He doesn't like seeing me in the standard sexist uniform for female employees—black crop tops, booty shorts, and fishnets. Thank goodness I get to wear high-tops and not heels.

"What are you doing here?" I demand, ignoring his question. Gribov doesn't get to have an opinion on any part of my life anymore, especially my wardrobe.

"Getting a drink."

"No!" I stomp my foot on the floor like an angry child having a tantrum. "You don't get to be here. In my space. My city. My life."

I stop and press my lips into a firm line to halt my trivial tirade. Especially since nothing coming out of my mouth makes any sense at all.

A coughing fit overtakes me as if on cue, and instead of keeping the hard, angry edge I had going, I immediately look like a distressed damsel.

Dammit! I turn my head to hack into my elbow.

Out of the corner of my eye, I see Pasha reach out, but I anticipate his move and smack his hand away.

"I don't need your help," I say between coughs. "I don't need anything from you."

Anger shakes each word, and I feel a meltdown coming on. But I'll never give him the satisfaction of seeing me break down over him again, not after the wedding debacle.

I speed to the opposite end of the bar to talk to the other bartender working tonight. "Danny, you've got a customer down there."

Pasha doesn't deserve any more of my emotions. No anger. No pain. He had zero for me, so why would I waste anything on him?

He predicted this scenario the night we parted ways after our extended day in San Juan.

He warned me.

He said I wouldn't like the person he was after the cruise. As puzzled as I'd been at the time, it all makes sense now.

The man I fell in love with was a fictional character named Pavlos.

Pavel Gribov showed me his true colors, which matched the colors he'd shown Auden years ago when she first told me about him.

On the cruise, he came across as someone who understood how much living life to the fullest meant—not just on vacation, but in the grand scheme of things. Now, I realize it was all part of his act to bring another person down to his level of misery.

Despite everything I've been through and everything I'll continue to go through, I wasn't a miserable person before I met Pavel Gribov, and I'd be damned if I turn into one after knowing him for one week.

Chapter Fifty-One

KRISTEN

"You're back!" I squeal, rushing toward Lena, standing behind the counter at the Olive Tap. When I reach my cousin, I lean over and hug her.

She texted me the night before to tell me she was back in town and would be working at the store while home from Grand Valley State University on winter break, where she's working on her master's degree.

"You can come back here, you know," she says, waving me to join her behind the cash register.

"Nah. Then Uncle George will make me start working here again, and I'll smell like olive oil all day," I tease.

"Do I smell like olive oil?" Lena grabs a piece of hair and brings it to her nose.

The answer is yes. She smells like olive oil after working in the shop all day.

I shrug. "It's not a *bad* smell, per se. Just a bit funky."

The doorbell chimes, alerting us to a new customer. Lena leans to the side to see around my head. "Oh, shit," she says under her breath.

Amused, I turn around to check out the customer who made her curse on her first day back at work in three months.

The amusement fades immediately when Pavel and his blond girl-friend walk in, talking and laughing.

No matter what I do, I can't get away. I'm destined to be haunted by the ghost of my fake boyfriend for the rest of my life.

My heart sinks, and my jaw tightens with each tender display of affection. Their easy smiles. When she places a hand on his forearm and laughs after something he says. The way his eyes light up when he looks at her.

He used to light up for me. He used to smile easily for me.

Nausea rolls through me, and I stagger away from the counter. Slowly, I shuffle backward toward the far wall in an attempt to slip away unnoticed. The last thing I want to do is make a scene. I don't want him to know my stomach twists at their vomit-inducing displays of affection.

Instead of the stealth getaway I imagined, my elbow hits a display of empty hand-painted oil bottles and sends one crashing to the floor. Splinters of glass fly across the painted concrete, and my mind immediately flashes back to the cell phone I dropped at Auden's reception. Though I squeeze my eyes shut, I know Pavel and his girlfriend saw me. Everyone looks when there's a commotion.

After a deep breath to regain my composure, I open my eyes and rush through the "Employees Only" door to retrieve a broom. It's not Lena's job to clean up my mess.

On my way to the utility closet, I see the girl catch Pavel's eye and nod toward me. He shakes his head, grabs her hand, and pulls her toward the door. She resists, standing firm and not budging.

At least she has some backbone. Though, I can't really give her high self-esteem points since she stayed with a guy who cheated on her for a week.

But that's her business, not mine.

A stormy look passes over Pavel's face, which I recognize as the childish pout he puts on when he doesn't get his way. But he doesn't stay. He leaves his girl behind to watch me sweep up the mess.

I'm left with the mess again—the mess he caused.

Stubborn. Childish. Completely Pavel.

I lift my eyes as I stretch for a piece of glass out of my reach.

The beautiful blonde's voice is soft when she says, "Is not what you think. He is not mine."

She shakes her head and closes her eyes as if apologizing. Then she removes the aviator sunglasses from the top of her head and slides them into place before walking out.

"That wasn't uncomfortable at all," Lena says. She bends over, holding a dustpan as I sweep debris into it.

"What do you think she meant by that?" I ask, glancing toward the door. "Why wouldn't she say more?"

"She was probably deterred by the multiple weapons you have at your disposal," Lena answers.

"Weapons?" I ask, confused.

Lena nods to a huge, jagged chunk of glass among the tiny shards on the floor and in the dustpan.

"You're sick, you know that?" I ask. "Arming myself with a broken olive oil bottle never crossed my mind."

Lena shrugs.

"But I'm not against slapping a bitch," I add.

The lame joke makes my cousin laugh. "That's my girl." She takes the broom from my grip and sweeps up the rest of the glass.

"Would you think I was stupid if I said I still had feelings for him?" I ask, hoping she'll give me her honest opinion, not just what she thinks I want to hear.

She saw us together on the cruise. She'd tell me if I was being played the entire week.

"You can't help who you fall in love with, Kristen." Lena pauses, chewing her lip as if contemplating her next statement. "But you guys only knew each other for a week. Can it really be that hard to get over him?"

"That's what I keep asking myself." I moan. "Why?"

"Well, it doesn't help that he's in town, ya know? I mean, you thought he lived in Charlotte. That would have been a clean break. But he's right here. In your face. On the TV. In the newspaper—"

"In my uncle's store."

"Yep." Lena walks over to the garbage can behind the register and dumps the glass. "When do you want me to say I told you so?"

"I'm surprised I didn't get that text months ago when everything went down at Auden's reception."

Lena looks up with a sad smile. "I can be a jerk, but not *that* much of a jerk."

Chapter Fifty-Two

PASHA

"You are a jerk!" Svetlana yells, her heels clicking against the pavement as she catches up to me. "Worse than that! A coward!"

Instead of acknowledging her, I turn my key in the lock and let myself into the house—her house. I thought about getting my own place, but doing that might jinx me, and I'll never get back to Charlotte.

Signing a lease would be too permanent, like pounding the last nail into my career's coffin.

She grabs my arm and pulls me back. "You have to work things out with that girl!"

I shake my head. "I can't."

"Why are you so afraid?"

"I don't want to hurt her anymore, Sveta! I'm done."

"So, everything is done, yes? Your career, too? Because you suck right now. Sorry, but someone has to say it. You're losing everything because of her." She stops and corrects herself. "No, not because of her. Because of *you*. Because you are too stubborn and thickheaded."

"Yeah, well, it's my life."

"No! It's not just your life. You are ruining hers, too."

I shrug because I didn't know what to say or do. "She doesn't want me anymore. It's been too long. I've had opportunities to apologize and tell her how I feel. To tell her the truth about everything. And I haven't."

"Every time she sees you, her wounds open back up." Svetlana lowers her voice. "You say you're staying out of her life because you care about her. If that's true, you must stay out of her life completely. Don't go to places you know she will be. Don't hang out with her friends. You must stop it all and leave her alone."

She's right. I won't let Kristen go. I knew Kristen lived in the apartment above the olive oil store. The only reason I'd gone in there with Sveta today was on the off chance that Kristen would be there and I might catch a glimpse of her.

I know the routes she takes for her morning runs. I've even taken the same routes to see if we would pass each other, thinking that maybe one of those times, I'd have the guts to talk to her.

But it wasn't fair that I never gave her closure. I didn't want to give her closure because I'm a selfish bastard.

Svetlana reaches out and brushes my hair to the side. Her touch is soft, like my mother's. "Can you stop thinking the worst of yourself for one minute? Try to see yourself how Kristen sees you. How Irina and I see you. How your mother saw you."

"How's that?" I ask, so overcome with emotion that my voice cracks on the words.

"You are an amazing man, Pasha. A man that we are all proud of. A man that would do anything to make the people he cares about happy. Are you perfect? No." Svetlana smiles. "But who is?"

Chapter Fifty-Three

KRISTEN

"I LOVE YOUR PLACE, KK!" AUDEN SAYS WHEN SHE WALKS IN THE door of my humble one-bedroom, one-bath apartment.

Auden stopped to visit me before heading to Bridgeland, where her grandparents live.

"I know. It's awesome, right? I'm grateful to my Uncle George. That wonderful soul is only charging me three hundred a month."

"What?" Auden sets her purse on the kitchen table. "That's a steal for this area."

"I know. The family discount is amazing." I open my fridge, checking out what I have to offer. Not much, but there are three bottles of wine and a bottle of vodka on the counter. I grab a lime from the bottom drawer. "I have wine or vodka to offer."

"Vodka club, please," she answers. She moves my laptop bag off the couch and sets it on the ground, clearing space for us to sit.

"With three lime wedges. I don't even have to ask." I wink at my friend, then start cutting the lime.

"Have you talked to Pasha?" Though Auden's tone sounds casual, the question holds the tension of watching someone walk over hot coals.

"You call him Pasha now? I thought you hated him."

"That was the past. There's a lot I didn't know."

"Yeah, well . . ." I grab two glasses from the cupboard and set them on the counter. "You knew enough. He *is* a sadistic liar who gets off on making people miserable."

"That's just his stupid defense. He's got so much going on inside that he needs to work out."

I know! I want to scream. Instead, I fill our glasses with ice. "I really can't handle you being on his side."

"I'm not on his side," Auden assures me. "I promise. He's an immature prick. And the shit he pulled on you was majorly fucked up."

As she speaks, I fill our glasses with club soda and vodka and hook three lime wedges on each rim.

"But? I know there's a 'but,' because the Auden I know would be helping me key his car," I say, handing her a drink and sitting next to her on the couch.

"There's no 'but.' I can't make excuses for him. I don't know what would possess him to lie like that. Especially since he obviously loves you."

"Loves me?" I glare at her. "Did you just say loves me? He used a fake name, a fake job, a fake—"

"He didn't use a fake name or a fake job. He is Pasha, and he is an Aviator."

"Have you been talking to my dad?" I ask before taking a sip.

"No, why?"

I shake my head. "I led the charge with pitchforks when he tried to break you and Aleksandr up. But he royally fucks with my head, and you just sit there, 'Oh, he's immature, but he's got a lot going on.' Well, I have a lot going on, too, Auden!" Tears spring to my eyes. "We understood each other. I fell for him—*really* fell for him. He's the first person who made me think that I might be able to have a future with someone. He was okay being with me, even knowing I was going to die someday sooner than any of you."

"Stop, KK!" Auden sets her drink down and puts her hands on my shoulders. "He's not okay with that! *No one* is okay with that. Stop saying those things." She wraps her arms around me and gives me a savage squeeze.

Auden used to have a melancholy outlook on life before she met Aleksandr. She'd lost her mother at a very young age, and her father was never in her life. She didn't think she'd find love. She didn't think she'd trust someone enough to drop her walls.

I'd always told her that she had to stop being so defensive and let people in before she could ever enjoy life.

Enjoy life. Live in the moment. Allow yourself to love. To care. All that bullshit I used to spew because I didn't realize how much it hurt to love someone.

"I can't handle it when you talk that way." Auden runs her hand over my hair, which brings another wave of tears to my eyes. "I'm on your side, KK. I want you to be in love. I want you to have your happily ever after."

Seeing Auden, my repressed best friend, showing this kind of emotion sends me into a tailspin. For the first time in years, I let myself cry on my friend's shoulder. Literally. Auden's bony shoulder digs into my cheek, but I don't care. Tears flow onto her worn gray Aviators T-shirt, creating two wet spots.

Auden pulls down the pink fleece blanket draped over the back of the couch and covers our legs. "He's miserable if that makes you feel any better."

"It doesn't make me feel better," I admit. "I don't want him to be miserable. I'm not a horrible person. I want to get over it."

"Did you love him?"

"I could have loved the person he created. From everything you've told me, he's a complete douche in real life. And he reinforced that with his deception on the cruise."

"We all have our defenses."

"I don't!"

"Haha. Haha. Hahahahahahaha." Auden mocks me with a ridiculous fake laugh.

"I'm a completely open book."

"Bullshit, KK!"

"What are my defenses, then?" I ask, knowing Auden won't hold back. She'll hit me with the brutal honesty we've come to expect from each other.

Auden takes a deep breath. "Evan screwed with your head so much you're afraid other guys won't want to be with you after they find out you have CF."

"CF is my life. I don't keep secrets."

"Not true. You don't date anyone long enough for it to come up. And you do that on purpose."

"Why complicate short-term matters?"

"Why did you tell Pasha? You told him everything. And a week-long vacation is just about the shortest term you can get."

"Because he walked in on a treatment. I couldn't lie at that point," I say, defending myself.

It's only a half-truth because when he walked in on me, he didn't bat an eyelash at the treatment, nor did he ask me about it. He wasn't fazed at all. We discussed everything in detail later.

"Then why are you so mad at him?"

"I'm pissed that he led me on with lies. He should have told the truth upfront. So, I had the choice if I wanted to get involved."

"You are absolutely correct that he was a douchebag for being deceitful. I'm not taking that away. But look at what you had with him. Look at what kind of relationship you found when you both opened up. I mean, he's such a different person since you two met."

"What we had was amazing. It was like nothing else I've ever felt. But it was a lie. And I never want to feel that way about someone and have it blow up in my face again."

Annoyance coats Auden's dramatic exhale. "You've gotta get over this bullshit. You don't want guys to fall in love with you because you don't want to cause them pain when they lose you."

It's impossible to have secrets when you have a friendship like Auden and I have. It's like she lives in my head, waiting to pluck my unspoken thoughts out when it will make the most impact. The fears a confident, carefree Kristen would never say out loud.

Maybe it isn't as complicated as I thought for someone close to me to connect the train tracks from the moment my high school boyfriend broke up with me to this point in time. Since we were so young, it sounds stupid, but when Evan told me he couldn't stay with me because he knew my life had an expiration date and he couldn't handle it, he devastated my world.

So I built a wall. Because he was my first boyfriend, he was the baseline for my experience of how guys would handle finding out the details about what goes into dating someone with cystic fibrosis. He couldn't handle it, so I automatically assumed no guys would want to handle it.

"What about your happiness, KK?"

"I'm happy," I say, wiping away a tear.

"You're too busy trying to protect others. Do you tell your parents not to love you? Did you tell me not to get too attached?"

"I did, but you followed me around Central State like a tail I couldn't cut off."

"Yeah, well, of course I did. You're hot, confident, and smart. And you walk slow."

I laugh out loud.

"Let people make their own decisions. Not everyone is Evan."

"Thank God."

"Mother-effing dickweed."

"I love you." I wrap Auden in a bear hug.

She speaks softly. "You could be happy with Pasha. He loves you. And I know you love him."

"It's not love. We didn't know each other long enough to fall in love."

"Well, it was almost love. You wouldn't be this upset if you didn't have super-intense, almost love-like feelings for him."

"Yeah, except it was one-sided. He had that beautiful blond girl-friend the entire time he played me."

Auden wiggles out of my arms and gives me a what-the-hell squint. "Do you honestly think I'd be telling you to get with a guy who's had a girlfriend the entire time? I mean, seriously, would we even be having this conversation?"

"Who is she, then? I've seen him with her multiple times since your wedding. Once was when they were locked out of his house."

"The beautiful blonde you're talking about is not his girlfriend like I told you. It's Svetlana Kruzova, his sister's best friend. And that's *her* house, not his." Auden leans back on the couch. "Stupid fucker got sent back to the Aviators during the first month of the season. He'd already given up his apartment because he thought he'd be in Charlotte for good. He didn't have a place to live, so he moved in with Svetlana. Temporary solution."

"Moves in with a gorgeous blonde with the body of a Victoria's Secret model. How convenient."

"Check your jealousy at the door, *chica*. Number one: Svetlana is like a sister to him. They've known each other since they were children. Number two: She's the daughter of Igor Kruzov, one of the most famous Russian hockey players of all time, who died just after she was born. You'd know that if you followed the greatest sport on earth."

I stick out my tongue.

Before I met Auden, I could barely tell you the name of a hockey player other than Gordie Howe, who was a very famous Red Wings player, I'm told. I'm not much better now, but I remember a few things she's pounded into my head.

"Number three," Auden continues, "Svetlana is engaged to Arkady Zukarov, the Washington Capitals star player. That girl is not trading hockey royalty for Pavel Gribov."

Was it really that simple? That easily explained?

"There's nothing between them?" I ask.

Auden leans toward me, grabs one of my hands, and brings it to her lap. "Look, I've had my issues with Gribov. You know that. But I would never tell you to give him another chance if I knew he was a two-timing douchebag. I'm not telling you what to do. You know him a lot better than I do. Hell, you know him better than anyone."

I thought I did.

"Do you think he was telling the truth about the real stuff? Like his past?" I ask. Before she has a chance to answer, I continue. "I need honesty here."

"Yes. I believe he was telling the truth about all of that. Pavel's parents weren't the only ones killed in that accident. Sasha's parents were in the car, too."

My stomach drops. I didn't know that. Pasha didn't go into detail about the accident itself. I lower my head. "I'm so sorry."

Auden takes my hand. "I also believe he was being honest with you because of what he told me and Sasha when he came to apologize."

"He apologized to you?"

"He apologized for a lot, actually. He said he was sorry for trying to break us up and ruining our reception." Auden sweeps hair out of her face. "But he surprised us when he apologized for blaming Sasha's parents for the accident. Because Sasha's dad was driving, Pavel took out all his anger and grief on him. He asked for forgiveness and said he wanted to rebuild their friendship."

I put a hand over my mouth. "Aleksandr's dad was driving when their parents were in the accident?"

Auden nods. "Aleksandr said that losing his parents wrecked Pasha." Auden shakes her head. "Which I understand, ya know?"

Auden lost her mom when she was six years old. She's learned to trust and to grieve in a healthy way now, but when you grow up with intense trauma, it shapes who you are as a person. And it's hard to see outside the pain without help.

Suddenly, Auden springs up from the couch. "Almost forgot." She crosses the room to retrieve her messenger bag from the kitchen table. She digs around and hands me a plastic grocery bag. "Sorry about the wrapping. This is how it was given to me."

"What is this?"

Auden shrugs. "I don't know. I didn't open it." She pushes the bag at me.

Inside is a cylinder-shaped object bundled in brown paper. I unroll it slowly. On my lap, snuggled in the bed of brown paper, lays the green glass bottle Pasha threw into the bay in San Juan. I squeeze my eyes shut.

This has to be a dream. That bottle couldn't be sitting on my legs.

When I open my eyes, it's still there. Still stuffed with the faux parchment paper he'd written on and shoved inside.

"Ooh, pretty. What's that from?" Auden asks, leaning over to get a better glimpse.

"Pasha and I threw bottles into the water in San Juan." I shake my head in disbelief. "How did he get this back?"

My thumb caresses the cork at the top of the bottle. It doesn't feel right to open it, but I know that's what Pasha wants or he wouldn't have sent it with Auden. My stomach tightens, dying to see what he'd written.

I tug out the cork and bang the top against my palm. The paper had unrolled inside and won't fit through the opening. If I want to get it. I'll have to break it.

"You open it from the bottom," Auden says quickly when she notices me struggling. "Totally forgot I was supposed to tell you that."

"Thanks." I squint at the bottle and see a line near the bottom. After I unscrew it, the paper falls out. I lift my eyes to Auden's before I start reading. She nods and smiles, giving me courage. But when I look down, the message is written in another language.

I look to my Russian translator best friend for help, handing her the note.

Thank you for accepting and understanding me. A week by your side, embraced by your enthusiasm and light, changed me. Spending time with you, a strong, independent woman, helped me see the good inside myself. I see who I am and how I can be moving forward.

You will live a long, wonderful life. You will find a man who deserves you. One who will take you on adventures—but always keep you safe. One who will appreciate your strength and courage and never dim your bright spirit. One who will love you more than he loves himself. I wish it could have been me.

Live well, my sun. I will always carry your beautiful spirit in my heart, guiding me to be a better man.

My heartbeat quickens, and tears blur my vision with every line she translates.

"The Aviators are playing at Martin Arena tonight," Auden says, returning the letter to me. She ducks her head under the strap of her messenger bag, adjusting it on her shoulder before fastening it across her body. "Just saying."

A teardrop rolls down my cheek when I lift my head to look at her. "You think I should go?"

"Yes. I think you should get off your ass and work it out with him. Because after meeting you, he's been a different person. And he's almost as wrecked without you as he was about his parents' car accident."

Auden pauses as if contemplating whether or not to share her next thought. "His career is suffering. I'm not blaming you for that, believe me. He's never been able to handle grief. And he still can't. Losing you was like losing his mom again. You two were the only ones who ever told him he was a good person. *I* certainly never did. And I feel horrible for judging him before I knew where he was coming from. Instead of trying to understand him, I brushed him off. Pretty hypocritical, eh? Since I hated when people did that to me."

My heart hurts for Pasha. The reactions he got from other people were something he brought on himself, with his arrogance and standoffishness. But that was his defense, his way of keeping people away and not letting them get too close.

Though I know Pasha doesn't want to turn out like his father, I realize now that he uses the things he'd learned from him to keep his heart safe. I figured he'd be pissed if I pointed that out to him.

Pissed and hurt. I didn't want to do that to him. I'd rather help him see how much better life could be if he softened a little. If he allowed people to penetrate the walls.

"Okay." I wipe my face with both hands, smearing tears across my cheeks. Then I jump up and wrap my arms around my best friend.

Auden's body tenses, steeling herself for a massive squeeze. But I don't crush her with my arms. Instead, I take her face in my hands and smother her cheeks with quick kisses.

"I love you. I love you," I say each time before my lips descend on her.

"Get off me, you freak!" she says through giggles. She wriggles, trying to bust out of my hold.

"Nope." I stop the silly kisses but don't let go. "I've missed you so much."

"I've missed you, too." Auden relaxes and lets me hug her. "Now go take a shower and wash the stale smell of heartache away."

Chapter Fifty-Four

KRISTEN

LESS THAN AN HOUR AFTER MY SHOWER, I'M HEADING TO MARTIN Arena. I tune my radio to AM 1130, the sports station that carries the Aviators games. Thank goodness Auden told me that; I would've been pressing the scan button on my radio forever.

Within seconds of listening, one of the announcers says, "Aviators' former leading scorer, Pavel Gribov, just dropped his gloves against Dalton Ward, the Ice Frogs' resident enforcer."

"Gribov picked at Ward last night, trying to get him to fight, and it's just not like him," another announcer adds. "I mean, Gribov's no stranger to trouble. His chirping usually makes him a target. But dropping the gloves is really out of character for him."

"Ward lands a jab," says the first, "but look at Gribov! He's got Ward by the jersey. Gribov with an uppercut. Gribov with a right and another right. Ward's helmet goes flying. He's trying to hold Gribov off, but—oh! Gribov with another uppercut and four quick rights!"

"Wow! Where's Gribov been hiding that uppercut?" jokes the other.

"Pavel Gribov has found his rhythm, folks. Ward's on his back. And there's the linesman."

"I'll bet Gribov gets the instigator penalty on top of the automatic five for fighting here. He was jabbing at Ward, and that's what started it all."

"Yes, he was, Don," the first announcer notes. "This is so surprising. When Pavel Gribov started the season in Charlotte, I never thought we'd see him in an Aviators uniform again. But over the last two months, he's got more penalty minutes than points."

"Well, he's obviously got some pent-up aggression. Maybe he can turn that energy around and get his scoring back on track."

"And you were right, Don—Gribov gets the extra two for instigating. Aviators coach Rick Vincent won't be happy about this turn of events."

"I'm surprised Gribov hasn't been benched yet. Vincent isn't known for letting his players get away with this kind of hotheadedness."

I turn the volume down when a commercial for a local tire company fills the air, replacing the hockey announcers. Though most hockey terms are almost entirely foreign to me, I know what a penalty is and what fighting is.

What is he doing? Why is he screwing up his entire career? It can't be about me. I refuse to believe that I have that much power over his mental state. Elite athletes are trained to be more disciplined than that.

Rain pelts my window as I drive down I-75 toward downtown Detroit. The navigation system's robotic voice keeps me on course, though I know the way. I've been to Martin Arena once for a concert.

What am I planning to do once I get to the arena? How am I going to get in? I don't have a ticket. I don't think there's a lobby you walk into. If Martin is anything like Robinson, the old arena, the doors have to be opened from the inside. Unless, of course, you worked there and could use a separate entrance.

Separate entrance . . . Boom. I'll drive around to the lot where the band tour buses park. It has to be the same lot where the players park their cars, right?

Five more minutes and I'll be there.

Five more minutes, and I'll see Pasha.

Five more minutes, and I'll ask for his forgiveness.

Technically, it'll be more since I'll have to wait until after the game to talk to him.

The rain comes down harder, and I flip my wipers to the highest speed—the annoying speed that doesn't even help because if it's raining hard enough to use it, you can't see no matter what. I grip the wheel tighter and lift my foot off the gas pedal.

A second later, everything goes black.

Chapter Fifty-Five

KRISTEN

My eyes flutter open, and I inhale sharply. The hospital room looks as familiar as my childhood bedroom, bringing almost as much comfort.

If I'm in the hospital, it means I'm alive.

I reach up and touch the mask covering my mouth and nose, filling my lungs with pure oxygen—another familiar staple of my experiences in the hospital. A hot pink fleece blanket lay draped across the lower half of my body on top of the thin, white standard blanket.

The accident flashes through my mind. A car traveling in the left lane on I-75 swerved hard and crossed over the other lanes of traffic. I jammed my brakes immediately, which probably made me hydroplane in the torrential downpour.

The back of that car clipped the front of mine and sent my car spinning. But I don't remember anything after that. I must've passed out when my forehead hit the steering wheel. I reach up, touch my face, and wince at the soreness and swelling.

When I look around the room, there's no one there, but my mom's purse and my dad's jacket and book sit on the chairs near my bed. According to the clock across from my bed, it's just before noon. They must've left to grab lunch.

The door to my hospital room is open a crack; through that opening, I see a familiar figure pass. Then I hear his voice, demanding the nurses tell him which room I'm in. I can't hear the responses, but it doesn't sound like he's getting the information he wants.

"I will open every door of every room here. I need to see my wife!" Pasha threatens.

Wife? More lies to get what he wants?

Surprise, surprise.

Only this time, his lie doesn't piss me off. The fabrication gives me hope that he'll forgive me despite never having made it to Martin Arena for my grand please-take-me-back gesture.

Seconds later, the door hinge squeaks, alerting me that someone entered my room. The first thing I notice is the smell of his body wash. The sandalwood and amber scent floods my head with unforgettable memories of our time on the cruise. I squeeze my eyes closed to halt any tears those memories bring.

Instead of opening them again, I relax and pretend to be asleep—or, ya know, unconscious.

I know letting him believe I'm unable to communicate is horrible and selfish, but I want to hear what he has to say. He didn't know I was on my way to the arena to apologize. And despite the fact that we'd run into each other three times in the last month, he didn't make any effort to apologize or talk about rekindling our relationship.

I need to know why he asked Auden to give me the message in the bottle. And why he's running around the hospital like a madman.

This moment is the closest I'll get to being at my own funeral. Even as I have that thought, I realize how much it makes me sound like a super-morbid nutcase.

"Kristen," Pasha whispers. He slides his fingers over mine and squeezes my hand. "KK, please open your eyes."

Silence fills the room. Pasha's firm grip and sweet, warm scent keep me grounded in the moment—in safety.

"You will not go down like this. We will get eaten by alligators or smash on the ground after we skydive together. This—this is not the way." Pasha's breathing rate increases, and I hear him sniffle.

It breaks my heart.

Then I hear another distinct squeak; this time, it's a nurse wheeling a cart into my room.

"What are you doing in here?" Her voice gets closer and closer. "Who are you?"

My throat aches, dehydrated by the dry air I inhale from the oxygen mask through slightly parted, chapped lips. I try to speak, knowing that it'll blow my cover, but only a hiss escapes, and the attempt hurts so badly that my eyes fill with tears beneath their closed lids.

A drop slips out, passing down my face and over my swollen cheek.

Trapped inside my own lie. I'm no better than Pasha is.

Chapter Fifty-Six

PASHA

"I AM VOLUNTEER HERE. ON CHILDREN'S FLOOR," I EXPLAIN TO Kristen's nurse. It doesn't mean shit in this situation, but I hope it will soften her stance on the hospital rules.

"That doesn't explain why you're in this room," the nurse responds calmly but sternly.

"She will wake up, yes? She will not stay this way. She will not die this way?" I ask, my voice shaking with the words. "She *cannot* die like this."

"I can't discuss her health with you unless you're family."

"I am her husband," I say, hoping my tone's complete and total confidence will make the lie convincing.

"Her husband, eh?" The nurse taps away at the portable computer she wheeled into the room. "No notes about a husband in here." She pauses. "No ring on her finger."

"Secret wedding. On cruise." I won't give up. I'll say whatever I have to until she lets me stay.

"I'll let you sit with her until her parents return to confirm your story. But I can't tell you anything about her condition. I'm sorry."

I nod. "Thank you."

I squeeze Kristen's hand as the nurse performs a series of tasks.

From countless hours here with other patients, I know there's a routine to each nurse's visit. I wait for her to leave before I begin speaking.

"Everything I did is wrong. I should have been honest. I want you to love me. But I fuck this all up," I say, gently massaging Kristen's hand as I speak. "I cannot think. I cannot play. I will lose my career soon. I cannot function without you."

I stop talking but keep working on her hand, sliding my fingers along each of hers and kneading her palm with my thumbs. I have no medical background, but I read that physical contact helps some people respond.

I can't stop my brain from returning to the intimate moments we shared. I'm not even talking about the sex. I ache for the intimacy of being with her—someone I trust and understand.

I slide my palm over her head, touching her softly. Then, using slightly more pressure, I push the hair off her forehead.

"I love you, KK." I lower my lips to her swollen cheek, pressing softly. "I spend all this time pissed off. When my parents die—" I stop and take a deep breath. "When my mother die, I forget how to live. I forget how to be happy. I do not let myself care about anyone. I do not want to love someone when every time I do, they die. Then you run into me on track and everything change. I never meet anyone who make me so happy. You understand me and care about me. And then you tell me you will die. Like everyone, but sooner."

The chair's metal legs scrape against the floor as I scoot closer to the bed.

"I think and think, KK. I think about only you. What is the Aviators record? This I do not know. How many goals I have? Probably zero. A ghost cannot score." I take a deep breath and exhale slowly.

"When you tell me about how serious your disorder is, I am scared, but I want to be here for you. I only care about my life when you're in it. I—"

I pause, trying to think of the correct words. "English. English. Fuck." I've never had to use English to express my adoration for someone. It's a test of my vocabulary.

"I will love you every day you have on this earth. I will live to make you happy. I want to be this person for you. You deserve the happiest life. And this life includes me. We will do this together. We fight. We live. We love. We do not think about the bad. Yes, I'm afraid to lose you, but if I spend every second of life in love with you, I know I lived my best."

"Who are you?" A woman's voice rings through the room.

I turn around, expecting to see another nurse to sweet-talk into allowing me to stay.

Instead, I see a replica of Kristen—same eyes and cheekbones— only this woman is twenty years older.

And she brought a Greek army.

Chapter Fifty-Seven

KRISTEN

PAVEL DROPS MY HAND AND PUSHES BACKWARD IN THE CHAIR. "I AM Pasha."

Oh, boy. I fight to keep my eyes closed, trying not to show that I've been faking.

"She's not in a coma. She's just sleeping." Mom's voice is soft, a tone I never imagined it would have if she ever met my Russian boyfriend.

"Is she okay?" he asks.

"She's bruised, and she'll be very sore, but she's fine." Mom brushes my forehead and slides her hand over my hair. "I'm surprised she's not awake yet."

"I am," I confess through the oxygen mask. Not because I want to give myself up but because I don't want to hear my mother grill Pasha obnoxiously.

Heads swivel toward me—more heads than I realized at first. My parents, grandparents, Lena, and Pasha all stand in my room. It's like a clown car unloaded while my eyes were closed.

I make no apologies as I lift the mask off my nose and mouth. I shrug and look at Pasha. "I wanted to hear what you had to say."

Instead of responding with anger, as I half expected, Pavel laughs.

"This is not Greek boy. Why you say you meet Greek boy? You lie to us, Kristen? You lie to us?" screeches my grandmother, whom I call *Yia Yia*.

I knew she'd be the one who'd have the biggest problem with Pasha. I was pretty sure that if my parents ever met him, they would give him a chance, at least until things got serious. Then I'd have some begging to do.

But *Yia Yia* would have none of this dating-outside-of-my-culture business. In her view, it wouldn't work—couldn't work. I have a deep-seated feeling that she would never *let* it work.

"Russian Orthodox boys similar to Greek Orthodox boys, yes?" Pasha asks. "I am not so different."

"Russian boys *nothing* like Greek boys," *Yia Yia* spits. She puts one hand to her chest and reaches behind her back with the other, blindly searching for a chair. Pasha slides one toward her.

"Can we have a minute?" I ask since I know Yia Yia's "heart troubles" are pure drama and nothing to worry about.

Pappoús, my grandfather, puts a hand on her shoulder to guide her out of the room, but my tiny, feisty grandma shrugs it off. "You tell him goodbye, Kristen," she warns, shaking her index finger at me.

Pappoús says something in Greek in her ear. She scowls at him but allows him to lead her toward the exit. My mother and father follow them.

"I have no doubt *Yia Yia* was one of the best Greek tragic actresses as a girl," Lena whispers, leaning in to kiss my forehead. "And I told you he'd be trouble."

"Thank you. An I-told-you-so is exactly what I need from you right now," I tease.

Lena squeezes my arm and gives Pasha a quick glance before leaving the room.

As soon as the door closes, Pasha asks, "Why you fake death?"

Chapter Fifty-Eight

PASHA

"I DIDN'T FAKE MY DEATH," KRISTEN SAYS DEFENSIVELY, CROSSING her arms over her chest.

"You know I am scared. You should open your eyes."

"I wanted to hear what you would say if you thought I was on the verge of dying."

"This is fucked up," I say, though I have to admit I'd do the same thing in the same situation.

"So is getting sent back to the minors and fighting people," she counters without apology. "You have a career to think about. You're replaceable, Pasha."

I stagger away from the bed, stunned she'd call me out like that. Then I remember who I'm talking to, and it shouldn't be much of a surprise.

"It wasn't an insult," she explains. "It's the truth. All athletes are replaceable. You need to be your best at all times."

"How can I be my best without you?" I ask.

"You were the best before me."

"I say this again. How can I be the best *after* you? I cannot think. I cannot sleep." I drop into the chair next to her bed and take her hand.

"I can't handle a pathetic dude."

Has she always been this frustrating? I lift my palms up in frustration. "Why you are mean?"

"I thought you liked my honesty."

"You are too much like me. This is how I sound?"

"You told me I should have sucked your dick and left."

I laugh, then immediately throw in a fake cough to hide it. I'm such a jerk.

"See! You love how blunt and honest you are." Kristen coughs.

Unlike mine, her cough is real—and it freaks me out. I lean closer, my heart jumping into my throat with every hack. Kristen closes her eyes and pats my arm.

"The days we spent together on that cruise were the most amazing of my life. I'd never felt so free to be myself. I didn't have to hide. It was like being with my best friend," she says.

Someone knocks on the door, and, as if on cue, Auden pokes her head in.

"Am I interrupting?" she asks.

"Yes," Kristen and I answer simultaneously, but Kristen waves Auden forward. I get up and step aside, giving her some room.

"Oh, good. Your grandma sent me in to break you guys up," Auden says.

"How's that for karma, eh, Pasha?" Kristen lifts her eyes to mine.

"I deserve this," I admit, shaking my head and casting my eyes to the floor. And I do. I still regret trying to break Auden and Aleksandr up during one of the lowest points of my life.

"But I'd never do it." Auden puts a hand on my shoulder. "Aleksandr loves you too much."

I straighten and glance at the door. "Where is he?"

"In Charlotte, where you should be."

"I will be back soon," I whisper. Auden and Kristen both fall silent for a moment. "Talk!" I demand so they'll stop looking at me like I'm a fucking sick dog. "Do not feel bad for me. I am asshole here."

Auden grins. "I didn't mean to bust in, but I had to make sure you were okay."

"My two best friends are at my bedside, and my family has their ears pressed to the door. I've never been better," Kristen tells her.

"I'll get them away from the door," Auden says.

"Oh, good," I sigh. "Because I need to get laid."

Auden's nose and mouth scrunch in disgust. "I'll pretend I didn't hear that." She stoops down and presses a kiss to Kristen's forehead. "How can you like this pig?" she asks after straightening. But on her way out of the room, she winks and squeezes my forearm.

Kristen speaks as soon as Auden is gone. "So where do we stand? Because I really like you. A lot. I haven't stopped thinking about you. But I need you to be all in. Be honest. Be blunt. I like Pasha when he's using his powers for good."

"Yes. I want all of this. And I only speak truth from now on." I grab my hair and groan. "Why you do not speak Russian? Is easier to communicate."

"I like to make it hard for you." Kristen reaches out and skims her hand over the front of my jeans.

"Yes. You have no problem with this." I lean over and kiss her softly. My heart speeds up, elated to have my lips on hers. Kissing her again feels like being on a breakaway. The same excitement and exhilaration rushes through my veins.

"I'm not breakable," Kristen whispers.

"No, but you are not ready for me to jump you in hospital bed."

"You're not the boss of me." She hooks her fingers into my waistband and pulls me toward her.

I try to brace myself, but I don't have time, and my full body weight falls on top of her.

"Owww!" she moans.

I immediately lift myself onto my hands. "This is what you call karma. And now your grandmother will bust in and kill me."

"She'll get over it." Kristen stretches her neck to kiss me.

"This I do not agree. She hate Russians. What did we do?"

"*Yia Yia* hates anyone who's not Greek. Do a few shots of ouzo with her, and she'll get over it."

"The stuff Panikos made me drink on the cruise that tastes like black licorice?" I make a face at the memory of that shit.

"Learn to love ouzo if you want to be with me," Kristen teases.

"I would drink gasoline to be with you."

"Well, that just seems stupid." She laughs. "Good thing we're in the hospital."

Yes. Good thing. Because being here means she's alive. And I will spend every second she has making her life the best it can be.

EPILOGUE

Pasha

TWO MONTHS LATER

"Kristen."

"Kristen!" I shake her shoulder, rousing her from the last few minutes of sleep before her alarm goes off. I can't help it—I'm too excited to wait.

"Hmm?" she mumbles without opening her eyes.

"Mike Kingston just called me."

"Who?" she asks.

"Mike Kingston," I repeat. "The Monarchs coach."

Kristen opens her eyes and bolts upright. The sheet falls, revealing her bare chest. I smile in appreciation at the greeting. Kristen leans over and presses her lips on mine. "Morning."

I push her hair away from her face. "I'm going back to Charlotte. Tonight."

"It's because they traded Malone, isn't it?" she asks.

I love it when she pretends to know hockey. A few months ago, she couldn't tell you what a hat trick was; now, she's in the running to replace my agent. I appreciate that she takes an interest and tries to learn because she knows it's my career, my passion.

Two days ago, the Monarchs traded Travis Malone to the Florida Panthers. He was the second-line center, but they had to give up a strong player to get the veteran defenseman the team needed.

Trading Malone opened up a position at center. This might be my chance to stay in the NHL—for good.

Kristen places her palm on my cheek and holds my gaze. "This is it. I can feel it."

Her confidence in me fills me with pride.

"You want to feel something else?" I ask, lifting my eyebrows.

"Yes," she answers without hesitation, and I tackle her back onto the bed.

Because that's exactly what she loves about me—my ability to take a serious moment and turn it into something sexual.

Since Kristen's car accident two months ago, I've been lucky enough to wake up next to her every morning I'm not traveling with the Aviators.

Because we both like to take things fast, I moved out of Svetlana's house and into Kristen's apartment almost immediately. We tried to live separately—two doors away—but realized it didn't make sense when we spent every free second together anyway.

"Live in the moment" is one of her mottos, and we jumped right in.

No regrets.

EPILOGUE

Kristen

THE SUN BEATS DOWN, PENETRATING MY HAIR AND BURNING MY scalp, a reminder that I should've worn a hat for today's run. I'd done an olive oil treatment on my dry locks this morning, which increased my scalp's sensitivity. And I probably smell disgusting.

I slow to a jog when I reach the corner and look both ways down West Second Street. Just as I step out into the road, a man jumps out from behind a lamppost and runs straight into me.

"Geez!" I scream as he wraps his arms around me, saving me from hitting the ground. "Why do you like doing that so much?" I ask.

Pasha kisses the top of my head. "Reminds me of how we met. When I fell for you." It almost makes his weird habit of jumping out and scaring the shit out of me sound so sweet.

"Are you packed?" I ask, looking both ways again before resuming my run.

My super-awesome athlete boyfriend easily matches my stride. "I will throw things in my bag and go."

"You could be in Charlotte for a while this time," I remind him.

"You can bring the rest of my stuff when you move there with me."

"What?" I stop running.

"If this is it—the real thing—would you move to Charlotte with me?" Pasha asks.

His question gives me all the girly feels. Of course, I want to move to Charlotte with him and spend the rest of my days frolicking barefoot in the sunshine of our love.

Okay, maybe that's a little much, but the random dorky thought is the first thing that came to my mind because he wants me to be with him. He's not trying to push me away. I broke down that defensive wall, which made me feel complete, happy, and alive.

I almost blurt out an answer without thinking, but I don't have the luxury of making big decisions—or any decisions—without thinking.

What about my job? What about my doctors? What about health insurance? Technically, my parents still carry me because the management group I work for doesn't offer insurance, and it's cheaper than getting an individual plan.

Before I can answer, Pasha starts speaking again. "I talk to lady at the Cystic Fibrosis Foundation in Charlotte. She give me information on best doctors in North Carolina. I know you must go there often, and I will take you. Every time. I will drive you anywhere. And Auden will be around in case you need someone if I am on road trip. My first priority is I keep you healthy."

Warmth rushes from my cheeks all the way to my toes. "Your first priority is hockey."

"Life—*your* life—is more precious than hockey. I can get another job. I cannot get another you."

"Stop talking like that. I'm strong and independent. I'm not going to be a burden on you or your career."

"You are not burden, Kristen! You are my life now. Hockey is hockey. I will play my ass off to make you so much fucking money we can afford a live-in doctor." Pasha pauses. "Female, of course."

"Of course!" I roll my eyes.

"I didn't mean it that way," Pasha explains. "I will get old lady. But no man will be in our home. You are too tempting."

"How did such a sweet conversation go south so fast?"

Pasha ignores me. "You like this idea, yes?"

"There're still a lot of things I have to think about, and I need to talk to my parents," I say.

Pasha nods, waiting for my answer with wide, eager eyes.

"But I want to try it out," I tell him honestly. "I want to be with you. I want to support you."

Pasha sweeps me off my feet and spins me around. "We take this one day at a time."

There's nothing more perfect than jogging through the streets of Royal Oak, Michigan, on an unseasonably warm day in February.

Well, sure, breathing in the salty scent of the ocean while jogging around the track on a cruise ship in the Caribbean would have been better.

But I'm not complaining because I have the love of my life jogging next to me.

Thanks for reading UNSPORTSMANLIKE CONDUCT!
I hope you love Kristen and Pavel!

Need another bad boy Russian hockey player and hard-working heroine to root for? Viktor and Lexie take angst to the next level when their steamy tryst ends in a surprise pregnancy in BLUE LINES. Download BLUE LINES today!

Turn the page for an excerpt of Blue Lines...

BLUE LINES EXCERPT

VIKTOR

UNLIKE SOME OF THE OTHER GUYS, WHO ARE CONSTANTLY TUGGING at the tightness of their collars, I feel entirely at ease at lavish parties like this.

My family owns The Russian Dining Room, a historic restaurant in New York City. We spent many evenings celebrating well into the night. Russian celebrations can last for days. Though, I'm not sure if that's normal or just us.

Either way, we know how to party and it's always done with elegance. That is one of the unique things about my family.

My father made international headlines when he defected to Detroit from the former Soviet Union to play hockey. Ivan Kravtsov was the first player from the USSR's Central Scarlet Army to leave without permission.

He doesn't like to talk about it. Though I've been able to pry some details out of him, most of what I know about it is from articles on the Internet. It was well-documented for the time since it was major historical news.

My uncle and aunt, Kirill Antonov and Anastasia Antonova,

escaped a short time later. Their story, though not documented like my father's, is just as thrilling—maybe even more so.

Mafia, money, murder—the background of how everyone in our family got to America sounds like something straight out of a suspense novel.

They came here to have a better life and to raise their children with opportunities and freedoms they didn't have.

Which brings me back to the lavish parties. They celebrate the difficult choices they made and the good fortune that came from those choices at every opportunity. And they raised all of us—my sisters and cousins—to appreciate every luxury we enjoy here in America.

As I exit the bathroom, I'm fiddling with my cufflink and accidentally bump into someone. When I look up to apologize, it's Lexie. Her head is down as she smooths her shirt against her trim stomach. Her hair glistens as if she had to wet it to get it to lay flat.

"Sorry," I say, bracing her by placing my hands on her biceps.

"I'm so sorry, sir, I—" she stammers before looking up. Once she sees me, a relieved sigh escapes her lips. "Oh, it's just you."

I lower my arms. "Just me? What does that mean?"

"It means I have more leniency bumping you." She pats my shoulder as if consoling a child before sweeping past me. "No need to get offended, Viktor."

"Someone's going to get hurt if we keep running into each other like this," I call out. "I can think of much better ways to touch each other."

She shakes her head without turning around.

Dropping my original mission to rejoin the guys, I spin around and follow her. The urge to have Lexie in my bed tonight is greater than the urge to listen to Luke rehash last night's game against Philly.

Please, Luke, tell us again how we need to capitalize on the Power Play.

She must know I'm a step behind because I catch her looking at me from the corner of her eye. But she doesn't stop or glance back.

I love a challenge. It's been a while since I used my primal impulse to hunt.

"Are you lost?" she asks as she rounds the corner of a long bar. She grabs a ticket printing from the machine behind her and scans it before scooping ice into a stainless-steel tumbler and then adding vodka and cranberry juice.

"Yes. Lost in thoughts of you." I place an elbow on the bar and lean toward her.

"Oh my gosh!" She rolls her eyes while screwing the cap on the vodka bottle. "Does that line ever work?"

"It's true. I can't get you out of my head, Lexie. I've been thinking about you since the first time we met. You realize that by now, right?"

"Really?" Her lips curve into a playful smile as she shakes the liquids and ice in a stainless-steel tumbler. "I didn't realize you had any recollection of the night we met."

"Well." I scratch the back of my neck while twisting my lips. "I mean, I think I do."

Her eyes narrow slightly, toying with me. "You remember the night you got to the Beaver already so drunk that I wouldn't serve you, *and* I had to pay for your ride home?"

Her words spark a memory, but not everything comes back to me. I rub the back of my neck and laugh. "I wondered how I got to my apartment."

"You didn't know how you got home?" She quickly lifts her gaze to mine while straining the drink into two frosted martini glasses.

"Nope." I chuckle. I always thought one of the boys took me home. Never even questioned it. "Sounds like I owe you a ride."

We both pause, realizing the sexual double entendre in my comment. Her cheeks heat up with a rosy tone as her gaze burns into me, lust seeping out like molten lava. She wants me just as much as I want her.

The question isn't *if* we'll have sex, but *when*.

KEEP READING

BE KIND. LOVE HARD.

At the beginning of my career, I vowed to give a portion of royalties from each of my books to charity. I choose charities that are close to my heart and that are involved in my books in some way. Visit the Be Kind Love Hard page on my website to learn more about each charity.

A HEARTFELT THANK YOU TO EACH ONE OF YOU
SOPHIA X

A portion of the royalties from the sale of UNSPORTSMANLIKE CONDUCT will be donated to the Cystic Fibrosis Foundation.

For information on the Cystic Fibrosis Foundation: www.cff.org

#BeKindLoveHard

REVIEWS ROCK!

THANK YOU so much for taking the time to read UNSPORTSMANLIKE CONDUCT. I truly appreciate every single one of you. If you enjoyed reading UNSPORTSMANLIKE CONDUCT as much as I enjoyed writing it, it would mean the world to me if you would consider leaving a review on Amazon.

(If you really loved the book, copy and paste the same review to Bookbub & Goodreads!)

SOPHIA X

PLAYLIST

Complete Playlist on YouTube: SophiaHenryOfficial

I Lived - One Republic
Shape Of You - Ed Sheeran
Duele El Corazón – Enrique Iglesias
Reggaéton Lento - CNCO
El Perdón - Nicky Jam (feat. Enrique Iglesias)
Whenever, Wherever - Shakira
Behave - Frightened Rabbit
Fall Into These Arms - New Politics
One More Whiskey - Tom Sartori
Wild Ones - Flo Rida (feat. Sia)
Favorite Liar - The Wrecks
When You Were Mine - Night Terrors of the 1927 (feat. Tegan & Sara)
Club Can't Handle Me - Flo Rida (feat. David Guetta)
Piece of Me - Britney Spears
Anna Sun - Walk The Moon
Toxic - Britney Spears
Honest - Kodaline
Not Over You - Gavin De Graw

Lose Control - James
Laid - James
Shattered (Turn the Car Around) O.A.R.
The Loneliness and the Scream - Frightened Rabbit
Unsteady - X Ambassadors
The Adventure - Angels and Airwaves
R U Mine? - Arctic Monkeys
I Bet You Look Good on the Dance Floor - Arctic Monkeys
Adrenalina - Wisin (feat. Jennifer Lopez & Rocky Martin

DON'T MISS OUT!

Sophia Henry's mailing list is the place to be if you like steamy romance novels that tug at your heart strings. Stay notified of new releases, sales, exclusive content. sophiahenry.com

MERCH STORE

Choose kindness and love with everything you've got. It's not just a motto. It's a way of life. Grab some motivational or bookish merch today! shopkrasivo.com

ALSO BY SOPHIA HENRY

FOREIGN EDITIONS

FRENCH

DUO SAINTS AND SINNERS

SAINTS

SINNERS

ROMANS AUTONOMES LIÉS AUX SAGAS

EVEN STRENGTH

Saints & Sinners/Aviators Hockey Crossover Novel

SAGA AVIATORS HOCKEY

JINGLE BALL BENDER

BLUE LINES

GERMAN

MATERIAL GIRLS SERIES

OPEN YOUR HEART

LIVE TO TELL

CRAZY FOR YOU

RUSSIAN

SAINTS AND SINNERS SERIES

SAINTS

SINNERS

ABOUT THE AUTHOR

USA Today Bestselling Author Sophia Henry fell in love with reading, writing, and hockey all before she became a teenager. After graduating with a Creative Writing degree from Central Michigan University, she moved to warm and sunny North Carolina to enjoy the remainder of her winters.

She spends her days writing steamy, heartfelt contemporary romance novels hoping they resonate with and encourage others. When Sophia's not writing, she's hanging out with her two high-energy sons, an equally high-energy Plott Hound, and two cats who want nothing to do with any of them. She can also be found watching her beloved Detroit Red Wings and rocking out at as many concerts as she can possibly attend.

Sophia Henry's mailing list is the place to be if you like steamy romance novels that tug at your heart strings. Sign up at sophiahenry.com.